From the reviews of Richard Aronowitz's first novel, Five Amber Beads

'After several cinematic treatments, and the literary success of Bernhard Schlink's *The Reader* and Jonathan Safran Foer's *Everything is Illuminated*, one might wonder whether fiction has anything new to say about the Holocaust. Through his shimmering use of the language of art Aronowitz has shown that it has.'

Christian House, *Independent on Sunday*

'Richard Aronowitz's *Five Amber Beads* is another first novel, and a good one. Charley Bernstein, the narrator, is an art detective who tracks down paintings stolen by the Nazis. His mother came to England as a Kindertransport refugee and married an Englishman. Charley has assumed his mother's Jewish surname ("amber" in German). In New York, after an accident, he wakes up in a ward with an old man who has lost his memory. He is European, perhaps German, and was clearly involved in the Second World War. But how?'

John Sutherland, *Financial Times*

'Haunting extracts from the diary are interwoven skilfully with Charley's reflections as he and his wife accompany Christopher on a journey into the past. Familiar subject matter, perhaps, but the writer's distinctive poetic voice offers a welcome fresh perspective.'

Rachel Hore, *The Guardian*

'Aronowitz portrays with elegance and thoughtfulness what it means to lose one's sense of self.'

Simon Baker, *The Spectator*

'Told in almost poetic language, the novel contributes to our understanding of the human need for restitution.'

Margaret Studer, *Wall Street Journal Europe*

IT'S JUST THE BEATING OF MY HEART

IT'S JUST THE BEATING OF MY HEART

Richard Aronowitz

FlambardPress

First published in Great Britain in 2010 by Flambard Press Ltd
Holy Jesus Hospital, City Road, Newcastle upon Tyne NE1 2AS
www.flambardpress.co.uk

Typeset by BookType
Cover artwork © Andrew Foley
Design by Gainford Design Associates
Printed in Great Britain by Cromwell Press Group, Trowbridge, Wiltshire

A CIP catalogue record for this book is available from the British Library.

ISBN: 978-1-906601-13-3

Flambard Press wishes to thank Arts Council England
for its financial support.

Flambard Press is a member of Inpress.

The paper used for this book is FSC accredited.

For my father, Ronald Arthur Mercer

'The distracted person, too, can form habits. More, the ability to master certain tasks in a state of distraction proves that their solution has become a matter of habit.'

Walter Benjamin, 'The Work of Art in the Age of Mechanical Reproduction', 1935

'Oh must you tell me all your secrets
When it's hard enough to love you knowing nothing'

Lloyd Cole & The Commotions, 'Four Flights Up', 1984

Chapter One

The valley is divided by light. The sun etches shapes into its far side, with its thick stands of beech and oak, while our house is already in shade by five o'clock. Our side of the valley is steeper, with open expanses of arable land at the top of the escarpment and a footpath behind our house, leading from the gate at the top of the garden into a copse that forms its natural border. If you sit quietly on the beech-wood bench by the back wall of our cottage when the sun has gone down, you can hear the rustling and rummaging of badgers as they forage for grubs and earth-worms, beetles and shoots. Sometimes, the bark of a fox breaks a silence so complete that the stars seem to sing with an eternal static charge in the night sky.

I have been walking around like a ghost. Rooms lose their atmosphere, their warmth, when I enter them. It is as if someone has died. In some sort of endless way they have. My wife is dead to me. She died when she left our house, our home. I cannot stop calling it our house, our valley. There has been no 'us' for more than twenty-one months. Bryony was ten when her mother took her away to live in Bristol early on Christmas morning the year before last. Twenty-five miles and a million lives away. A car passes on our lane once every two or three hours. The nearest house is perhaps two hundred yards away; a holiday home that the owners from London only live in for three months of the year.

Bryony, already tall like her mother but with my dark-brown eyes, visits for two weekends each month, emptying the house of its loneliness. Linda leaves Bryony on the wooden bench in Stroud railway station's quiet ticket office at precisely five o'clock every other Friday evening. She waits and watches until she sees my Volvo pull up in the station car park and knows that Bryony will be safe, then makes her unseen getaway. We never speak face-to-face. I find my daughter clutching her small rucksack to her chest, with her head buried in whichever book she is reading at the time. I return her on Monday morning at eight o'clock sharp, each of us trusting the other with our daughter without question or hesitation. Linda has always disappeared up the wooden stairs of the bridge that links the two platforms by the time that I walk into the ticket office to collect Bryony, going back to her car in the far car park and her journey on the motorway back to Bristol. We can never cross paths. We trust each other beyond words with our daughter, but cannot trust each other with ourselves.

What happened to us? Even now I cannot begin to explain it to myself; I cannot shape it into words that do not jump around the page like frightened mice. All I know is that I wake up each morning in an empty bed. The pillow beside mine is cold; Linda's presence has not left its mark there. I want to hit the bottle, to pour vodka onto my cornflakes, to put shots of whisky in my morning's first cup of coffee. Alcohol was just a way for me to relax after work, a lubricator in stressful social situations, when Linda and Bryony were in my life. Linda had a different take on it and perhaps she was right: it has become my life now. It has been like this since they left me.

Bryony has just turned twelve and likes one of the boy bands whose name I forget and whose members look only a little older than her. She likes boy bands, animals of every kind (she says that she wants to be a vet), and walks in the countryside. She does not like the empty bottles that she finds in the glass-recycling bin outside the back porch. 'Dad, you promised you wouldn't drink between my visits,' she says. 'That's *not at all*, Dad. Why can't you just drink orange juice or Ribena like me?'

'I had guests round for dinner last Saturday, Bee. We shared a bottle or two of wine, that's all.'

'Well, I've told you before and I won't tell you again. Mum will never have you back otherwise.'

'My not having a drink won't make any difference, Bee. Things are a bit more complicated than that. What about going on that walk?'

There were no guests and she knows it. Bryony goes to the cupboard by the back door to find her pink Wellington boots and pulls them on over her woolly blue socks. She sighs with the effort then asks me to find one of her favourite denim jackets that she leaves here for her visits. 'Shouldn't you wear a jumper or something underneath, over your sweatshirt?'

'*Da-ad*, I'll be fine,' she says. 'It's not *that* cold. Please stop fussing.'

We walk up the narrow lane, which has been known for generations as Folly Lane, although the folly itself is long gone. This single track runs from the lower part of Stroud up through an area of council housing then continues on upwards, snaking along the side of the valley, to the top of the escarpment. Woods of oak and beech are interspersed with fields of corn and wheat, rye and barley up here. The landscape has not changed much for centuries, for the three hundred years since our cottage, the Stone House, was built. It has probably not changed much since the Norman Conquest and since the Magna Carta first named the lords and landowners of the local demesne.

Bryony has a favourite walk, which also remains un-changed and immutable. Beyond the ancient deciduous woods, the tarmac road peters out to grit and gravel. It leads nowhere in particular, but deeper and deeper into a no-man's land of pasture and rough ground, grassland sparsely populated by the odd burnt-out car or abandoned hulk of rusting farm machinery. Farther on, there are managed woods of spruce and fir that the local Forestry Commission nurture and then cut down, nurture and cut down.

We first came on this walk as a family, once we moved here full-time in the early nineties when Bryony was two and a half. We began this walk as a family and I ended it alone. Aloneness is relative; you can be with someone, share your life, your home, your bed with them and still feel as isolated and uncared for as these rusting tractor parts and ploughs. I think that this is how Linda felt towards the end: she felt that she had lost me. Aloneness is relative; Bryony holds my hand tightly in hers as the woods become denser and darker. The path hides under a thick blanket of needles; sounds are muffled, dampened down by the laden branches and the soft ground. No one else seems to come here, although the hoof-marks on the pathways betray their use as bridle-tracks and conduits for cattle. Occasionally you meet a dog-walker on the path that skirts the edge of the fir woods, but once you enter them you are always alone.

From the top of the escarpment we descend towards the bottom of the valley down a steep path; the trees thin out here, giving way to meadowland again and the clear sounds of a stream. We sit and rest on the trunk of a fallen tree, a great elm that stood, dead upright, for two decades following the Dutch Elm Disease epidemic in the seventies, only to be felled by the storms that swept this part of the country in the late eighties. Bryony picks up a handful of limestone chips and small pebbles of flint, tossing them casually one by one into the shallow stream. They sink down into the clear water and embed themselves in the sandy soil of the streambed.

'Dad,' she says, 'do you ever come down here without me? Do you ever bring anyone else here?'

'I come here sometimes in the very early mornings,

before I go off to London to work, but I've never brought anyone else with me. It's just for you and me, Bee.'

I did, just once, come here with someone else, but that is a story for later. The way Bryony thinks of these woods as our special secret makes me feel that I betrayed her somehow, by bringing someone here who meant something to me.

It is September and we set out on our walk in the half-light of an early autumn evening. The wind, which was only a gentle breeze when we left our house, has caught its breath and blows the full force of its lungs at us. We get up from the bleached and desiccated tree-trunk and begin our walk along the stream, up to the far end of the valley. There is a large, Georgian Cotswold stone house here, with high redbrick walls surrounding it that are covered in ivy and patches of lichen and moss. A long drive lined with alternating plane trees and beeches leads from the house up to the lane that runs across the head of the valley and through the woods towards Stroud. High wrought-iron gates keep out unwanted visitors and the house stands out against the deep greens and browns of the woods high above it and the light greens of the valley grasses like a fortress.

What exactly the story is with the woman who owns the house is apparently open to some debate amongst the scattered cottages and houses along Folly Lane. She never goes to the monthly Neighbourhood Watch meetings that they arrange; nor for that matter do I any longer. I was told that she did not give any money towards the fête that they organised for the Queen's Golden Jubilee lower down Folly Lane on the outskirts of the town, which closed the road for a day, but was quick to write to the local councillor to complain at the inconvenience of the closure. The only thing that people seem to know is that she is a widow and that her married name is or was Fenshawe. We knew that death had visited the house one weekend three winters ago when a hearse was seen emerging from the great length of the drive, its black metallic body filled with a load of inert flesh inside a fine oak coffin. A death notice appeared in *The Times* soon after, with a request for no flowers and asking for letters of condolence and cheques made out to Cancer Research to be sent to Mrs Fenshawe, Court House, Folly Lane, Nr. Stroud, Glos. I have seen her just once; she was coming out of her drive in a smart black hatchback and looked too young and too attractive, with long black hair and clear, pale skin, to be widowed. With an unnecessary flick of her hair and the car's indicator, she pulled out of her drive and was gone down the lane. Even then, I wanted to find out more.

Bryony hugs her jacket against herself as we walk up the last stretch of the valley path, completing the circuit back to the lane at the side of our cottage. The sun is setting in the west, dipping down beneath the horizon and the Bristol Channel. Perhaps Linda is watching the sun sink beneath the land from her modern brick house in the cul-de-sac that Bryony tells me about as I take Bryony into the porch and help her pull off her boots. Linda used to love our walk.

I have not had a drink for almost twenty-four hours, although the drinks I have not had are beginning to add up in my mind. While Bryony watches Saturday-night television in the sitting room, I cook us a simple supper of pasta and tomato sauce and prepare a green salad. Bryony hears the popping of a cork and comes into the kitchen as I pour my first glass of red wine. I roll it around my mouth, over my tongue, like a polluting, intoxicating blackberry mouthwash. I swallow, and a million nerve-receptors begin their dance.

'Dad, you *promised* me.'

'What did I promise you?'

'That you wouldn't drink.'

'No, I said I wouldn't drink *between* your visits. You're here, Bee. It's okay. I'm only going to have one or two glasses.'

Bryony goes back to the television and I go back to my glass, sitting at the kitchen table. Sounds of laughter and lightweight conversation drift in like litter from the sitting-room, the tinnitus of contemporary life that is designed not to penetrate the brain, only to numb the senses with the banality of it all. An electric anaesthetic; a static discharge. The wine makes me immune, inviolable, strong. I am not an alcoholic. I have days off drinking and can control my intake. It is just that I really like it. It is just that I think about it a lot of the time. It is just that I do not want to stop the drinking surge that I began when they left me. It is just that I am often frightened that I want to die.

In the meantime, I live alone. Bryony rescues me from loneliness for perhaps five days a month. I keep myself busy working, pushing myself to commute by train to London four days a week rather than finding a midweek room in town; the work itself is always a challenge, even though at forty-five I know what I am doing. The art business has never been tougher: a slow recession does that to you.

We eat in silence, Bryony engrossed in the talent show that has now taken over the screen; while I am too tired to demand that she comes to eat at the table at the other end of the room. She is growing up: it seems barely any time at all since I was giving her baths with rubber ducks, washing her fine hair and reading her bedtime stories. Now she will not even let me into her bedroom.

What I do for a living is a little like watching a child grow up: I find young artists fresh from art school, having learnt the rudiments of their craft for three or four years, but with little sense of how to make a go of it in the uninterested 'real world'. Reality bites, the bills come in and they have no way of paying; they get fed up with surviving on a diet of roll-ups and builder's tea, and they come to people like me for advice, support and – that elusive word – *success*. I am not a public relations guru or a marketing man. I am an art historian, or at least that is what I try to tell myself. I explain to prospective buyers in my small gallery in St James's, just south of Piccadilly, that I have learnt from the past and seen the future. The future is contemporary art. But it is not true, of course. The future is the future and art has very little to do with it. Art is not reality; it is not even a version of reality. Art is a luxury good, a necessary evil. I make a living, I used to make quite a good one, out of the venality of collectors and the vanity of artists. Or should that be the other way round?

The successes came regularly in the late eighties and early nineties: Jake Andreiou, Corinne Carr, Sandra Langdon, Max Jones . . . The trouble has always been that success makes artists stray to bigger and more famous galleries: Gagosian, Haunch of Venison, Marlborough. The ones with real clout. I am just a bit-part player on the art stage in the capital; my gallery is like a nursery for tender seedlings that have been left wilting in dark obscurity and need plenty of light and constant watering to bring them round. Suddenly, with no apparent reason or obvious talent for life, some of these etiolating milk-saps spring to noto- riety or sudden acclaim, while others see their talent shrivel in the full glare of the sun and fade away, back into the topsoil of the welfare system. Let's put it this way: the supply of needy seedlings seems to have dried up lately. Perhaps they are taught *business management* at art schools these days. Perhaps success is on the curriculum now.

I survive on past achievements and a reputation for a golden touch that is, uncharacteristically for gold, begin- ning to tarnish. I am no metallurgist and certainly no alchemist these days. My base metal stays base. A few of my artists have remained faithful, however, Jake being one.

Since he started making sculptures out of refuse, garbage found in skips and on weed-strewn building sites, his career has begun to wilt. No one wants this rottenness in their homes. Jake will just not go back to painting the canvasses that made his name. Nothing seems to stop this inevitable death from setting in. Out with the old and in with the new. It is ever thus in the art world.

The cheap red wine is having its way with me and I like what it is doing. It softens the edges of reason. It makes me feel as if I am packed in bubble-wrap; a cocoon that renders the world incoherent. Bryony's programme is in garish colour, almost Technicolor, and I do not like what it is doing to my eyes.

'Bryony, it's time for bed,' I say, without slurring. 'We're going to have an early start tomorrow, if we're going to meet Helen and Clare at Burford.'

'*Da-ad*, I'm nearly thirteen. Mum lets me stay up to ten on weekend nights. It's only *nine* o'clock,' she says, looking at her luminous plastic watch.

'You're not *nearly thirteen*, you little liar, you've only just had your twelfth birthday. We'll make a deal: you can stay up till half past nine, then bed. No reading; lights out.'

'*Da-ad*, I'm going to tell Mum that you're depriving me of my education. Mr Troughton says that we should read whenever we can.'

'Mr Troughton doesn't have to get you up on dark mornings when you're in a grump. Mr Troughton doesn't argue with you about bedtimes.'

After Bryony has gone up to bed, I move over to one of the two plain, off-white sofas that Linda and I bought when we were first married. I wash the covers quite regularly, but they never really come clean now. I sit on the sofa nearest the television, next to the indentation that Bryony's body has left behind. I could pretend that I am as alone as I feel, but there is another presence in this house that needs me.

I wake up lying awkwardly on the sofa and the green display on the video is showing two twenty-five. The wine bottle is empty and a man on the television is attempting to explain gravity to his audience of drunks, insomniacs, night-porters and, perhaps, the odd Open University student. One long, brown collar threatens to take off between the aperture of his beige v-neck and his pale throat, with its bobbing Adam's apple. It attempts to undermine the point that he is making about gravitational pull.

I need to get to bed. It used to be a time that I loved: after the apartness of the day, coming together again with Linda as if we were twins that had suffered an enforced separation. We had our own language; our own way of holding each other at night.

When I take the empty bottle out to the bin by the back door, I hear a sudden movement and see a flash of eyes in the undergrowth at the top of the garden. It is a fox, perhaps hoping to find food in a bin full of glass.

Chapter Two

Knock, knock, knock. Knock, knock, *knock*. A brief silence, then the play of bare feet on the floorboards and a soft thud as Bryony lands on the far side of the bed by the door. She is already dressed and has her old Walkman on.

'YOU DIDN'T ANSWER, SO I JUST CAME IN,' she blurts.

'Bee, turn the volume down; you're shouting.'

I feel as if someone has detuned the television; there is a snowstorm in my head. It must be the heating: I must remember to switch it off at night; it always makes you so dehydrated.

'Dad, what's the time? You said we were going early.'

The alarm clock is saying, impossibly, ten thirty. I cannot believe she did not wake me earlier; I never lie in beyond seven thirty or quarter to eight.

'Bee, give me twenty minutes and I'll be ready. We're not meeting them till twelve; we'll be okay. We'll just have to drive quickly.'

I never drink in the morning, even if I often feel like doing so. My friend Tim persuaded me to go to AA meetings about a year or so ago once it had got to the stage that I was drinking perhaps a bottle of red wine every night when I got back from London. I felt such a fraud: like a hypochondriac who self-diagnoses and misconstrues all of the symptoms. I did not seem to drink like all of the other AA regulars, the bull-necked, crew-cut passive-aggressive lorry driver; the morphine- and alcohol-fuelled surgeon; the signet-ringed golden boy from a local family seat who had drunk himself to the edge by twenty-one. I felt like a liar when I said 'My name is John and I'm an alcoholic.'

I did not believe it, and nor did they. Alcohol is a symptom, not the disease, with me. I gave up on AA after three visits, and have kept on drinking.

An American cartoonist once wrote: 'Another day, another pair of underpants.' Mine are green this Sunday and the jumper that I wear is blue. *Ennui*. That is another symptom of my disease. Each day is so similar to the last that you often forget who you are or where you are in time and space. The months and years go by like something glimpsed out of the corner of your eye and before you know it you are waking up too late.

Bryony is waiting by the car on our gravel parking area at the side of the cottage when I come downstairs, tapping unheard rhythms onto the roof of our old red Volvo estate.

The drive to the wildlife park in Oxfordshire takes almost one hour. Bryony tells me about school in Bristol, about her project on Marilyn Monroe for General Culture.

'I wonder if *she* wanted to be a vet when *she* was growing up,' she says.

'I very much doubt it. I can't imagine her having liked biology, chemistry and all those things you'll need if you want to be a vet.' I avoid the obvious joke about anatomy. I still remember how to behave in company. I often think that my daughter is more mature now than I am. Loneliness seems to make me infantile; my connection to other people, to society, to bloody *civilisation*, seems to have rusted up, corroded somehow. It needs easing, lubricating with drink: alcohol is my WD-40.

The afternoon is enjoyable enough. The mother of the two girls, who seems to ignore Bryony completely and only talks to me and who calls herself Poppy for some reason, even though her given name is Alexandra, is one of those jodhpurs-and-gin women in their early forties, with laughter lines around her eyes and a face, not pretty so much as handsome, that has seen more than its fair share of cross-country hacks and holidays in Barbados. She split from her husband three years ago and does her best to commiserate with my more recent and incomparable pain. We met twelve or so years ago at antenatal classes and our families somehow stayed in touch. The girls gossip happily amongst themselves and spend as much time talking about boy bands and mobile phones as they do looking at the animals.

We say goodbye in the car park, although we end up tailing Poppy and her girls in their Range Rover all the way to Cirencester. The girls turn around every hundred yards or so, it seems to me, to wave and make faces at our car and Bryony waves back at them, grimaces or laughs, beside me in the passenger seat.

The morning after the Paddington rail crash in 1999, the car park at Kemble, the station that serves Cirencester, was littered with iced-up, abandoned cars whose drivers from the town or from this area of Gloucestershire had been injured or killed. Women just like Poppy vie for parking spaces in Cirencester's narrow High Street car park that runs up the centre of the road like a spine. They drive four-by-fours, or sports-utility vehicles, to use the American parlance, although I doubt that these women ever use them for anything more than their endless trips around – or up to – town, with a lower or an upper case 't' depending on whether we are talking about High Glos or London. With a lower or an upper case 'm' for man depending on what kind of chap they are sharing the journey with. With the possible exception of Poppy, their relationships and sex lives seem as healthy as they invariably are of body: these types go on for years, decades; nigh on centuries. I am meant to be at my prime, but I feel desiccated by my lack of contact with woman with a capital 'W'. Dried-out by bodily isolation.

* * *

Dawn breaks grey and windblown over the valley, with a striated sky like the evanescent markings of a mackerel caught in a fisherman's nets. I have been awake since before five, watching the back garden's night-life and the slow coming of day. I wake Bryony at seven and prepare breakfast while she gets dressed upstairs. I used to listen to the *Today* programme on Radio 4, the mellifluous language of the presenters soothing me into my day. Now, I cannot bear all the words: their prolixity seems an empty exercise, a verbal trap. I turn to music channels instead; pop or rock, depending on my mood: back to my teenage years again, with an AOR or MOR twist rather than anything more hard-core or alternative. I hate all that shouting and screaming. I like singers who can hold a tune.

We used to have breakfast together, Linda, Bryony and I. A little unit; I thought of it jokingly as a holy trinity without the religion.

'Dad, have you got any Sugar Puffs? Will Mum be waiting at the station when we get there?' The familiar questions of every other Monday morning, reminding me that Bryony is on temporary loan to me.

The sun flickers through the high hedgerows as we drive down Folly Lane to Stroud. The clouds have been scoured from the sky by the wind and the strobe of light through the hazel hedges sets the pulsing rhythm of headache free in my head, which lasts all day.

At Stroud railway station, I park the car and take Bryony to the waiting room on the down-line side of the platforms. I leave her with a kiss on the forehead, reading her book on budgerigars and their diseases, and climb the steps that lead to the covered wooden bridge over the tracks and back down to the London side of the rails. The shuttle of the loom begins again.

I resist the temptation to watch for Linda coming to collect Bryony. I know that she will be there precisely at eight o'clock, but so is my train and my view is obscured as it pulls into the platform. I get on at the back end of the train, down where the carriages are less crowded with commuters, and where I can have some space to myself. As the carriage pulls past the ticket office, I see Linda bending down to hug Bryony. Her hair is shorter; it used to be halfway down her back when I last saw her, one day when I could no longer resist the temptation and I got to Stroud earlier than usual on a Friday afternoon, before the appointed time of five o'clock precisely, waiting out of sight behind a parked car to see her for the first time in more than six months. That was four months ago, it must be. Now her hair is shoulder-length; it seems to have gained a new lustre and shine. My heart slips like a landslide; I can feel it roiling in my guts. I want to see her all of the time or none of the time.

Paddington station is awash with passengers and people waiting for them. By half past nine, I am wide-awake but also numbed with lack of sleep and tiredness by the early start. The litany, the rosary, of stations is counted off: Edgware Road, Marylebone, Baker Street, Regent's Park, Oxford Circus, Piccadilly Circus. I get off the Tube and cut down Piccadilly, turning off down a narrow passageway opposite the Royal Academy. Hordes of tourists form a queue that stretches right around its great courtyard, waiting their turn to see its latest exhibition. If only I could put an A-board advertising my gallery outside its illustrious front doors.

My gallery would take up roughly one quarter of the Royal Academy's lobby space. It is up on the first floor of a building on Duke Street, whose galleries tend towards the 'Square-Rigged Schooner on a Rough Sea' and 'Sheep on the Wold' school of painting. I show rubbish, and so do they. Mine is *meant*; theirs is unintentional.

Penelope, my gallery assistant, greets me with a cup of strong black coffee as soon as I walk through the door, just as she does each day Monday to Thursday when I am in the gallery. I work at home on Fridays.

There are the usual administrative tasks to go through, telephone calls to return, letters to answer, bills and invoices to pay. My headache will not let up, despite the painkillers slowly spreading through my veins, and I want to be anywhere but here.

Jake Andreiou comes in at two o'clock to discuss his latest project: a series of intricate imaginary towers, helter-skelters, lighthouses, castles in the air, constructed out of refuse and waste metal. I want to be a refuse *refusenik*, but his arguments about contemporary art museums around the world queuing up for this kind of hybrid installation and sculpture convince me, despite myself, to give Jake one more chance. He is a nice guy and we have history, as they say. I still want to help him. I will only be able to exhibit a few of the pieces in my gallery, such is their monumental scale. I know of no private collector who could house them with ease, unless they were placed out-of-doors. They might disintegrate in a heavy rainfall or a high wind.

Penelope is obviously pleased about my commitment to another show of Jake's work in the spring. I think that she secretly quite likes him.

'Did he tell you that the great man himself had shown interest in his new work? He got a phone call last week in his studio?'

'He mentioned it, yes. That's great for him, but I'll believe it when I see it. These collectors are bloody fickle; one minute you're all the rage, the next you're untouchable.'

'Well, I *certainly* don't think he's untouchable.'

'Penelope, don't distract him, he's got a lot to do by February.'

When I get off the train at Stroud around eight o'clock that night, I walk to the one gallery in town for their opening of *Modern British Artists and the Abstract Idiom*. The gallery is hidden away in a courtyard in a beautiful seventeenth-century Cotswold stone building. I am among the first guests to arrive, and the ranked glasses of sparkling wine perspire with dewy freshness. Downing a few of these glasses will be a cure for my headache if ever there was one, an excellent primer for the taxi-ride home and the night ahead on my own.

The gallery soon begins to fill out on both exhibition floors with worthies and art-lovers from the local area. The large-format abstract canvasses somehow remind me of migraine auras, amoeba-like shapes that float and swirl against throbbing, impastoed greens, violets and oranges that dominate the compositions. I wander through the clusters of people with their knitted clothes and brows, wondering whether I should walk back to the office of the local taxi firm on the approach road to the station or stay for a couple more glasses of wine, humiliating myself as I look for some-one to talk to.

I first catch sight of her out of the corner of my eye. It is that certain shade of deep brown, almost black, hair that I find irresistible. She has her head turned away from me, but I feel almost sure who she is before she turns around. She is standing with her head bent slightly to one side and holding a glass in her hand. She is noticeable because she is one of the only people in the room who is actually looking at the pictures. A kindred spirit, even if this body of work is far from my kind of thing.

I decide that the best approach is to go to stand next to her and pretend to scrutinise the painting, then to engage her in conversation. She can have no idea who I am. She takes a sip of red wine as I walk up beside her to look at the large lime-green- and puce-coloured canvas on the wall. She seems to wince very slightly, but it could be from the wine.

'That's a fine one, isn't it?' I say, without slurring. She laughs, but does not reply.

'I'm sure I've seen you before somewhere. Do you ever go to galleries in London, by any chance?' I try again. I am the original source of uninspired chat-up lines.

'Which one, in particular?' she asks. She has a voice like melting butter.

'My small contemporary art gallery in Duke Street, St James's. Not far from the Royal Academy up on Piccadilly.'

She does not seem impressed that I run my own outfit, or even to have heard the details of what I have said. 'I hardly ever go to galleries up there these days. I'm not really in Town that much any more. I work as a solicitor for a firm in Cheltenham and it's quite busy at the moment.' She turns to face me as she says this and her eyes and lips are like a blow to the solar plexus.

'Are you from around here?' I ask.

'I grew up near Cheltenham.'

'Does the place have a name?'

'It's in the middle of nowhere. I don't imagine someone like you'd ever have heard of it,' she replies.

Just as I am about to reply that I know this county like the back of my hand, like the soles of my feet, like the soul of my being, a well-groomed man perhaps fifteen years her senior comes up and touches her elbow. He leans over her shoulder, slightly flushed, and says, 'Coming, then?'

'I've just been talking to this nice man about art and things. Philip Howard meet Mr–?'

'Stack, John Stack, as in hay.' She looks at me blankly as I say my name and the man smiles and turns away. She has no idea that we are near-neighbours. She touches my arm and says, 'I've got to go.' She is led away by him to the door of the gallery and disappears. She did not, I realise, tell me her name. She did not need to; I already know it or, at least, I know the last part: Fenshawe.

Chapter Three

It starts off sweet and gets bitter, than goes back to sweet again. Pernod and blackcurrant, sweet cider and snakebite. Those were the drinks that I started off drinking with my friends in the local village pubs around Gloucestershire when I was about fifteen years old. I moved on to lagers and real ales, always just social drinking, when I was at university in London in the late seventies, at King's College where the queens and lefties went. Now that my drinking has advanced from hobby to professional pursuit, I will probably graduate to sherry, brandy, port, dessert wine, perhaps even scrumpy cider when I am in my advanced dotage. I am sure to develop a sweet tooth again; people who drink usually do. It is that or the effervescent thrill of methylated spirits, I suppose.

I am still at the bitter-sweet stage. Drinking is to me what golf is to a golfing pro or skydiving is to a skydiving champion. I want to master it, to hone my sipping, my savouring, my guzzling skills each day. It gives me a buzz like no other.

Those eyes, that mouth. Can you fall in love with someone while you still love someone else? The house is marooned in silence as I try to access my gallery emails. Many Fridays at home I spend like this, daydreaming or walking across the fields to one or another pub for a quiet pint or three, making truncated conversation with the barman or sitting in the snug bar trying to read a book. I ring in to the gallery perhaps twice for a progress report from Penelope or her assistant, Rowena, the assistant of an assistant who works on Fridays and Saturdays and who looks like a young woman from a Northern Renaissance masterpiece, but actually lives in Hackney. I have too much time on my hands and, if it is one of the two weekends each month when Bryony is not coming to stay, it stretches ahead of me like a dead calm at sea.

October, the heart of the autumn, is the month when I perhaps love Gloucestershire the most. Trees have always been the things that have rooted me to this place: the great canopies of elm and beech, the ancient gnarled trunks of oak and hawthorn, the generosity of walnut-tree and chestnut.

It is nearly three o'clock on this particular Friday afternoon in October when I decide to go for a long walk through the woods. I would like to get a dog, but my being away from the Stone House so much means that this cannot happen. I do not know the other households in our hamlet well enough to ask them to keep an eye on it during the days when I am in London.

Someone or something has been ringing our home telephone in the late evenings since July, perhaps once or twice each week. I pick up the receiver and all I hear is the quiet, rhythmical breathing of silence and static. I wonder whether it is some automated sales line with a fault, a glitch, a ghost in the machine. At first, I hoped that it might be Linda. I still hope that it might be her, those nights when the telephone rings and no one is there, but I know that hope won't make it true. Perhaps I should report the glitch to the fault-repair or nuisance-call lines in the front of the telephone book. I think I would rather that the telephone still rang. Out of the silence, out of the blue.

The weather is cold and clear and the woods sigh in the breeze. The stream is very full and dams of moulding leaves and twigs do not impede its flow. I cannot resist it. I want to go and see her house again; to be near beauty in this pallor of autumn twilight.

The iron gates are shut. Darkness is coming down and the Cotswold stone façade of the house looks back at me blankly, darkly through the iron bars of the gates, with only one light on in a window high up in the eaves. This place is absolutely silent; only the wind gives it a sense of time, of movement, of texture.

I do not know how long I have been standing at the wide gates when something makes me turn to face up the drive behind me. The great march of plane trees and beeches makes an abrupt right-hand turn about one hundred yards from the house, up towards the head of the valley. Car lights are flickering through the darkness of the trees. The sounds of the engine, from this distance, are dissolved by the wind.

The car is almost invisible; only its headlights and the bonnet that they define betray the roughness of the drive-way as it bumps slowly down the slight incline, then turns left and heads towards me as I retreat into the trees at the side of the house. She must not see me. She would not understand why I am here, not yet.

The gates slide open and the car crunches onto the gravel forecourt of the house. She was not driving. She was the shape in the passenger seat beside the driver on the side nearest to me, I am sure of that. I am also sure that my secret is safe, that she did not see me. It is fairly dark and I was well hidden by the trees. Car doors slam solidly, expensively, twice. It is her house but not her car. A bright light comes on at the front of the house as I follow a small animal track up through the wood. Why am I always on the outside; out in the cold?

It is already past five thirty when I get back to the Stone House, after my long walk up through uncharted stretches of the wood. I am not scared of the dark. When I was a boy of fifteen or sixteen and first went out drinking in the pubs in the villages around Stroud with my friends, I used to leave them at closing time and walk home across the common-land or through the dense woods or empty fields around the town as midnight turned into the early hours of morning.

What would I have done if she had seen me? What would I have said? Perhaps I would have stumbled off up the driveway, making a fumbled and ambiguous gesture of confusion and apology as the headlights caught me in their glare. But she would not have seen me; not because I was well-hidden, but because the solipsism of beauty makes it so. They never seem to see you.

Bryony calls for a short bedtime chat at eight; otherwise, the evening is very quiet and slips away down the gentle neck of a bottle of Fleurie from 1985. I miss Bryony more when she calls; the alienation effect of the telephone makes her not being here all the more real.

I cannot stay stranded like this. Saturday morning crackles with sunshine and frost underfoot.

When you are a newly single or divorced woman, married couples tend to avoid inviting you around or having you to stay, for fear that you lead the man astray. When you are in the same position as a man, married couples are only too keen for you to come over for the weekend; the men for someone to discuss finance, football, filth or school fees with, depending on their class and their proclivities, and the women to complain about their men in a gently mocking, sexually faithful way, to make you feel a little better as a man.

Tim and Joanna are such a couple. They live the right side of Swindon in the Wiltshire countryside. They have two children and are very rarely doing anything at the weekends or at night, except avoiding making more children, and there is a palpable cheer in Tim's voice when I ring him to ask if it would be alright to come over. Tim sends a muffled 'Jo, it's Jack. Is it okay if he comes over this *afo* and stays the night?' out into the ether. I do not hear her reply, but he says 'Of course, matey' in any case.

I went to school with Tim for five years, one of those middle-ranking public schools that inspire chips on shoulders and poor use of language. Tim's insistence on calling me Jack, ever since the second year when we met, is typical. He is a St Botolph's Academy man through and through.

The drive through the Gloucestershire countryside into Wiltshire is beautiful. I avoid using main roads where possible, relying instead on instinct and the occasional reference to my road atlas as I drive through a maze of high-hedged lanes, Cotswold dry-stone-walled roads and blind turns. A woman getting lost is the next passer-by's friend. A man getting lost swears blind that he knows where he is going and refuses to wind down the window. God knows what I would do if the lane ended in a ploughed field or petered out into pastureland. Turn back, I suppose, and try the next turn in the maze. It reminds me of a friend's cat when I was a child: it became senile and the family found it walking forwards, but going nowhere, in a hedge. It had been missing for some days.

I find my way, however. My muddy car pulls up in their driveway. Their two children, one boy and one girl both around seven or eight, run out and ask if I have brought any presents with me. 'Not unless I've hidden them in the boot,' I tease them. I do not think that they get the joke.

'Presents, presents,' they shout, leaping around the back end of the car.

'I must've forgotten them at home. I promise to bring them with me the next time I come.' They do not hide their disappointment. They let it out all over their faces as only children do. They always call me Uncle Jack, which is a little strange, as I do not have any brothers or sisters.

It is only late lunchtime, but Tim and Joanna have opened a bottle of red wine. We sit in their conservatory while the children play elsewhere in the house. It is all a bit *cheap*. The conservatory looks as if it is made out of some kind of plastic and the wine tastes as if it has been bottled in it. Theirs is an artifice, a facsimile, a simulacrum of an existence. Still, they treat me like family and make me feel at home.

'So, have you got anyone in your life at the moment?' Joanna asks.

'What, you mean apart from my artists?' I reply.

'Anyone *female* and *un*-artistic,' Tim adds.

'Not at the moment. There's no one at the moment,' I say.

'I think you have to try to put the past behind you somehow. I don't mean forget, just give yourself the chance for a new life with someone,' Joanna says.

'How's the drinking, by the way?' Tim asks, pouring me another glass of wine.

'It's going quite well, doctor,' I reply.

'No, seriously,' he says.

'I am being serious. By the way, talking of *adult* things, I did sort of meet someone. A near-neighbour, although she doesn't know it.'

'What do you mean?' Joanna says.

'Well, I met her out of context, only for two minutes, though. She doesn't know that I live in Stroud and that my intentions are wicked.'

'Does she even know your name?'

'I told it to her, but I'm sure she's forgotten it.'

'How will you make her remember?' Joanna asks with a slight *non sequitur*.

'It'll involve walking.'

'Spring-heeled Jack,' Tim says. 'It'll involve actually talking to her as well, I presume?'

'I suppose it will,' I reply.

'What d'you mean, *walking?*' Joanna asks.

'She lives down in the woods.'

'What, like some kind of hermit?' Tim says with his fourteen-year-old's laugh.

'Not many *inclusas* are holed up in a large Georgian pile,' I reply.

'Not many *inamorata* are completely unaware that they're the object of someone they don't know,' Joanna surprises me with her vocabulary. 'It sounds a little like stalking.'

'It'll only be like that until she wants me to be around. She won't be able to resist me in the end.'

By nine o'clock, the children are asleep and we have been drinking red wine for seven hours. A cavalry, a cavalcade, a motorcade, a menagerie of drunks are staggering through my brain. I feel that my tongue, my teeth, my words are being juggled by a mime-artist as I try to speak.

'You're so lucky to have each other,' I garble. They both smile encouragingly.

'What I mean is, you deserve each other.' They both laugh.

'Luck has nothing to do with it; not with my looks and charisma,' Tim says, his voice not cracking.

'And I was young and naïve,' Joanna adds.

Neither of them seems drunk; when I count the bottles on the table, their fractions fall heavily on me. What have I *not* to be drunk for? About two months to go until Christmas Day, the second anniversary of Linda's leaving, and I am still on my own.

That day; God, that day. I had gone out for a quick drink on Christmas Eve after the gallery closed for the holidays. I went out with two other gallery-owners from St James's, both bachelors with no particular homes to go to, and a quick drink turned into a very long one. I had looked at my watch at eight o'clock in a pub on Duke Street, with its fake fire and its exhaled bonhomie from the crowd of drinkers sucking in the freedom of a week off work, and promised myself that I would get the ten past nine to Stroud. The next thing I knew, after two shared bottles of champagne in Black's on Dean Street, with its real fire and its pack of media fakirs, it was past eleven and the last train had departed Paddington. No black cab would take me home. I negotiated a fee of two hundred pounds from an Algerian mini-cab driver on Shaftsbury

Avenue and we got to the M40 by half past midnight. I tried to ring Linda to apologise, but there was no answer on her mobile. I dared not try our home telephone, for fear of waking Bryony. I left a short message saying how sorry I was, but she did not call back.

What a Father Christmas I made, stealing into the house at two thirty and tiptoeing with lead boots up to Bryony's room to kiss her goodnight. I had meant to help Linda make her stocking, but she had had to make it on her own. Bryony was sleeping peacefully, the moon sending a chink of light through the curtains onto her pillow and cheek, and I thought then that I had never seen anything more beautiful. I went up to bed, my hangover already developing and the house ice-cold before the heating came on again at dawn. Linda stirred and woke. She simply asked me, with her eyes turned to the wall, to sleep on the sofa downstairs.

In the morning, on Christmas Day, she told Bryony that they were going to visit her sister in Bristol for the day.

'What about Daddy?' Bryony asked.

'Daddy will join us tonight,' Linda answered. Even at ten years old, Bryony knew that her mother was lying to her.

Chapter Four

I am certainly not ugly. People are always curious to know what other people who they haven't met look like. It sometimes seems to be all that they care about. How else to judge a book than by its cover? I am just over six feet tall and have dark brown eyes: Bryony inherited them from me, as I said. My hair is light brown and on a scale of physical attraction between, say, Rudolph Valentino and Rudolf Hess, I would fall somewhere in the middle. I think that I am like a rough diamond: polished on the inside, but a bit uneven and jagged around the edges. I need knocking into shape, a spit and a polish and a spin on the grinder's wheel.

People might assume that I would have an educated English accent, as a man who spent his later boyhood in the well-heeled shires and went to one of the country's minor public schools. That is the type of voice that they would hear in their mind's ear, as it were, when chancing upon my name on my gallery website or seeing my photograph in the back of my old school's yearbook from those days. It is true that I did go to school in this country from the age of twelve and lived here full-time from about fourteen, but my parents were both American. My accent is caught somewhere in the mid-Atlantic, like my childhood. St Botolph's welcomed me into its stone-cold embrace during term-time after I left my prep school in Massachusetts. During the holidays, *vacations* as my fellow Americans would of course call them, I went back home to Washington where my father worked in government. When he was posted to the embassy here we lived in

Belgravia at a very smart address where they entertained a great deal. I was an only child and had a habit of sneaking downstairs to their parties to drink from neglected glasses. If only they had noticed, they might have done something about me then.

Both my parents are dead now. They went back to Washington at the beginning of the nineties after nearly twenty years here, but did not get to call it home again for very long. Washington, D.C. has one of the worst rates of murder in the United States. D.C. might stand for the District of Criminality, the Death of Conscience, or perhaps the Disease of Control. Of course, my parents did not die in a violent way; old age got them first.

Where did Gloucestershire fit in? My parents bought a holiday home, this very house, to escape from the hubbub of the city. We came here most weekends and my mother and I spent much of my school holidays at the Stone House when we moved to England full-time. After Washington, where no one walks and where asphalt and concrete spread wider than the reaches of even the mightiest oak wood, Gloucestershire amazed me. The very *age* of the settled land astounded me; the Iron Age earthworks up on the common-land above Stroud compelled me to walk their contours again and again. I admit that I fell in love with the place and did not want to leave; to go back to school at the beginning of each term or back to the States, even if that was only twice a year to see our extended family and our Washington house. I adapted very quickly to life in England and no longer called the house that I had grown up in over there *home*. I made friends, both at school and here in Gloucestershire, and knew where I wanted to be.

London again: if a tabloid newspaper were to make a crass analogy for this city, it would be a wife-beater. It cannot stop hurting you, dominating you, breaking you down. You cannot stop loving it, needing it, coming back for more.

Jake Andreiou brings in his digital camera to show me some images of his refuse *folies de grandeur*. They are progressing well for mounds of garbage. Penelope joins us for the very intimate presentation on the screen of Jake's telephone and seems to like what she sees. They remind me of a particularly hard kind of confectionery, or of towers of Babel made out of an incoherence of fused flotsam and jetsam.

'We've got about three and a half months until your show in February,' I say. 'We've got to work out what to charge for them, for the smaller and the larger ones.'

'It's pretty much up to you, but it takes me weeks to source the materials and design and build each one,' he says.

Jake is typical for a struggling artist: he charges for his time and materials, like a builder or a plumber. The conceit of Imagination, the mirage of Creativity, the aura of Genius do not shuffle on, from stage left, until they meet with lasting success. Then the premium is on the idea, not its execution.

It is Friday and a beautiful October afternoon. Mine will be the loneliness of the long-distance runner, until Monday comes around the bend in the tracks again. I will not be as lonely as I would like to see myself, however, as Bryony will be deposited by Linda at five o'clock at the station for the weekend. I have something that I need to do before then. I am going down to the house in the woods again. I just need a couple of glasses of red to steady my nerves.

The façade of the house is bathed in sunlight and the iron gates are thrown open wide. I am standing in the aperture of the gates, wondering what to do next. Should I simply walk up to the door and ring the bell or press the buzzer, hoping that she is out and all of this has been some strange mistake or case of misplaced infatuation, or should I wait and hope that she sees me and comes out to ask who I am and what I want?

'Hello?' It is said as a challenge.

I wheel around, already turning a deep shade of crimson, I am sure.

'I-I-hello,' I reply as I am turning to face that voice.

'Ah, the Canadian dry,' she says. 'I was wondering when you were going to show up.' She laughs and those hazel eyes shine as if she means that laughter.

'You can't have been *expecting* me?' I say, in what sounds to me like the high-pitched whine of a puppy eager to please its mistress.

'You knew *exactly* who I was when we met in the gallery. Neighbourhood Watch, you see. There's a photo of you in all of the old brochures that they used to keep shoving through the door, until I told them to stop.'

'But I was on the committee ages ago,' I say feebly, still completely out of sync with the reality of it all. 'I haven't been involved for a couple of years at least.'

'Before your wife–?' she begins.

'There are spies everywhere,' I cut in. 'Neighbourhood bloody Watchers. And I'm not Canadian: I'm American, well sort of.' I try to regain some ground. 'And I certainly wasn't dry that day; had to make that appalling show more palatable somehow.'

'Yes, I noticed,' she replies. 'The paintings were, how can I put it, a little *bacterial*, weren't they?'

She looks me straight in the eyes as we conduct this pantomime of a conversation and she has a pair of secateurs in her left hand. She seems so self-assured, so in possession of herself, and I feel that I am going to sink into the ground with childish embarrassment, or turn to stone with fright. I hope that she cannot smell the wine on my breath.

'Now that you're here, you'd better come inside. No use in standing in the driveway all afternoon,' she says to break our momentary silence, as the birds sing in the trees around us.

'I only came down to introduce myself. I don't want to keep you from what you're doing, if you're busy.'

'I think that the pruning can wait. It's a losing battle anyway,' she replies.

The hallway is furnished in what could be described as the *World of Interiors* style. Celadon-green vases tower against pale Georgian shutters, stripped bare; what look like Afghan or Turkish carpets are spread over naked flagstones; a giant grandfather clock cranks out the minutes and the hours. I can see no pictures, no art, however.

'Us New World types, we go crazy for history like this,' I joke, switching my accent from vague burr to something approaching New York Jewish. She laughs again, a lovely full-throated laugh that plays around the house like the sound of a silver bell. 'No seriously, it's beautiful,' I say.

'A lot of dusting and upkeep,' she replies. 'My late husband bought it before we were married. I can't seem to let it go just yet.'

'I'm sorry,' I say lamely.

'About the house?'

'About your husband.'

'That was a long time ago,' is all she says.

I am trying to look at her as an intelligent, mid-thirties professional woman who is speaking to me openly, articu-lately, rather than as an object of my pent-up male fantasies.

'Would you like a drink?' she says. 'I can offer you tea, coffee, or something stronger if you'd like?'

'How did you know I'd come?' I reply.

'I suppose I thought that curiosity would get the better of you. People around here are very *curious* about me, because I live alone down here in this somewhat notice-able house.'

'It killed the cat,' I say.

'What did; tea or coffee?' she replies with a smile.

'I'd love a coffee. Milk no sugar please. It's a little early for a drink, isn't it?' I say, lying rhetorically.

'So, how does a quiet American end up living on his own in an out-of-the-way Gloucestershire village?' she asks, as we drink our coffees in the sitting-room, which is flooded with light from the high windows.

'That's a long story. Basically, I like it here. And I married an English girl.'

'Two good reasons,' she says with a laugh. Her laugh sounds slightly forced now, as if she is straining for jollity because she is sorry for me somehow, or because there is some spectre in the room that both of us can see but do not want to admit to seeing for fear of alarming each other.

'I must have been coming to Stroud for almost as long as you've been alive,' I say. 'My parents worked over here and bought the Stone House when I was in my early teens.'

'So, you're almost one of us,' she replies softly.

'Did you grow up around here, then?'

'I meant *British*, not part of the local menagerie. But I did, as it happens. In Cheltenham.'

'The posh end of Gloucestershire,' I say, as if competing in some dumb-comment competition.

'It's not all Regency houses and spa water. It has its rough underbelly as well.'

'Yeah, I'm sure. Like South Central LA or Crown Heights,' I say to tease her.

I am not good with birds, but I think that it is a black-bird's voice that sings to fill in the lull in our conversation. She looks over the back of the sofa, out through the double doors onto the large garden at the rear of the house. We are sitting on the same mahogany-coloured Chesterfield, but wide apart, turned towards one another. I am trying to concentrate on not spilling my coffee from its cup into the saucer. My hand is trembling slightly. She smells of lily of the valley and her white teeth look as if they could skin me alive.

'Where does the art business fit in?' she says suddenly to break the silence.

'I show a small group of contemporary artists, but make my living by finding things at auction and selling them on at a profit to my clients. I just need a couple of hits a month to keep going, depending on the margins.'

'You're not working today?'

'I've been taking Fridays off for a long time,' I reply.

I look at my watch while she walks into the kitchen to clear away the coffee cups and the coffee pot, and am surprised to see that it is already nearly three o'clock. 'Talking of taking off, I'd better get going soon. I'm meeting someone in Stroud at five.'

'Well, it's been nice to meet you again. I'll come and surprise you up at the Stone House some time,' she says, coming back into the room.

'I'd like that. "A good neighbour is a friend for life," as they say,' I intone in my mock-New York accent. 'By the way, you haven't told me your first name.'

'It's Nicola. My name's Nicola, pleased to meet you,' she says with a laugh as I walk over towards the gate, the gravel crunching underfoot.

Back at the Stone House, I shut the sitting-room curtains against the last remaining light draining out of the after-noon and finish the bottle of red in the near-darkness of the room. Did I make a fool of myself? I no longer seem to know how to behave as an adult in the middle of his life. I cannot seem to talk without making stupid jokes. Her beauty only made things worse. It is easier to talk to ugly people; they embarrass you less.

I call the cab company in Stroud and at four thirty a car sounds its horn outside the house. I never drink and drive.

Bryony is waiting on her usual bench at the station and is still reading her book on budgerigars.

'What happened to your hair?'

'Mum said that I could have it cut in a bob.'

'It makes you look like the girl from the film.'

'Which film, Dad?'

'You haven't seen it. It's called *Léon* and it has a girl in it who's about your age and also has a bob. She's very beautiful, like you.'

She rolls her eyes, as if I have made a silly joke.

Chapter Five

The café where I have brought Bryony this Saturday lunchtime is a scrum of activity. The striped red and blue rugby
shirts of Stroud Town Rugby Football Club, worn by un-
athletic supporters whose paunches are magnified by the
taught horizontal bands across their midriffs, mean that there
must have been a match today. There is a run on fried-egg
sandwiches and tea the colour of rusting iron in rainwater.

We crush ourselves into a corner table by the fire escape
and order toast and jam and tea for two. Bryony disappears
to the lavatory and a man, who has not noticed her in the
melee, asks if he can sit opposite me.

'I'm afraid not. I'm with my daughter, she's just gone to
the bathroom.'

'You mean the "toilet"; we're English here,' he jokes sar-
castically.

'And proud,' I say sharply back.

When Bryony returns, I lean forward conspiratorially and
whisper to her about the man. She giggles and sneaks a
quick look over at him, then eats her toast. The man looks
at me openly, rudely on and off for the rest of the time that
we are in the café; he stands propped against the counter
to eat his sandwich and stares over at me in between bites,
when he focuses all of his energy on making sure that the
egg does not drip down his front.

The weather is icy and Bryony does not want to help me
in the garden after lunch. She stays in the warmth of the
house to watch Saturday-afternoon television.

I rake up a subdued horde of frozen leaves like the devil counting in his lost souls. Once disturbed from their secure resting-places, the breeze moves them over the ground and makes them hard to capture. Pigs are squealing on Plawhatch Farm down the valley. They are either being mated or killed.

'Dad, you know that tree-house that I used to play in at the top of the garden when I was little? Let's go and see if it's still there.' I jump; she was so quiet that I did not even hear her come out of the house.

'That's a good idea, darling. I haven't looked for it for years.'

We walk slowly up to the top of the garden, through the sloping stand of ash and sycamore that form the upper limits of our space before it gives way to farmland, hand-in-hand as we did when Bryony was still a little girl, not this half-child, half-wise thing that she has become. The tree-house is dilapidated and sagging forwards out of the high tree. The ladder has fallen and is rotting in the grass.

'You're a bit grown up for tree-houses now, aren't you, Bee?' is all I can say to comfort her.

All of the next week, the commute is slowed by an early fall of snow that settles to ice on the tracks. I have to wake at five on the four days that I go into the gallery. The journey takes three hours each way in this weather. A bottle of red each evening knocks me out by ten o'clock and I sleep, sometimes on one of the sofas, until the pre-dawn chorus starts to sing its blacked-out song.

There is a problem in the gallery. One of my two banks wants to foreclose on their loan that I took to buy a group of pictures at auction. I had a client in mind for them, but the deal fell through and now I have stock on my hands that I cannot yet shift. On Wednesday, after some anxious telephone conversations, the bank gives me three months to settle the outstanding amount of eighteen thousand pounds. I have until just before Jake's show, as it happens, to sell the works, or to find another way of repaying the money. Ten years ago it would have been easy; that amount of money would have meant much less to me.

There is one piece of *good* news at least: the critic, Charles Everard, has agreed to write the foreword to Jake's small exhibition catalogue. Having a well-known voice to say-so Jake's work will, I pray, mean a few sales. I cannot afford the show to be museum-like: pored over by goateed critics and public alike, whilst not one piece actually sells.

By the end of the week of snow, I am weighted down, muffled by tiredness. Sometimes I think that it would be easier to live in London, but I cannot leave the Stone House. It is what I know, where I come from. The US is a mirage, a construct of my past. I feel no connection, no affinity, no *love* for that country, that place. Washington? Who would feel at home there? Politicos, hacks and weirdoes, no one else. When I last visited, before my parents died, everyone thought that I was a Brit. Perhaps I am now, British that is. The Republican has been washed right out of me. Republicanism has never been a hit in this country: look at warty Oliver Cromwell and how he is thought of today. This is a country of Queen Mother-mug-supping publicans, not republicans.

Friday early morning and the hedges are alight with snow in the dark. I need to breathe, to get some fresh air into my lungs. By eight o'clock I am already out walking as if in a fugue state, letting my body take me where it wants to go. It follows the road into Stroud, although that is the last route that I would want to walk on such a beautiful day as this. It follows the road into Stroud and stops for a rest at a sharp, steep downward bend in the road about a mile from the Stone House. The tarmac gleams with black ice and I cannot bear to stay here long. The trees overarch the road to form a green tunnel, which is dark and oppressive and speaks of that fatal collision between man and nature, even as the sun shines in the sky above the gloom.

I continue downhill towards the town then turn off up a footpath still covered in a thin layer of untrodden snow. It would do me so much good to be able to walk this landscape with someone again, someone *female* and *unartistic*, as Tim and Joanna joked. There is one set of footprints in the snow behind me; there will be one pint glass at the pub table at lunchtime; there was one bowl and one spoon in the kitchen sink this morning. I am bloody fed up of speaking in monologue.

I head up to Bisley, which is a four-mile walk from here across the frozen landscape and nestles high up on the Cotswold escarpment. This morning is one of those crystal-clear days when the air pricks your throat with its rawness and you can see for miles. I feel like one of those figures in a Caspar David Friedrich painting, dwarfed by the nature around him and yet a part of it. Hopeful, yet somehow flawed. Fully alive, yet tragic.

In the Bear Inn, the publican says, 'I haven't seen you or the missus around here for a long time. You used to be quite the *regliers*,' as he pours me a pint of bitter.

'Times and habits change,' I dissemble, patting my belly, as if to indicate that I am taking better care of myself and that life is somehow still the same, only with less beer and less of his company.

Linda used to love this pub: its honey-coloured Cotswold stone walls, the highly polished horse-brasses, the dark oak country furniture, the winter evenings in front of the fire in the snug bar. Sometimes we would walk here and back home again on weekend evenings, taking Bryony with us in a carrier on our backs when she was still little and walking her slowly hand-in-hand-in-hand between us when she was able to manage the distance. Linda always drank sweet Somerset cider, or the bad house red that they serve here. Her face was radiant in the heat from the fire.

I order a second pint, then a third. The barman asks, 'Not working today?'

'I never work on Fridays, they're sacrosanct,' I reply. 'My wife had something wrong with her sacrosanct,' he says. 'She had to go and see the osteopath.' He laughs and laughs.

When I get back to the Stone House towards four o'clock, there is a rolled sheet of paper pushed into the letterbox. It is a note on cream-coloured headed wove in a precise, almost copperplate hand:

THE COURT HOUSE, FOLLY LANE, NR. STROUD, GLOS.
Dinner sometime? Nicola F.

No supper and a bottle of red. The night comes down like black ink in water.

I am just dropping off to sleep when the telephone rings. A branch taps against the windowpane in Morse code. I lift the receiver on the bedside table and put it to my ear: the quiet inevitability of static.

'Hello–? Hello–?' There is the susurration of silence.

'*Hello?*' I repeat more loudly.

'John . . .' It is said very quietly, as if from another dimension. It is said in what sounds like Linda's voice. 'John.' There it is again, almost inaudibly.

The line goes dead suddenly. I dial 1471 and another woman's voice says: 'The caller *withheld* their *number.*' I dare not call back. I cannot call back: I do not have Linda's home number. I only ever call Bryony on her mobile. It always seems to go to voicemail these days.

I lie in bed listening to the sounds of the night and wondering whether I imagined that voice. I lie in bed listening to the steady thump of my heart and knowing that it still misses her as dangerously as forgetting to beat. I lie in bed missing Linda with all my heart, but all I can see is Nicola's face in my mind's eye. How fickle men are. I cannot get to sleep until almost dawn.

Chapter Six

'Hello. 'Sthat Nicola?'

'Speaking. *John*? No one else lives here, you know,' she says with a lightness to her voice that could be easily addictive.

'Thanks for the note. You've got very nice handwriting.'

'That's alright. What about the contents?'

'I'd love to. I was trying to pluck up the courage to ask you the same question myself.'

'It took you a while,' she says. 'You've been away?'

'I'm sorry; the last ten days have been very hectic in London. What about that little Italian in Stroud, my treat?'

'Is she now?' she laughs.

'What's it called? La Tragedia? La Treatoria?'

'*Il Trovatore*.'

'That's the one. What about this Friday at eight? I'll pick you up in a cab.'

'Will you now?' she laughs again.

I am thinking about her all of the week at the gallery and as I shuttle back home again. I hardly know her. She is *gorgeous*. When did I last hear anyone laugh in my presence *in a good way*? She lives alone. Is she secretly deranged or mad? Her lips; she is *lovely*. My thoughts go round like a game of swing-ball. I send them out into the ether and they come back at me with a lateral wallop but go nowhere.

Jake says that the works are ready; that he can do no more for the show. He invites me to his studio on the Wednesday and I find myself in some godforsaken council-estate-strewn road off Brick Lane that afternoon, dodging dog turds and their progenitors. An East End dead-end leads to his first-floor co-op studio like a sentence ending in a hackneyed cliché.

Music is blaring from behind a steel door: something bass-driven from my side of the pond. Jake is hammering what looks like a steel tent-peg into the base of a two-foot-high piece made up of scrap metal. He makes a syncopated rhythm in diametric opposition to the thrum of the music.

'Angel of the Suburbs,' he says in his Estuarine twang.

'Are you Romanian somewhere along the line? Brancusi was a great sculptor,' I shout over the noise.

'Andreiou's Cypriot. My dad came over in the fifties. He worked for the Post Office,' he says as he walks over to the stereo to kill the music.

'Let's hope that this show will *stamp* your reputation on the London scene.'

'Boom *boom*,' he says. 'John, that was truly dreadful. Do you want a drink? I've got whisky or lager.'

'I'll have both, please: one to chase the other.'

'I didn't know you were a tippler, John. You always seem such the controlled English, er Canadian, gent.'

'*American*. And gents, I can promise you, know the Twelve Steps better than most.'

'Sounds like the Brownshirts out a-marching again,' he says with a grin.

'Twelve Steps, not goose-steps, you prat,' I say, walking around the Angel. 'This is strong, *tectonic*.'

'Thanks. As you can see, there are plenty more like that.'

'Where are the full-size ones?'

'In the courtyard. We'll need a hoist and a flatbed to get them to Piccadilly.'

'Getting them up to the first floor will be interesting. They'll have to take that large window out and get them in that way.'

We take our drinks out to the courtyard, reverberating down a set of iron fire-escape stairs attached to the back of the building. Jake's sculptures out here remind me of the aftermath of a giant explosion in a metalwork shop or smithy; or of what would happen if the sudden inward force of gravity were applied to constellations of weightless, icy asteroids and intergalactic waste. They would collapse together like this horde of golems in a post-modern Big Bang. Jake's sculptures are the collision of objects frozen in time. The human presence, the *ownership*, is long gone. We are left with accretions of found metal waste that tower around us like strange giant cacti. They are as weightless and remote as those asteroids and meteorites.

'These should give the critics something to write about,' is all I can think of saying in the way of praise.

I have not had a woman since Linda. That is not entirely true: I have not had a *relationship* since Linda. I made a fumbled pass at Rowena, the Titian-haired assistant-of-an-assistant at the gallery. She seemed to reciprocate and came down to stay for a weekend at the Stone House. It was in the spring, about six months ago. I felt so terribly lonely. I just wanted some human contact, the warmth of skin on skin. I kept thinking that she just felt sorry for me. I kept talking about Linda. We had very un-erotic sex, more like a penetrative cuddle, just once that weekend. She said that she liked an older man. I realised that she was still only in her twenties; still learning, still learning. I talked about Linda, have I already said that? At the end of the weekend, I told her that it would perhaps be better if we were just friends. She seemed relieved. She said, 'So have I passed the boss test now, then?' 'What test?' I replied. Now she only works the days that I am not in the gallery. I pay her a part-time assistant's wage nonetheless.

Nicola, *Nicola*. It must mean something in Latin or Ancient Greek. I wish that I had paid more attention to the Classics at school.

Christmastide, as the marketing men probably brand it in their mad bubble-speak, has already reached the West End. The lights on Oxford Street and Regent Street hypnotise the hard-of-cash and lure them from the English regions to spend their money on things that their children will soon grow tired of, or that will have sunk into obsolescence and be superseded before the year is out and Christmas comes round again.

The lights pulse and flicker with the ebb and flow of the crowds. What to buy for Bryony, the girl who wants nothing but to be my daughter again? What to do about Nicola: should I bother to buy her something, or is it presumptuous of me to hope that we will meet again after our first date, nearer Christmas when present-giving to virtual strangers might seem a little less strange? The lights pulse and flicker and I cannot decide.

Christmastime, mistletoe and wine,
Children singing, what a waste of time . . .

That eternal Peter Pan with his tight trousers and sun-fried skin seems to be singing in his piped voice. The mall echoes with his canned delivery and there can be no greater prophylactic against creative seasonal present-buying than a concrete shopping centre drowning in the halitosis of the crowds, as if emanating from Peter Pan's own goaty, foetid throat. London is only good for shopping if you are a tourist or if you have a lot of money, and then only if you do not need to work for it *and* shop here.

On Thursday evening I get back to the Stone House by eight. The snow and ice have melted away; the earth smells of decaying plant-life and the air of winter bonfires and the smoke from numberless hearths across the valley.

The woods are pitch-black after my supper of tinned lobster bisque and red wine. I walk carefully down through the trees, only switching on my torch at the most precarious sections of the twisting animal paths that lead down to the house. The lights are on up on the top floor. I sit on a damp, slug-infested fallen tree-trunk on a steep bank roughly level with the top of the building, but can see no movement inside. I wait and wait until almost eleven thirty. These old opera-glasses from my mother are beginning to hurt my eyes.

I just want to feel close to her. Sometimes it is so lonely coming back to my empty cottage. Scanning from left to right along the back of the Court House, there is a large bedroom on the top floor with its lights on, although I can only see a corner of a bed and a wardrobe, and next to it there is a room that I cannot yet identify, as it is in darkness. I guess that it might be a bathroom. In the third room, the most clearly visible from this angle, there are shelves and shelves of books: a small library or study, and what appears to be an exercise machine. It is a work-out room for body and for mind.

I have been waiting more than two hours on this damp log and my breath condenses in the air as the temperature falls. The bottle of red wine, as if turned by Christ's will to white wine vinegar, needs an outlet. Obeying some ancient sense of decorousness, despite the complete darkness at this distance from the house, I face away from the Court House and piss into the undergrowth.

When I turn around again, she is standing in the open bedroom window in what appears to be a white silk dressing-gown, blowing smoke from a cigarette out into the night. I did not know that she smoked.

I am only about fifty yards away and dare not move. I know that she cannot hear me, but sounds travel for miles at night. After two minutes, me breathing quietly and my heart pounding in my chest, she flicks the butt-end out of the window onto the pea-gravel below, turns away from the window and extinguishes the light. She has not seen me. It is almost a moment of intimacy in the loneliness of the night.

Chapter Seven

Bryony calls before she goes to school on Friday morning. She sounds a little lost and sad. 'Dad,' she says in her small voice, 'one weekend when I come can we go Christmas shopping together?'

'Of course, Bee. I was planning that anyway. I'm looking forward to it very much.'

It is early, seven thirty or a quarter to eight, and I lie in bed with the receiver of the bedside telephone propped next to my head on the pillow. She tells me about school, about some boy in the class above her who she likes, and talks about animals, animals, animals.

'I saw a programme about orang-utans in Sumatra. They're *amazing*, Dad. That funny Australian man and his snakes and crocodiles: I want to be like him.' I listen and listen, drinking in her voice.

'*Dad*, are you there?' she asks. 'ARE YOU STILL THERE?'

'Yes, I'm here, Bee. I'm just a bit tired, that's all.'

I wake up with a cracking headache at ten o'clock. I must drink more water after drinking wine. The heating comes on at five and dries you out like a toad in the sun. I have an ache in the pit of my stomach. I feel queasy from the hangover and I am nervous about tonight.

The thrum of my headache drowns out thought. What should I wear? Should it be a smart suit and tie or casual jeans and jacket? Should I make a mature gentlemanly effort or display a boyish, relaxed ease?

Tim has a business appointment in the area and is coming over for lunch. I am meeting him at twelve thirty in the Bear Inn. He insisted on picking me up. I insisted on walking. He has always been there for me when I needed him most as a friend, but two or three pints or one or two hours in the presence of his St Botolph's Academy tie that he insists on wearing for work are enough for me at the moment.

Penelope rings from the gallery at eleven. Jake wants to know if I have heard any more about the catalogue text from Charles Everard.

'No, but I spoke to Charles a couple of weeks ago and he's on the case. Jake needs to relax; we've still got three weeks till it goes to print.'

'Jake *relax*? He's a real live wire, I can tell you,' Penelope says with mischief in her voice.

'Is he now? You can spare me the details and the blushes,' I shoot straight back.

Perhaps I could spend the rest of my natural life conducting all of my human interaction by telephone. Never mind that 'no-man-is-an-island' routine: I feel like some uninhabited isle off the coast of Chile or any one of a myriad of anonymous islets in a giant thousand-island archipelago in the seas off south-east Asia.

Tim is not an island. His family is something like a city-state, self-contained and self-determining; the Vatican, perhaps, but without the religion. It lets in visitors, but they are always just that: *visitors*. They can never belong, unless they are blood.

He is thumbing his palm-pilot and feeding some work-speak into his mobile when I get to the table that he has snagged in the Bear.

'Push up the bottom line and cost out the differentials . . . No, I told Fenella to adjust her Bloombergs . . . Yep, they've raised the bar to two percent collateral . . . What? I don't *care* what Quintin said. Can you wire through the spreadsheets. Uh b-bye-bye,' and with that his mobile is flipped shut.

'Sorry about that, old boy,' he says in his best Old Botolphian. 'It's all work, work, work.'

'Tell me about it,' I say, putting my walking-booted feet up under the table on the free chair next to him and downing in one gulp half the pint of Old Brock that he has bought in readiness for my arrival.

'How's the bank?'

'They've given me three months, until the end of February. Sounds a bit like a cancer prognosis.'

'D'you think you'll make the repayment?'

'I think I'll just have to shut the gallery after the March show and sell what stock I have at auction, probably at a loss. Having a gallery in London requires a lot of financial backing these days and that's been my problem. I'm also bloody fed up with the commute.'

'But all that time and *effort* you've put into it, Jack,' he says with genuine sentiment. 'It's a bloody shame, matey.'

'At least I haven't got a mortgage to worry about. All I need to do is cover food and bills.'

'It would've been different if Linda and Bryony were still around,' he says. 'You'd have fought for it tooth and nail. It would've been different.'

'But they're not, are they?'

'That's the bloody awful part, that's the awful part. Why do you always sound so *bitter* when you talk about Linda, rather than sad? Is it just an American thing?'

'It's a life thing; it's a life thing. I'm not bitter, I'm bloody *angry.*'

'How's the drinking?' he asks after a long pause.

'This pint's almost finished. I'll get us two more.'

'I'll have a half of orange and lemonade. I've got the company Beemer in the car park.'

'You remember when we used to come here in the school holidays and drink snakebites underage?' I ask. 'I wonder when things changed.'

'Life changed, I suppose,' he says.

'You know I was telling you I'd kind of met someone? I've got a date with her tonight in Stroud.'

'What's she called again?'

'Nicola.'

'Like the sexy Nicola Six in that Martin Amis novel?' he sniggers.

'Quite a lot like her, actually. But without the darts.'

'But with the stockings and things?' he says like a school kid.

'Who knows?' I reply. 'We'll see. She's got the looks and the figure.'

'Lucky you, I hope. She gets murdered, doesn't she?'

'What d'you mean?'

'In the book's version of events.'

'Don't worry, life won't imitate art,' I reply.

I order the taxi for seven thirty, knowing that the one firm in Stroud is always late. My headache is occluded by the three and a half painkillers that I have taken. It is like a partial eclipse of the sun: the pain is a bright disk burning itself onto the retinas. Its cure is a black planet exactly the diameter of the pain, but it has not yet aligned itself into perfect linear space to block out the heat, the searing intensity of the neuralgia.

I stand in the full-length mirror that Linda used to use to dress. Looking at my white figure naked, not at all flabby but undefined by lack of exercise, I feel like a pale ghost staring into a two-way mirror with Linda on the other side. I have the strange feeling that the minutes and the hours that she might have spent in front of this mirror have somehow imprinted themselves onto its surface. I feel embarrassed for myself as she watches me.

I decide to wear a suit and tie to show her that I am making an effort. Do I mean Nicola or Linda? I am no longer sure.

The taxi arrives at ten to eight and we are already late as we bump down the long drive of the Court House. The gates are shut and there is a moment when I think that they are firmly locked; that she has forgotten and must be out. It is just a tricky gate-latch, however.

The taxi driver turns the car around laboriously and heads a short way up the pitch-black drive, then stops. The car's lights illuminate the trees, whose trunks cast long shadows along the verges of the drive like the legs of a procession of giant figures who are watching me. I am stranded on the gravel in front of the gates like an orphaned child begging for food at the local manor. The car's poor engine chokes out a low growl behind me.

'John. I won't be a second.' I cannot tell where her voice is coming from. Its timbre has the texture of chocolate left too long in the sun.

One half of the large oak front door suddenly opens and the electric light from inside casts an anamorphic rectangle of light out onto the forecourt of the house. Nicola is transfigured in the doorway, rummaging in her black patent-leather handbag for something. She pulls out a set of keys and turns to face me, flashing me an almost shy smile. She is wearing a simple, knee-length green dress the colour of good jade and made out of a material that looks like cashmere, and has a thick white woollen waist-length coat wrapped around her shoulders. She pulls the door shut behind her and locks it twice, then hides the keys under the stones surrounding a water-butt to the left of the door.

'I always know where they are then,' she says.

'You look very nice. Sorry I'm a bit late. Our chauffeur is waiting.'

'D'you think I might be a bit overdressed for Il Trovatore?'

'The good citizens of Stroud won't know what's hit 'em. You'll knock 'em dead.'

'You look very smart yourself. Have you come from a business meeting or something?' she asks.

In the taxi, she tells me about her week and leans in

close to me as she looks into the driver's rear-view mirror to put on some lipstick. I try to stifle an erection.

Stroud is asleep when we get there and it is not even a quarter to nine. The clock on the Town Hall appears to have stopped. Every pub that we pass on the way seems to be full of people, but no one is out on the street.

'It's-a de *fut*-bol,' the waiter says as he shows us to our table in the half-empty restaurant.

'What football?'

'*Whad-a fut*-bol?' he says incredulously in an exaggerated Italian accent, even though I have seen him around the town since he was a child and he is no more native Italian than a Starbuck's caffè latte. 'It*a*lia versus England, that's what.'

'Who are you supporting?' Nicola asks with a twinkle in her eye.

'Who I support? Come on-a,' he says. 'Basta. Whaddya drink?'

'A bottle of your best red, please. Preferably light and fruity. How's the old man?' I ask him. '*When I was a child he used to do odd-jobs for my parents,*' I add in a whisper to Nicola as an aside.

He walks off with a sour look on his face. I hope that he does not spit it into my food.

'So, hello again,' I say, smiling and leaning forwards to pour her a glass of water from the bottle on the table.

'Yes, hello,' she says. 'It's nice to see you again.'

'It's a little strange, isn't it?'

'What is?'

'That we never met each other before.'

'A small village can be a big place in this country,' she says.

A different waiter brings the wine and asks which of us would like to taste it.

'Women have more sensitive palates,' I say. 'Nicola, you taste it.' She takes a large sip from the glass, draining the small amount of wine, and swallows. She winces as if she has just eaten half a lemon, then bursts out into a beautiful smile.

'It's actually rather nice,' she says. 'You're the expert on alcohol, though, aren't you?' she adds, still smiling.

We have almost finished the first bottle by the time that the main course arrives. Nicola's cheeks are slightly flushed and I order a second bottle as the waiter pours the last dregs of the first into her glass.

'Have you stayed in this area your whole life?' I ask.

'You say that as if it were a crime.'

'It would be a blessing,' I say. 'I love it here. I'm in love with Gloucestershire.'

'I went away to university to study Law in Edinburgh and worked as a junior in a practice for about four years in Bristol, but later on my husband, my boyfriend as he was then, wanted to settle down around here. I'd introduced him to the area. He was a bit like you; worked in London, but came back at weekends and one or two evenings during the week.'

'How did you lose him?'

'What did he die of, you mean? Let's stick to plain English. It was cancer: a brain tumour at forty-one,' she says gently. 'Just over three years ago. He was eight years older than me.'

'That's *terrible*,' I say.

'I've always gone for older men.'

'I'm so sorry.'

'What, about the older men?' she forces a dry laugh.

'I'm sorry about your husband.'

'You don't want to talk about your wife, do you?' she says quietly.

'You probably know the story. Her name was Linda. Our marriage had stopped working. It was my fault. Perhaps I'd been drinking a little too much: work pressure and all that crap. She was angry with me and drove our daughter away on Christmas Day the year before last. That's how it happened.'

'I'm so sorry,' she says echolalically. 'I suppose all people like us can do is to try to get on with living,' she whispers and suddenly leans forward, placing her hand softly on my right shoulder in a gesture of support and solidarity. Her face is so close to mine. I feel myself flushing and beads of sweat begin to break out on my forehead and upper lip. There is that smell of lily of the valley again. She has *eau de nil* eyes that could charm snakes.

'What sort of area of law d'you work in?' I ask to calm myself down when she has drawn back to her side of the table again.

'Oh, family law mostly. Things like wills and conveyancing, with the odd divorce settlement thrown in sometimes. I've never been hugely ambitious about developing my practice. I've always thought of being a solicitor more as a job that uses my brain than as a career with some great outcome just over the horizon.'

'You must've been pretty academic to get into law at university. Your grades must've meant something in the eighties or whenever it was.'

'Is that a leading question by any chance? I'm thirty-six, if you're asking, and was an A-grade kind of girl.'

'I was never that keen on academic work. I just felt that I should at least *try* to go to university to reward my parents for all the school fees they paid.'

'I didn't think private schools were such a big thing in the States?'

'They're not that common, but I went to public school here when my parents moved over for work.'

'What was it called?'

'Oh, I'm sure you've never heard of it. It's a minor one called St Botolph's Academy, just outside Taunton.'

'There are so many minor ones, aren't there? I went to a good old-fashioned girls' high school,' she says.

'Was it like this on your first day of college? I seem to remember all we did was talk about where we went to school and what A-level grades we got.'

'It does seem vaguely familiar,' she replies with a laugh.

The other waiter comes to clear away the remnants of our meal. Nicola has hardly touched her linguine and I have only eaten two-thirds of my *Quattro stagioni* pizza. When he has taken away our plates and cutlery and brought us another bottle of red, I take a large gulp of the delicately blackberry-nosed wine and plunge into the dangerous currents of conversation again.

'Have you met anyone else since your husband's death?' I seem to blurt out very suddenly.

'You don't beat around the bush, do you?' she says and laughs again, perhaps a little nervously this time, then takes a delicate sip from her glass. 'Not being one to scare the children, I've had the odd man ask me out on a date, but nothing too serious. It has always felt a bit soon to get serious with someone again.'

'That makes sense,' I reply. 'And I agree about you not scaring the horses, for the record.'

'Oh, I don't know about *horses*, I might scare them wit-less. I only guaranteed that I wouldn't make *children* run for the hills.' She seems to slur slightly when she says this and almost leans too far back in her chair as she laughs. Her 'What about you?' as she rocks forward again catches me off-guard.

'I, er, no. It's not been that long.'

'No one at all in a year and a half to help you through your grief?'

'No one at all, I'm telling the truth,' I reply. 'I'm not so sure that being on your own is what nature intended. I've never felt so lonely.'

Another taxi picks us up at half past eleven and Nicola leans her head far back on the headrest as we are driven back to the Court House. I think that I have got her a little drunk.

'Had a good night then, sir?' the taxi driver asks.

'Yes, thanks. It was very nice.'

'Are you a tourist to these parts, sir?' he asks, as if he has driven straight out of the Middle Ages.

'No, I live here,' I reply. 'It's home. My accent's just not from around here.'

When we get back to the house, I pay the driver and Nicola opens the right-hand gate like a somnambulist. I retrieve the keys from beneath the water-butt and let us into the hall. Nicola slips off her coat, walks down the hallway into the sitting-room and slings it onto an armchair. She whirls around once in her jade-green dress, giggles then collapses onto one of the two sofas. She is a beautiful whirling dervish.

'Make us a drink; they're on the sideboard in the kitchen,' she says, putting her feet up on the upholstered arm of the sofa.

I come back into the room two or three minutes later, with two clinking glasses of Whisky Mac in my hands, and she is sleeping like a child dead to the world. I do not know what to do. I cannot simply leave her there and abscond into the night like a breaker-and-enterer.

I lift her gently under the waist and nestle her head against my shoulder. She is as light as a bird in my arms. I carry her slowly up the two flights of stairs and her breathing remains the same; soft and slow and regular. I know where her bedroom is and nudge open the door with my foot. The curtains are open onto the woods and the bright moon, high above the dark trees, illuminates the bed with its soft white counterpane of light and shows me the chair, the wardrobe and the dressing-table that make up a part of nearly all versions of normal life, everywhere.

I place her on the bed and suddenly have a vision of myself as some middle-aged imitation of a B-list action hero, no longer in the public eye and going to seed. I have to smile. I sit on the chair to catch my breath and watch

Nicola sleep for a moment then tiptoe out of the room, down the stairs and out of the front door.

As I am closing the door softly behind me, I could swear that I hear her calling 'Call me', but it could simply be the wind. It is simply the wind whispering in the trees now that the breeze has picked up.

Home alone again. Nicola has eyes that could charm snakes. She has eyes that could charm snakes.

Chapter Eight

I cannot get her out of my mind. Drink doesn't erase her from my thoughts; going for long walks only intensifies my thinking about her. I want to take her out again and see what happens. It seems to me that there might be *something* there, that she might like me at least a little. Perhaps these are just the illusions of a lonely and desperate man. How am I going to break through those emotional barriers of bereavement and loss?

I have only spoken to her once since our evening out in Stroud. I really want to see her again. She will help me to hang on. It is strange how quickly one develops an instinct for these things. It is almost like going back to a more primitive way of life where it is all about survival: the hand-to-mouth of taking emotional support where you can find it, drinking in physical contact when it finds you.

I call her number several times one evening, but she does not answer. She must still be at work. I tell myself that I will try one more time then give up for tonight.

I call her again just after nine o'clock and this time she answers the telephone.

'Nicola, it's John Stack. How're you?'

'Hello, John Stack. I'm fine, although I only got in from the office about twenty minutes ago. We're preparing something for a very demanding client and even when you're a partner, your colleagues expect you to stick around into the evening.'

'I usually don't get in until well after eight Monday through Thursday. This work thing is not all it's cracked up to be, is it?'

'Well, it has its moments,' she says. 'It has its moments. So, how're you? What's been happening?'

'I'm okay. You know, gallery stuff, commuting. I've been for a few walks. They could make a movie of my life.'

'No less riveting than many, I imagine.' She laughs.

'I guess not, but it could do with a *little* more excitement these days.'

'I know the feeling,' she says.

'Would you like to go out somewhere again, perhaps to Cheltenham this time? Say, Friday week? There's an exhibition opening at the museum there. We could go and have a look, then get some supper.'

'That'd be nice: I think I'm free. D'you want to pick me up from the office? You might have to wait around a bit. I'll give you the address nearer the time.'

'I'll get a taxi over to you. The museum's laying on drinks and nibbles.'

'I guess I'll be driving us back home then,' she says and laughs.

'Or you could leave your car, we get a taxi back to Stroud and I drive you back to Cheltenham to pick it up on Saturday morning?'

'That's a bit presumptuous, isn't it?'

'N-no, no – I only meant I'd come over to yours and collect you in the morning.'

'I'm only joking,' she replies and laughs again.

'I'll call you to confirm early next week, then?'

'That would be great,' she says.

I am a visual person. Wolfgang von Goethe called himself an *Augenmensch*, an eye person, and that is how I view myself. I like looking at things: it is as simple as that. I see things that other people might not see. I notice things that other people might miss: the value in an old painting with yellowed varnish hidden away in a country auction, the quality of an emerging artist who has been overlooked by the mainstream, minute flaws in perfect-looking marble, ugly secrets behind the veneers of beautiful people. I want Nicola to have something wrong with her. She seems too perfect.

On Tuesday I put Penelope in charge of the gallery for the day and do not take my usual train to Paddington. I have spotted what could be a very good Old Master painting in a catalogue for a sale this Friday at a small auction rooms in Dorchester. I am going to drive the ninety miles across country to have a look at it.

The drive takes me nearly two and a half hours. The weak early winter sun climbs steadily over my left shoulder as I head south. The hedges, trees, fences, lamp-posts, and houses form a stream-of-consciousness narrative that speeds up to a blur or slows down to intelligibility with the flow of the traffic or the twists and turns of the road.

I get to Dorchester just after midday. I have been to the auction rooms before and find my way to them without getting lost. They are so far from the big London auction houses. There are no liveried doormen waiting to greet you, no lacquer-haired blondes of a certain age on the front counter who look like the ex-girlfriends of faded pop stars. This is where normal people come to buy an antique or an inexpensive painting to decorate their homes. This is where dealers come to spot items of quality that the inexpert eyes of the cataloguers at the auction rooms have failed to single out for greater scrutiny. The normal people have no chance when the dealers decide that they want something.

The small painting does not look like much at first. It is hanging in one corner of the large ground-floor showroom. The cataloguers have described it as 'Seventeenth-century Flemish School. A still-life of pears and apples on a pewter dish.' They have obviously not spotted the monogram tucked into the extreme lower left corner just inside the edge of the frame, a black cursive script on a near-black background. The apples and pears shine with preserved life. I am pretty certain that it is a late work by the Dutch still-life specialist Willem van Aelst. The estimate is only £400–600. If my instinct is right and the hand and monogram are his, it would be worth at least a hundred times that.

It is a quiet view and there are only three or four other people wandering around the showroom, clutching copies of the catalogue and making occasional notes in the margins with the pecking nibs of their pens. I leave a commission bid of one thousand, two hundred pounds with a young male clerk on the front desk who tries to strike up conversation with me in a thick Dorset brogue. I wish that I could leave a higher bid, but I cannot afford to risk more money on a work that I cannot spend weeks researching.

I will know by Friday afternoon whether my bid on the painting has been successful. It could mean my being able to pay back my business loan to the bank on time. The paradox is that my cash-flow problems are making me less willing to take risks and there are bound to be other dealers who spot the work and know more about Old Masters than I do. If they think that it is right, they will take much bigger punts on it than I would be happy to take.

I need to try to supplement my gallery income by finding sleepers. In a contemporary art market that is booming like never before, my small stable of artists is spectacularly failing to find wider recognition. My own success as a gallery-owner seems such a long time ago, but it is less than a decade since the shows that I organised in my small space were making it onto the arts pages of national newspapers and journals. That was when the money was good. The reviews and the money have rather dried up now, like a streambed in summer.

If I have to close the gallery, I must make sure that Penelope and the flame-haired one will be alright; that they have other things to go on to. They will need advanced warning if I am going to abandon ship. I owe that to them at least.

I do not get back to Stroud until nearly four thirty. There is an accident on the road just north of Salisbury and my stomach lurches as I hear the sickening sound of sirens growing louder behind me, then see the ambulance on the wrong side of the road, overtaking the long queue of traffic behind and ahead of me. Each vehicle is slowing down as it passes the spectacle of the crashed car which has mounted the pavement and hit a dry-stone wall. Two paramedics are standing at the back end of the car and talking into their radios when I finally get past the site. All that I can see of a human presence in the crushed mass of metal at the front end of the car is the bare arm of the driver that has been extruded through the gap where the driver's-side window used to be. I cannot contain a rising tide of panic. My stomach spins and bile shoots up my throat. I feel like I need to be sick.

The sky is already darkening when I get back to the Stone House. The local birdlife twitters and chirrups quietly as it beds down for the night in the branches of trees and the thick parts of hedges. Their sounds soothe me, sing me a lullaby. The evenings are when I feel it most, this chill of loneliness.

Wine warms this coldness, this frozenness in my bones. The first glass takes the edge off the chill, the second ignites a fire that spreads its warmth outwards from my belly; by the third glass I feel that I am in perfect company. Everything else seems to fade into nothingness. Even Nicola seems to cease to exist.

Chapter Nine

The painting sold for two thousand, eight hundred pounds. Somebody got lucky, or else will have an attractive but pretty worthless picture on their walls that they might have to sell on at a loss.

I am collecting Bryony from the station tonight and I cannot wait to see her. It feels like a long time since I last saw her face. No one ever told me that you could love your children this much, to breaking point. I think that I love her even more than I loved my wife; it is an unqualified devotion. I don't think that I could ever let go.

I know nothing of her life in Bristol, other than what she tells me. I do not get to be a part of that world. Linda made it clear that she did not want me to get involved with Bryony's education when she moved schools. I think that she would be angry if I tried to intrude on Bryony's parents' evenings or sports days. Even though we do not speak any more, I feel that she always deposits Bryony in Stroud as if she is very reluctant to let her go, to give her up so that she can spend time with me for a few days. I know that she watches and waits to make sure that Bryony is safe before she drives away. I wonder what she feels when she looks at me.

Linda blamed me so completely when things went wrong that her sister and parents sided with her without questioning the truth. I have lost the logic of the sequence of events that led to what happened. It keeps on escaping my grasp, running away with itself. How could sometimes drinking too much cause such grief?

Linda's family was very hard on me about what

happened. They have not forgiven me over the last two years. I used to hope that those blank phone calls might be one of them trying to get in touch, to overcome themselves and their precious anger that they must tend like fragile flames. Now I am not sure that I could face speaking to them again, going over the facts of the case. I might lose myself in the details.

Bryony is there as usual on the ticket-office bench when I arrive at five o'clock. She is talking to a little old lady in a thick, grey woollen overcoat who is sitting beside her with a Highland terrier at her feet. The dog has a stained moustache and trembles with febrile life, trying to attract its mistress's attention. No one else is around, only the man in the ticket office who is sipping something from a plastic cup and printing out what are perhaps reports from his machine.

'Bee, hello. Let's go,' I say as I bend to give her a kiss on the forehead. The old woman seems to ignore me, but Bryony stands up and hoists her small rucksack onto her back, then says goodbye to her bench companion. The station master nods at me in familiar greeting from behind his glass screen as we head out into the car park. He has a sad, faraway expression in his eyes, as if he is looking right through me to something dark or frightening at the back of his mind.

Sometimes it is difficult to know what to do with Bryony. Sometimes I feel utterly lost; I do not know how to keep her entertained. I feel that I have to make such an effort to keep her on my side, to resist the gravitational pull of her mother. Sometimes Bryony is dead even to me, the father that she always adored, when she comes to stay. She seems not to know that I am there. She is absorbed deep inside herself, reading or watching television.

I wonder whether Bryony could learn to accept Nicola

in my life, whether she could understand that it is important that I am not alone. I will not even mention Nicola to her until I am certain that things will work out between us.

We spend a very quiet weekend together, Bryony and I, like we did sometimes when we were a family and her mother might have gone away for a night or two to see her aging parents, to spend some quality time with them on her own before they let go of this life. What can you do with a twelve-year-old girl who is by now used to hanging out with her girlfriends in Bristol's shopping centres, to talking about pop music, boys, accessories, homework assignments, about things that you cannot know or relate to? At least she still loves animals and nature; she has been taken out of the countryside, but the countryside has not been taken out of her. All that we can do is to drive down into Stroud on Saturday afternoon to look at the clothes shops and to visit the organic café in a courtyard off the pedestrianised high street for a cup of tea; to head off on a long damp walk in the wintry woods on Sunday morning as a mad cacophony of church bells rings out across the shire.

I call Nicola on Monday evening and she still sounds keen to go out on Friday night. There is a spark of an unidentifiable *something* in her voice; perhaps she just wants someone to entertain her and it has little to do with me being the one to give her some company for the evening. My desire to spend time with her is less undifferentiated. She is the first woman I have met since Linda left who I have really liked. I can imagine us having something together. I feel guilty when my mind wanders in the direction of pleasure, of possible happiness. I punish it with drink and do not stop until these thoughts are beaten down again.

* * *

The taxi picks me up from the Stone House at six o'clock on Friday evening. The taxi driver is the first person I have talked to face-to-face all day or, rather, I address myself to the back of his head as we make our way towards Cheltenham. I give him Nicola's directions to her office and we get there by a quarter to seven. Her firm are on the first two floors of a Regency townhouse not far from the high street. I ask the taxi driver to wait with the engine switched off while I get Nicola.

She is wearing a black skirt, cut just above the knee, and a white silk blouse under a black jacket that matches her skirt. She looks like she has just been in court. She is dressed to kill. She introduces me casually to a couple of her colleagues – a young man who must be a junior solicitor and a serious-looking, broad-hipped older woman who has a pursed look like a devout Christian – and points out her office to me behind a glass partition wall. It looks very neat and tidy. She opens the door to her office to retrieve her patent-leather handbag and pale-green overcoat, appearing momentarily like an exotic creature trapped behind the glass of a terrarium. She is rushing slightly because she knows that our taxi is waiting outside the front door. Her colleagues seem vaguely curious about me, but do not say much and I do not give them any real opportunity to ask me questions about what I do for a living or where we are going tonight, as we exit the main office door less than five minutes after I first entered it.

'They seem nice,' I say as we are getting into the taxi.

'They *are* nice,' she replies as she pulls her door shut behind her. 'Matt's our new litigator and Joan's our office manager. She's been at Sturgess McCarter longer than I have. She's part of the furniture.'

'She's certainly very well upholstered.'

'Now, now,' she says and laughs. I see the driver trying to stifle a smile in the rear-view mirror.

'Where to now, sir?' he asks.

'The museum and art gallery. D'you know where that is?'

'I've even been *in* there once or twice, sir. The kids and missus like it. Didn't trade in my life for the taxi licence.'

'It's a good place, isn't it? Full of interesting things,' Nicola chimes in diplomatically.

'I just meant I don't know the name of the road, that's all,' I add.

'We'll have you both there in no time,' he says, turning sharply down towards the promenade. He is probably jealous of me for Nicola's looks. I feel obliged to give him an extra five pounds as a tip and salve to my conscience when he deposits us at the front steps of the museum.

The art gallery side of the museum organizes regular exhibitions, both those dedicated to dead artists, who are easier to manage, and solo or group shows of works by living ones who some art-lovers might label as 'contemporary'. These artists often have aspirations to solo shows at leading commercial galleries in London, but settle on non-selling exhibitions in small or medium-sized provincial museums as the next-best thing, so as to raise their profiles and to convince the London galleries to take them more seriously the next time that they submit work to them. What they all want, of course, is high-impact dealers representing them and high-gain selling exhibitions. Nice champagne at the opening, sprays of flowers in crystal vases, pretty girls in dresses handing out canapés, that kind of thing. What they want is hard cash for their years of labouring away in obscurity. Even on the opening night of their provincial museum shows, these artists probably feel that they have already failed in some way.

I have been following the career of George Branscombe for about a decade now. I had not meant to, it is just that I somehow got on to his mailing list and receive invitations and the occasional round-robin news update in the post once or twice a year. He paints in oils; figures and landscapes and interiors. He really is not bad. He is already in his mid-forties and will probably never get anywhere on the London scene.

When we get up to the main gallery floor in the High Victorian Gothic building with its rusticated exterior, there are twenty or thirty people standing around chatting with glasses of white wine in their hands, their backs turned resolutely away from the works on the walls. I fetch a glass of wine for each of us from the makeshift bar and begin to chaperone Nicola around the show.

'Don't they have any red?' she asks, smiling as she takes the glass from my hand.

'White wine doesn't stain like red does. They're not allowed to serve red in case the guests start splashing it over the works on the walls like crazy Abstract Expressionists.'

'Isn't that kind of unlikely in twenty-first century Cheltenham, of all places?' she asks.

'Risk managers would probably say their job is the art of the unlikely,' I reply.

'Still, I don't like white very much. It's always too sweet or too sharp, isn't it? Although this isn't too bad,' she adds, taking her first sip.

'We'll just stay for a couple of drinks; I've booked our table for eight thirty in any case.'

George Branscombe has a particular thing for the female nude. At least half of the canvasses in this show depict women in various states of undress. George is wearing a jade-green tweed jacket and a knitted yellow tie over a checked shirt and is standing in front of one of his nudes, gesticulating animatedly as he gets his point across. The attractive young woman in front of him seems deep in thought. I am not sure that she is actually listening to what he is saying. We walk over to stand in front of the painting, next to George and his companion. He leans over and shakes my hand, saying 'Thanks so much for coming.'

It is always interesting to hear what artists have to say about their own work. I am not sure that they are the best interpreters of what they do. They don't have the necessary *distance*. This particular nude has a pair of pert breasts and a torrent of auburn hair cascading over her left shoulder. She looks at the viewer coquettishly through deer-brown eyes. She is a touch too cartoonish to be seductive, but George seems to find her desperately compelling.

'She's my best life model, Stacy. She has this, er, *stillness*, it's quite breathtaking.'

'Does she model for you often?' the young woman asks, looking up at him suspiciously.

'As often as my wife will allow. She doesn't like my nudes very much for some reason,' he neighs with laughter. 'There're a few of her dotted around here,' he adds, pointing vaguely around the gallery. He pops a mint imperial in between crooked teeth. He glances in Nicola's direction furtively. I catch his gaze and he looks away at once.

'He's quite a catch, I don't think,' Nicola whispers in my ear as I take her elbow and steer her gently onwards through the gallery to a section of still-lives. 'Why is it that some men think that they're such a hit with the ladies when they're so obviously not?'

'Are you trying to tell me something by any chance?' I lean in and whisper back.

'No, not *you*,' she laughs out loud. 'I don't think you've got arrogance issues. Probably quite the opposite in fact.'

'What does that mean?'

'I think you're probably quite unconfident, deep down,' she replies.

'I have every reason to be. It's hardly been a vintage few years. I'm just going to get us two more glasses of wine,' I add hastily.

I have not talked in an intimate way to anyone for so long now. It is making me feel quite nervous. The chilled wine glasses perspire in my hands as I take them back towards Nicola. The gallery is filling out slightly, but it is hardly a thronging crowd.

'Here we are; we'd better find another taxi quite soon and get up to Birdlip,' I say. 'What d'you think of these still-lives?'

'His flowers aren't too bad,' she says. 'They're quite realistic; vibrant and fresh.'

'Perhaps they're expressions of his desire to deflower fresh young things,' I joke.

'Yuck,' she replies. 'I think I've gone right off them now.'

'They're quite *painterly*. He's certainly got technique, he's well trained.'

'You say that as if it's a bad thing,' she replies.

'Technical ability's probably at the bottom of the pecking order in the sort of contemporary art that makes it on the international market. It's all about the idea these days, the notion, the *angle*.'

'Perhaps I'm a traditionalist, but I like paintings that *look like* paintings.' She touches my hand with her fingertips as she says this and sends an electric charge through me.

We eat in the garden of a restaurant in the small village of Birdlip, high up on the side of the escarpment on the road back to Stroud. We are seated at a table under a powerful standing kerosene heater. Even though it is late November, the warmth that the heater gives off makes it feel much earlier in the year. As the crow flies, we are not far from the vertiginous hill on which the plummeting cheese-rollers come to grief each year, and the view down over the plain where Gloucester and Cheltenham sprawl is magnificent from this height. Stars prick out the fabric of the night sky.

I want to ask her who the man was who was with her when I met her at the gallery that time in Stroud. Does he have some kind of stake in her? This hope that something might happen between us: it might have already been erased by other entanglements that began long before we met. I cannot seem to find the right time to ask her about him. She has never mentioned him since, but I have no idea whether she is telling me the truth when she says that there has been no one serious since her husband died.

The terrace has perhaps ten pairs of tables, each sharing a heater, and they are all occupied by soon after nine. Most of the people seem to be office workers who have come up here for the food and the night-lit view, their designated driver quietly sipping a Coke or a lemonade, while everyone else gets legless by mid-evening on wine or beer as only the English do.

Nicola unbuttons her green woollen overcoat as the warmth from the kerosene heater becomes almost stifling. Her white blouse contours beautifully over her breasts. I have to keep remembering to look into her eyes when we speak. She is already on her fourth glass of wine this evening, having switched to red now, and cannot seem to stop smiling at me with a gently playful look in her eyes.

'So, you lured me out again,' she says.

'I seem to have, don't I?' I reply.

'I think we'd better eat something. I'm beginning to feel a little sloshed,' she says.

'It's necessary to unwind after a long week at work, though, isn't it? Not that I'd know about *long* weeks as such any more. How's your work going at the moment, by the way?'

'Christ, we're not going to spend the evening talking about the law and office politics, are we?' she laughs.

'I just thought I'd better ask. I only need the potted version.'

'Oh, it's all fine. It is what it is. I'm working on one or two interesting cases at the moment: family stuff.'

'Happy families or unhappy ones?'

'Very much the latter: they only come my way when there's been a divorce or a death,' she says.

The table at which we are sitting is small and there must only be three feet between us as we eat. She has the most amazing hazel eyes. She has the most amazing breasts. I do not know where to look. I do not know where to look first. The wine is untethering my gaze, loosening my tongue. She is trying to suck up *spaghetti carbonara* delicately through deliciously moist lips while I slice sections off my plump Gloucestershire Old Spot sausages. It is the closest I have come to sex for a long time.

'Enjoying your food?' she asks.

'I'm enjoying everything,' I reply. 'D'you want another glass of wine?'

'That'd be lovely,' she says.

We order coffee at around ten thirty. Even with the heaters on full blast it is getting cold now and some of our fellow diners have moved inside to the bar area, or are too drunk to notice. I settle the bill with the waiter who brings us the two cups of steaming coffee and Nicola suddenly leans across the table when he has gone and kisses me softly on the cheek.

'I-I, that was very nice of you,' I stammer.

'It was very nice of *you* to buy me supper,' she says and smiles.

'I'm sorry; I'm not being very coherent, am I?' I lean forward and say quietly into her lovely face. I hope that she cannot smell the alcohol on my breath from this lunchtime. Real ale followed by red wine is a potent combination and trumps toothpaste every time. I can feel a charge on my skin, as if she has touched a Van der Graaf generator and then kissed me as a practical joke. Her hand on mine, her hard pink nails tickling the hairs on the back of my hand, say that it is not a practical joke, however.

'Sweet forty-sixteen and never been kissed.' She laughs and touches my nose with the tip of her index finger.

'I'm still forty-five, actually, if you don't mind. Excuse me; can we get a glass of still water here please? Plenty of ice,' I say to a passing waiter.

'A little hot and bothered?' she laughs again.

'Nothing I can't handle. I'm just not used to female attention. I only ever get weird menopausal women staring at me on the Tube.'

'You have all the best lines,' she says and smiles.

I pull out a packet of Marlboro Lights from my jacket pocket and tap one out like a pro, offering it to her.

'How did you know I smoked?'

'I didn't. It was just an educated guess,' I reply.

'How d'you guess something like that? I don't have the teeth or the lines, I hope.'

'You certainly don't. You're a *stunner*, as the tabloids would say.'

'You have a terrible London accent, by the way,' she whispers, kissing me softly on the cheek again.

'Want to know how I guessed?' I say. '*Femmes fatales* always smoke, at least in the movies.'

'You're very kind, but I'm hardly one of those.'

I fumble with the matches and eventually get the thing alight. My bloody hands are trembling. She smokes the cigarette slowly, taking long drags and then blowing the smoke out of the corner of her mouth away from the table.

'I don't mind cigarette smoke,' I say.

'Nor do I,' she laughs. She is slurring very slightly.

In the taxi on the way back to Stroud, she leans her head on my shoulder. I kiss her forehead gently once or twice; she murmurs appreciatively, but seems to be fast asleep. When we get to the Court House, she wakes up with a start as if she does not know where she is for a second. I unlock the front door for her and make sure that she is safely in the house, giving her a goodnight kiss on the cheek, then get the taxi-driver to take me the half mile up the hill to the Stone House.

I do not go straight to sleep, but open a bottle of red

wine and sit on the sofa nearest the sitting-room window, looking out at the night. Nicola and I could really have a story together, if only she would let it happen. My stomach lurches with thoughts of Linda when I am thinking this.

Chapter Ten

'Hello, sleeping beauty,' I say when Nicola answers the phone at about ten o'clock.

'God, I'm sorry. I don't know what came over me.'

'I suspect sleep did,' I say.

'And a tide of red wine,' she adds and laughs.

'So, how are you?'

'I'm feeling a bit queasy this morning. I'm not used to drinking very much any more.'

'I hope you don't think I took advantage of your, erm, *high spirits*,' I say.

'I took advantage of *you*, if anything. With some men, I might've woken up in the morning to find someone un-wanted in bed beside me.'

'I was raised a good blue-eyed American boy,' I say.

'What, as in a smart-suited city-slicker with deviant sexual tendencies and a penchant for handguns?' she jokes slightly croakily.

'Oh, absolutely. Welkum t' ma *werld*,' I say, exaggerating my accent.

'I think I would've picked up on that by now. And you have brown eyes.'

'Are you feeling up to being driven into Cheltenham for your car? Are you feeling okay to *drive*?' I ask.

'Would it be alright with you if we waited until early afternoon, say around two? I don't think I'm fit to drive yet. My head's still exploding. I'm sorry if that's a pain.'

'I don't have anything planned at all. Another action-packed day ahead,' I reply. 'I'll see you this afternoon.'

There are so many things that I want to know about

Nicola, so many things that I don't dare to ask her. What was her husband like? How has she coped with his death; how did she bear the unimaginable burden of him dying slowly at home in front of her? When somebody loses someone they love, it is very hard for people to ask them such direct questions. There are just suppressed conversations, silent narratives. I need to understand how she has managed to survive it all. I still feel that I am drowning very slowly day by day, like a flying insect in a honey trap.

Nicola seems to have an inner strength, a quiet dignity, that I feel I was born without, or lost somewhere along the way. She has that lawyer's way of weighing her words carefully and not wasting them. I like that about her. She does not talk endlessly like some women do; she is not frightened of silences. I wonder if the fact that she is a lawyer helped her to sort things out when her husband died. I am sure it is good to know how things work in a crisis.

I cannot sit here waiting for the afternoon to come. The winter sun is shining in a pale sky and I need to get outside into the air. I walk up the path that runs past the Stone House and, rather than turning down into the woods towards Nicola, continue on through the endless ploughed fields. The path runs along the seam between the fields for several miles before the next village emerges from the high ground. I used to walk up here as a boy and never once suspected, lost in these limitless fields, my hands skimming the ripening heads of the crops as I walked in the summertime, how complicated life could become.

The very last walk that we went on with my parents before they retreated back to the States was up here. It was not long before Linda became pregnant, when we were happy. I was drinking very little then. I woke up each morning with a clear head and a sense of purpose. The gallery was just beginning to do well. My parents were both walking with sticks, but full of the joys of a Gloucestershire spring. They said that they were going to miss this place, this view, in ways that they could not begin to express. They seemed to know that they would not be coming back again.

I arrive just after two o'clock at the Court House. Nicola is looking paler than usual, as if she has spent an extended period in a room with no natural sunlight. She still smells delicious, of freshly pressed grapes, when I give her a kiss on the cheek.

'How're you feeling now?' I ask.

'A lot better; it was a bit touch-and-go this morning, I tell you. I'd forgotten that hangovers could make you so queasy.'

'Blame it on me. I shouldn't have let you mix white and red wine. That probably did it.'

'Women make their own choices these days, haven't you heard?' she says and laughs.

'Okay, they might do, but I should've warned you in any case. Trust me: I know what I'm talking about.'

'I'm sure you do,' she replies. 'Next time we go out for a drink I'm in your hands.'

'Is that a promise?' I reply with a smile.

'You can depend on it,' she says and winks, flirting with me playfully.

'I'll hold you to that, then.'

We get to the side road where she has parked her shiny black Audi around the corner from her office just before three. There is an awkward moment when she opens the passenger door to get out of the car and neither of us knows what to say. I am wondering whether to ask her if she would like to spend the rest of the afternoon up at the Stone House and have some supper with me. Perhaps she is thinking about asking me if I would like to come back to hers, or is distracted by another totally unrelated thought, one where I do not even feature.

'D'you want to follow me up to my house? We could watch a film and I could make you some supper,' I say.

She hesitates for a split second, before replying, 'That'd be very nice. I'll race you back there.'

She shuts the passenger door of my car with a careful slam and walks around to the driver's side of her car, gets in and starts the engine as I pull away.

As I am driving home I keep thinking that I do not know how to play this. What would Linda say if she could see me now? She would probably laugh at my clumsiness and awkwardness. It has been so long since I last dated anyone, about twenty years since I first got together with Linda, that I have no idea what I am doing or exactly what I want out of it all. I just know that I do not want to be lonely any more, that Nicola is beautiful and funny and might like me too. I keep asking myself what she could possibly see in me. It just seems so implausible, so unlikely that I deserve anyone like her. I feel guilty that I am abandoning Linda somehow; that the memory of what we had together should be enough to get me through when it simply isn't enough sustenance and it was Linda who left me.

We come to the divide in the road in the woods near Cranham at about fifty miles an hour, Nicola following closely behind me in her car that shines in the cold evening light like a hearse in my rear-view mirror. The black widow is chasing my tail like a panther running down a deer. I carry on towards Stroud on the main road and she suddenly flashes me with her headlights and veers off onto the right-hand branch of the road that will take her steeply down the escarpment to the valley below. Perhaps she thinks that she knows another faster route home; perhaps she has decided that she has other plans for this evening.

That black widow image keeps pressing itself up against my mind's eye as I watch the road unfold hypnotically in front of me. Her raven hair; her calm, manicured poise; the house, the car: it is quite some package that her husband left behind. An unpleasant thought enters my head and I cannot shake it free again: what if Nicola is really not what she seems to be? I wish that I could get to know her better before I fall in deep, but sometimes when you swim in the sea you just have to trust that the currents will buoy you up rather than pull you under.

Nicola's car is not outside my house when I get home. I pour myself a glass of red wine and sit in the sitting-room, looking out over the valley as night settles on the landscape. After half an hour, I have decided that she must not be coming. I am drowning that thought with a second glass of wine when there is a knock on the front door. I go to answer it, putting on the outside light and seeing a silhouette emerge from the darkness behind the frosted glass, and it is Nicola, with a flurry of apologies for having taken longer than she expected. In her hands are two white plastic carrier-bags filled with white cardboard cartons.

'I hope you like Chinese,' she says. 'I've bought enough to feed the Terracotta Army.'

'That's so kind of you. I *love* Chinese. I could eat a Ming horse. I'd given up hope that you were coming: I was going to send out a search party.'

'The service at Chi's is bloody slow, but their food's fantastic. Nice cottage by the way,' she says. 'Point me in the direction of the kitchen and some plates and I'll dish up.'

'You're my *guest*; you just take a seat in the sitting-room through there and I'll sort it out. Shall I just give us half each of everything? D'you want some soy sauce?'

'Yes please, on all counts,' she says with a tired smile.

'Coming right up,' I reply.

We eat side-by-side on one of the sofas, with our plates perched on our laps. I offer her a glass of wine but all that she wants is water. This is the first time since Linda left that I have ever had an evening meal at home with anyone other than Bryony. Our thighs touch sometimes as we eat our food. It is a little difficult to concentrate on the delicate flavours of what is on my plate.

'How come your parents chose this area?' she asks suddenly between mouthfuls, half turning to me and touching my arm with her hand.

'I think they were sent to the Quaint Cotswolds for a holiday once by friends of theirs in London, and fell in love with the place. My father had some money spare and bought the cottage.'

'What was it like, what *is* it like, to be an only child?' she asks, wiping her mouth carefully with the linen napkin that I have given her. I take her plate and cutlery and cradle them on mine, now that we have both finished our food.

'I don't know what it's like to have brothers and sisters. I was a bit lonely sometimes, I guess. My parents, or more my father, always seemed to be too busy to have much time for me. They just sent me away to school or gave me money. It's me against the world again now, and that's still a bit frightening.'

'Didn't you have any uncles, aunts, *cousins?*'

'I'm an only child of only children. My father did have one much older brother, but he died at eighteen in World War Two. When your parents go, that's pretty much it,' I reply.

'Well, we'll have to try to do something about your being lonely,' she says and suddenly we are kissing. Sweet-salt taste of her saliva mixing with mine; the warmth and softness of her lips, her mouth; the flickering of her tongue against the tip of mine. Our hands do not know where to put themselves. They begin on each other's faces and then cascade down the slopes of our shoulders onto the contours of our bodies, and on down. I want her kissing never to stop. She comes up for air like a delicious free-diver.

'God, I needed that,' she says into my mouth. 'You're a great kisser.'

'God, you're beautiful,' I whisper back. 'I didn't want

you to stop.' I feel flushed, light-headed, as if my brain is about to explode through the architecture of my skull. I feel like I did when I once snorted poppers as a student.

'I just need to freshen up; I'll be back in a minute, don't you worry,' she says, kissing me on the lips one more time.

'It's at the top of the stairs, first on the left,' I say.

While she is in the bathroom, I pour myself another glass of red wine and sit looking out of the window into the dark. The sitting-room light is reflected on the window-pane like a strident, artificial sun hanging in the night sky. I am still shaking from the thrill of Nicola's mouth on mine, the taste of her, from the memory of her exploring tongue and hands. She comes back down the stairs with the clatter of high-heels.

'I've just seen the time; I had no *idea* it was so late. I've got an eight thirty conference call in the office tomorrow morning. I'm really sorry, I'd better make a move and get to bed soon,' she says in one gout of language, stopping her descent on the last step of the stairs.

'Is everything okay?'

'Of course, why shouldn't it be? I've had a really nice evening,' she replies.

'It just seems a bit, er, sudden. Your needing to get home, I mean.'

'No, everything's fine. I just need some sleep. I'll make it up to you, I promise,' she says, putting her arms around my neck and looking into my eyes. I want to kiss her mouth again, but hold back. We are the same height when she stands on the bottom step of the stairs.

'All my stuff's at home. This was all a bit, um, *sponta-neous*,' she adds. Her breath smells of my mint toothpaste, as if she has tried to wash away the taste of me.

'I think I like spontaneous,' I say with a laugh. 'Look, I'll come with you in your car to make sure you get back safely then walk home through the woods. I could do with some wintry air to cool me down.'

When we have driven down the long track that forms the Court House's drive, flanked on both sides by the impenetrable darkness of the woods, I realise that we have done so in complete silence, as if we don't know what to say to each other now that everything has changed, now that the stakes are suddenly so much higher. I think that Nicola is waiting for me to say something, to let her know how I feel. I cannot find the right words; they seem to come out all wrong.

'Can I give you a ring in the next few days, once I know what's in my work diary, and we can do something just before Christmas again? I've had a lovely time tonight,' I say. I sound as if I am thanking someone for having been a good host after a particularly entertaining dinner party. I have become estranged from the language of romance, of lust, of love. Her face does not betray any disappointment at my performance. She simply smiles very slightly, looking up at my face with a quizzical half-frown forming around her eyes, and then gives me a gentle squeeze on the arm.

'Let's make it sooner than that,' she says.

She gives me a glancing kiss on the cheek, unlocks the heavy front door, pulls it open and then disappears into the darkness of her unlit house.

Chapter Eleven

On the train up to Paddington on Monday morning and all day in the gallery I cannot stop thinking about Nicola. I can taste the memory of her mouth, feel her hands on me. Penelope has a clutch of bills and invoices for us to settle and it is as much as I can do to concentrate on signing the cheques. The task is made harder by my knowledge of how little money we have in the business account.

'That hedge-fund manager came in again on Friday when you were at home.'

'Oh yes? Any joy?'

'He looked at quite a few pieces; I took him through into the storeroom as well. He's *so* rude. He wanted me to leave him alone in there to look at things; said I was putting him off concentrating by telling him about each work. He just needs to *bite* on a couple of the more expensive ones.'

'He can bite my backside before I allow you to leave him alone with the stock. I don't trust him. I've been wondering whether he might have been sent to snoop around here by the bank. Who says he's a hedge-fund manager anyway?'

'He does.'

'Exactly.'

'Last time you were out when he came in with his wife, or he said she was his wife. She looked like the type who'd be married to a hedge-fund manager. You know, Swiss-finishing-school Euro accent, brain the size of a walnut, Armani sunglasses in October?'

'Well, if he ever actually buys anything, I'll eat something. This Styrofoam cup, your handbag, I dunno, *something*.'

'I'll remember that,' she says with a laugh.

'Penny, I've been meaning to talk to you about something for a while,' I begin gently, after we have both looked through the post and drunk some more coffee that she has brewed in the kitchenette.

'When you address me by my name, I know it must be bad.'

'You know better than anyone else how difficult things have been over the last couple of years.'

'They couldn't've been any worse for you,' she replies, looking down into her coffee cup. 'Everyone's been proud of you for having got through at all: Jake for one often says how highly he rates you.'

'I don't mean so much personally, I'm really talking about the business. It's not viable any longer, is it? You can see the costs of running the space, the price these days of finding new stock, and you can see also what we take each month.'

'Are you trying to tell me something?' she asks quietly.

'Not you, *us*,' I reply. 'I'm trying to tell us both something. You and I *are* the gallery these days, although admittedly I own what's left of the stock. I think I've decided to call it a day at the end of Jake's show. It's not working for me any more, I'm afraid.'

'Sounds like you're breaking up with me,' she says with a wry half-laugh.

'I'm really breaking up with the last fifteen years of my life. I'm not exactly going out on a high, am I?'

'At least you've bloody well given it a good go.'

'This all means you've got nearly four months to find something else. You'll get three months' redundancy pay on top of that.'

'What can I say? I'm gutted, but I do understand your decision. I half expected it to come sooner than this, to be honest. Jake was even wondering at one point whether you might bail on his show. N-not that he knows anything about the gallery finances, of course,' she stutters. 'He was just wondering whether your heart was really in it all any more.'

'He's right, I don't think it really is, in the gallery I mean,' I reply. 'But we'll certainly go ahead with his show, after all the work he's put into it.'

'Good – and I do understand your decision,' she says again.

I cannot play it cool with Nicola, however much I would like to. I am already picking up the telephone to call her when I get back from London on Tuesday night. Again, she seems to be out the first couple of times that I call, but answers the phone on my third attempt to get through to her.

'I was at the gym in Stroud,' she says in her breathy voice when I ask her what she has been up to this evening. 'Got back about half an hour ago; I go about twice a week.'

'All those sweaty locals; I've never fancied that form of exercise with everyone watching you going through the motions on the treadmill or the rowing machine,' I reply.

'I was a sweaty local until I had a shower,' she laughs. 'It's the only activity that *gets* me in a sweat these days.'

'I don't quite know what to say to that. I'd like to try to help you remedy that situation; is that an appropriate reply?'

'It might be, it might be,' she breathes seductively, then giggles. 'But let's not put the cart before the horse.'

'I've never really understood that saying,' I reply. 'I don't think we have it in America. We're a post-cart kind of nation, unless you happen to be Amish.'

'I mean let's take it one step at a time, see what happens. There's no rush, is there?'

'Are you expecting me to answer that honestly?' I reply.

'I guess not,' she says. 'When it comes to anything to do with sex, men are rarely honest, in my experience.'

'Are you basing that on a lot of past case studies?'

'Hardly,' she replies and laughs dryly. 'I was married for quite a while, don't forget. There was no one else for some time before and a long time afterwards as well.'

'Likewise: I hardly know where to begin. Is that honest enough for you?'

'I think it is, yeah. I'm not quite sure where this leaves us, though, but at least we're being honest. I'm sure we'll muddle through somehow.'

'It's a bit like riding a bike, apparently.'

'What is – honesty?' she asks with a laugh. 'In a straight line, with the occasional wobbly bits?'

'Are you free for a drink or something later this week?'

'What about Thursday night? I have a meeting with a client that might go on fairly late tomorrow, but I'm definitely free on Thursday.'

'I'll pick you up about seven thirty, if that's okay,' I reply.

'Great,' she says. 'I'll see you here then.'

Nicola knows exactly what she is doing. She always appears to be in control. I cannot see her slipping up as a lawyer or in her private life. It seems almost unbelievable that she has suffered the loss that she has had to live with for the last three years. If someone did not know about her husband, they would think that everything was perfect in her world. She does not even seem to be carrying around that much *grief* in the confines of her head or heart. I suppose that everyone expresses that emotion in different ways. She laughs a lot; she is full of lightness. That must be the antidote that makes still living bearable for her.

The early December mornings are full of the icy, oxygenated air of winter that takes your breath away. On Wednesday I am up before first light, my head still thrumming from the bottle of wine the night before. I get dressed in my regulation jacket, shirt, tie and chinos and leave the house by six. It is as if my legs walk themselves with no government from my head. I have to go again to the place where it happened. I usually try to avoid it at all costs, even if that means a longer route into Stroud and back. Today I cannot resist the pull of that winding section of road and have to go and stand there once more, motionless like a statue as the sun rises weakly on the horizon. The asphalt surface is shiny with ice again today as the light filters down through the hard trees, just as it was that day, much later in the morning, when the seismic trace of tyre tracks in the frost led to the end of all I knew. I can still feel absolutely nothing. It is as if I have been switched off. A beetle is scuttling across the road as wide as a desert.

Thursday night does not come soon enough. The hours drag like heavy chains and I want to be anywhere else but in the gallery or on the train. The pattern of my working life for the last fifteen years suddenly seems meaningless to me. I have no idea what it has all been for.

I order a taxi to pick us up from the Court House at just before eight. I am still wearing my London clothes and pick my way down through the woods in thick darkness. If anyone came across me scrambling down these unmarked paths they would think that I was a lunatic on the loose. The full moon tonight is hiding behind heavy cloud and refuses to fulfil its part of the bargain. I am a lunatic without a moon. Its weak light spills out from behind the clouds only enough for me to climb down through the woods to Nicola's drive without colliding with any trees.

I am wiping the mud off the soles of my shoes on the iron boot-scraper mounted by her front door when she opens one half of the oak double doors. I have not even had time to pull the porcelain handle that connects with the old-fashioned pulley system, sending the sound of a bell clanging around her house.

'How did you know I was here?'

'Must be my sixth sense or something.' She laughs and gives me a quick kiss on the lips. 'No, I heard the sound of breaking twigs and thought it must be you or a deer.'

'And there was me thinking I could creep up on you at will without making a sound,' I joke and kiss her back.

'Why, d'you go in for that sort of thing then?' she asks, suddenly only a weak smile now caressing her lips. 'One night I was having a cigarette in my bedroom window a couple of months back and thought I saw someone sitting in the woods watching the house. I was a bit worried at the time, but must've been seeing things. It *was* pretty dark.'

'Why would anyone want to do that?' I say, cursing myself inwardly for having almost given myself away.

'God knows. Perhaps they were casing the joint, as your people might say, or they just like sitting in the woods at night, looking at Georgian houses. I guess I must've been seeing things,' she repeats. It is difficult to gauge how much she really saw, but she is playing it dead straight.

'I'm sure you must've been,' I reply, my heart inexplicably pounding in my chest. It would be almost impossible to explain to her why I had been sitting there for some hours in the dark, simply wanting to be near her.

The taxi arrives only ten minutes late. It takes us up the long drive, onto Folly Lane and down into Stroud. Nicola seems to have forgotten all about the figure in the woods. She presses close to me on the back seat; the lily of the valley on her skin and the warmth of her body next to mine making me forget everything else for as long as the journey lasts.

We go back to Il Trovatore again. The faux Italian seems to be having a night off and the restaurant is very quiet. The good citizens of Stroud and the surrounding villages must stay at home on Thursday nights.

I need to ask Nicola more about her husband, but cannot seem to find the right moment. She has learnt to avoid the subject of Linda and Bryony altogether. That is *terra incognita* as far as she is concerned, a distant continent of silence and unanswered questions. It is as if our pasts were erased when we met. I want Nicola to fill in the blanks of hers for me, to tell me how she survived her husband's death. Such questions are just too hard to ask; we need more time to get to know each other first.

'How's your week been?' I ask, as a waiter pours us each a glass of house red.

'Oh, quite quiet. Things always start getting quieter the month before Christmas in the legal business. People are too busy shopping to get divorced.'

'I thought Christmas was the peak time for break-ups?'

'Yeah, that's *at* or after Christmas,' she replies. 'The petitions for divorce start hitting our desks in the New Year.'

'Out with the old and in with the new. Don't you find it a bit *depressing* having to deal with divorces and deaths all the time? You must see some of the worst aspects of human behaviour.'

'Well, I'm not really implicated, am I? I just do the paperwork,' she says with a laugh.

'I guess not,' I reply. 'Still, it must be hard sometimes to keep your professional distance.'

'If I can help some woman get a fair divorce settlement,' she says, suddenly serious for a moment, 'when she's given up her career and stayed at home for years to look after the kids, while her husband goes off to work and sleeps with his secretary, then I'm pleased.' With that she beckons the waiter over again. 'Have you chosen yet, John?' she asks, raising her eyebrows and rolling her delicious eyes in mock jest at her own seriousness.

'You go first,' I reply. I have hardly even looked down at the menu on the table in front of me.

'I'm going to have the *spaghetti alla carbonara* and a *tricolore* salad, please. Is the pasta fresh?' she asks, as my eyes scroll down the interminable list of uninspiring dishes on offer.

'Of course, madam,' the waiter replies.

'And I'll go for the veal Milanese and a side order of chips. Can you make sure they're crunchy, please?'

'Very well, sir, madam,' the waiter says, nodding, when he has finished scribbling down our orders. 'Would you like any more drinks?'

'Shall we get another bottle of house red? Yes, let's get another bottle of red,' I reply.

'Your demanding American ways seem to be rubbing off on me,' she says when he has gone.

'Hardly – I've learnt not to expect service of any kind in this country. That way I find I'm never disappointed.'

'Have you always been so fond of drinking?' she asks. 'I mean, um, such *regular* drinking.'

'I'd call my drinking anything *but* regular. I'd say it was *extraordinary*,' I joke, with a lavish sweep of my hands that nearly sends my cutlery flying onto the cheaply carpeted floor. 'No, seriously, it became more, ah, regular when Linda and Bryony left. It is under control though, you know? There's really nothing to worry about.'

'I know; it's just if we're going to do this, whatever *this* is–' it is her turn to gesture expansively around the room with her delicate hands while trying to conjure up a visual image of *us* '–then I have a right to worry about you, to ask awkward questions.'

'There's no awkwardness about it, because it's really not a problem,' I reply, pouring more wine from the second bottle that the waiter has brought into our large glasses that bear the drying blood-red tidemarks of what we have just consumed.

'I'll take your word for that,' she says, raising her glass and tipping it towards mine. They chime together with a hollow ring.

* * *

Nicola falls asleep with her head leaning against my shoulder again in the taxi on the way back home. It is not even eleven o'clock. Red wine and her long working day seem to have that effect on her, even though we did not finish the second bottle and it was me who drank the lion's share. I want to spend the night with her, but will not push it yet. Her sweet breath rises and falls in tides in her chest as she sleeps on the short journey and I put my arm protectively around her shoulders. She stirs slightly but does not wake up. I have told the taxi driver to take us back to her house.

'Nicola, wake up, we're here,' I say gently when the car has pulled up in front of the gates. It is pitch-black and the automatic spotlight above the front door has failed to come on. She comes to the surface of consciousness slowly, like a diver coming up for air from a great depth, and rubs her eyes carefully as I pay the driver.

'I needed that,' she says, yawning as she opens up the house. 'The week seems never-ending these days. I can't wait for Christmas; I've taken too little time off this year.'

'Don't worry, I won't come in,' I reply then give her a kiss on the lips. 'You need to get your beauty sleep. No, that's not true; you've got quite enough of that already.'

'If you say so,' she laughs sleepily.

'I've got the day off tomorrow, but you've to go to work, don't you?'

'Afraid so,' she says. 'No rest for the wicked. D'you want to do something on Saturday night again?'

'I can't. I'm really sorry. I've got to go over to my friend Tim's in Wiltshire this weekend,' I lie. She looks disappointed in the half-light. 'Shall I call you before you go to bed to say I got back safely?'

'If you like,' she says, kissing me softly goodnight. 'I might be fast asleep by then, but you can try.'

As I walk back through the blacked-out woods, I suddenly know what I wanted to ask her but did not have the courage to say when we were face-to-face. I dial her number as soon as I get back home. She picks up after two rings, as if she has been waiting by the phone.

'I didn't get eaten by wolves,' I say.

'That's good. I can't see you as Little Red Riding Hood,' she replies, slightly muffled on the other end of the phone. She sounds as if she is lying down with the receiver resting against her ear.

'You should get to bed.'

'I will – I'm half there already. I'm feeling kind've lonely; I wish you'd stayed after all,' she says and goes quiet on the other end of the phone.

'So do I, you've got no idea how much. But we'll see each other at the beginning of next week, won't we? Nicola –' I pause then plunge in. This can only be a one-way street from here on in. 'I, I never do anything for Christmas these days, since Linda left. It's a dead day for me. Are you going away somewhere this year, or staying at home?'

'I was planning to go to my sister and her husband's in Banbury, but that's not set in stone. Why?'

'I-I know you might find this a little, erm, *premature*, but I was wondering if you'd like to spend it with me up here? I'd much prefer talking to you than staring into the fire.'

'God, you're a flatterer, aren't you?' She manages to laugh and yawn down the phone at the same time.

'You know what I mean.'

'Let me think about it,' she says sweetly. 'If I say yes, we'll do it down here. I know where everything is.'

We say goodnight and I take her answer as an almost-yes. I stay up late into the night, polishing off a half-empty bottle of red and watching for signs of life in the garden. The telephone rings at past twelve thirty and I rush to pick up the call, thinking that Nicola cannot sleep and wants to tell me something, No one is there, just the endless pulsing of static and silence.

'Hello? HELLO? *HELLO?*' I say, increasing the volume of my voice with each word until I am almost shouting. The line clicks dead.

Chapter Twelve

I pick Bryony up from the station at five o'clock on Friday night. Her book on budgerigars has been replaced by one called *Caring for Your Horse or Pony*. She hardly looks up when I walk up to her bench. She will read herself into a place at King's College to study Veterinary Sciences, I am sure of it. King's Cambridge rather than London, I hope. My *alma mater* was for the ABRACADABRAs rather than for straight-A students as she will be.

'Hello, little Bee, been here long?' I joke.

'*Da*-ad, you know Mum always brings me at exactly the same time.'

'Like *Groundhog Day*.'

'That was a funny film,' she says. 'The man looked like a sad, constipated dog. Treatment: one teaspoon of cod-liver oil in his food until symptoms are relieved.'

In the afternoon, I take her into Stroud for some Christmas shopping. It is 10 December and the steep high street is crowded with people who look as if they have been put together wrong. *This Man with his Neck-Brace is Brought to you by Benson & Hedges. Pop-Tarts Introduces for your Delight the Woman with Short Arms.* They crowd the street with their bull-necks, stiff backs and eye-patches like some Mediaeval parade.

Bryony decides that she wants to be an adult and walks arm-in-arm with me, rather than hand-in-hand. I hardly need to bend my head to talk to her, she is growing so tall. She is the spitting image of her mother. She still has sleep in the corner of one eye.

'God, you're turning into a very pretty young lady.'

'No I'm NOT, Dad.' She blushes profusely and unlinks her arm from mine.

'Yes you are, little lady,' I tease her and tickle her ribs as she tries to squirm out of the way. 'The boys will be flocking around you like seagulls before too long.'

'No they WON'T, Dad.' She giggles and slaps my hand away.

I have given her forty pounds. She wants to buy presents for Linda, for her grandmother on Linda's side, for her aunt, Linda's younger sister Jane, and for me.

We snake in and out of the shops up one side of the high street, then down the other. She does not know what she wants to buy.

'Tell you what: I'm going to get myself a take-away coffee and you a Coke. I'll wait on that bench up there on the left and we'll meet in half an hour. Make sure you count your change *before* leaving the shop. Keep your phone on.'

Bryony is nearly thirteen, I tell myself. You have got to learn to trust your children once they get to a certain age. It is a short high street; I will probably see her coming in and out of the shops as I drink my coffee on the bench. I need some gloves. It is getting colder by the day.

A small-town busker, no London Underground glory for him, strangles a penny whistle outside the Co-Op. He is wearing a Technicolor dream-coat of a smock, over what look like woven woollen trousers and open-toed sandals in the winter air. We are only about forty or so miles from Stonehenge and Glastonbury Tor, after all. This is the centre of the New Age.

I only have to buy presents for Bryony and Nicola. I think that Tim and family have given up expecting anything from me. They buy me a bottle of single malt for when I appear at some point between Christmas and New Year. That first Christmas after Linda was gone, I downed double doses of Valium with the whisky until the bottle ran out, then rang the taxi firm to bring me another one up from the town. I could not leave the house for nearly a week. Tim had to come to stay with me; he was a good friend to me then.

I wait and wait. Half an hour comes and goes and I have not seen her once. Forty-five minutes, fifty. I try her mobile every two or three minutes, but it is switched off. I am beginning to get worried now.

I walk up and down the road, in and out of the book-shops, the gift shops, the record stores, the clothing chains. 'Have you seen a girl about this tall,' I indicate with my hand, trying to modulate the tone of my voice, 'with wavy brown hair in a bob and brown eyes?'

'No,' the indifferent shop girls answer, chewing bubble-gum, the detritus of old bubbles at the corners of their mouths. 'It's him again. Dawn, he's asking about Bob summon. You seen 'im?'

'Nah.' There are different versions of the same story in all the shops in which I ask.

I try her phone and it is still switched off. It is more than an hour since she left. I decide to walk back up to the bench again where I said I would wait, which I cannot see from the bottom of the high street as the road curves slightly. The crowds obscure the view. My stomach lurches when I get there; I can already tell from a way off: the bench is empty. A pigeon is hopping around underneath it, pecking the life out of a piece of white bread. Where has she gone? Why is she doing this to me?

'*Dad?*' the tone of her voice out of the blue is tentative, questioning. 'Where've you been?'

'I've been looking for you.' I whirl around and face her, flushed with anger and relief. 'I've been looking for *you*,' I repeat. 'Where the bloody hell have you *been*?'

'Waiting on the bench, like you said,' she says contritely. 'I've been there for more than twenty minutes. I got bored and started walking up and down. Mum always makes me put ten pence in the fine pot when I swear.'

I hug Bryony as if I am going to squeeze the life out of her. I am so relieved. 'Which bench, darling?'

'Up there at the top of the street on the left,' she points with her right hand to a bench about one hundred yards away and on the other side of the road to where I thought I had made it clear, with child-proof precision, we were to meet.

'Don't do that to me again,' I say. 'My heart can't take it.'

On Monday morning, I feel desolate. That is the only word for it. Bryony is being taken away on holiday by her mother for a month before school starts again in January. I will not see her for a long while again.

'Have a lovely Christmas, Bee. I'll ring you on Christmas Day. Don't forget to keep your phone on. Your present's a surprise in January.' I cannot help choking up when I say these words.

The end cannot come soon enough for the gallery. I am not even going to try to sell the stock to pay back the balance of the loan to the bank. They can take what they want and shove it up their backsides, as far as I am concerned. I am fed up with the commute and the responsibility of it all. Jake's show will be my swansong, my clarion call before the walls of Jericho fall. I will deal from home. How hard can it be to turn over enough to pay for food and bills?

The catalogue text by Charles Everard arrives at the gallery by post ten days before Christmas. He has typed it on a typewriter with a jumping 'y' and a cracked 'a'. Who uses those machines these days, except as some anachronistic affectation? Penelope will have to type the whole thing up again on her computer.

They stand like giants amongst us, these metal men. They are mythic figures, creatures of the night of our primeval subconscious. Their blood has turned to bronze, iron, tin. Where do they come from?

Jake Andreiou (b. 1970) made his name at a young age in the mid-nineties with complex abstract canvasses, after graduating from Central Saint Martin's. What made those works remarkable was a skein-like complex or meta-structure of splashes, serifs, dribbles, drips and dashes of oil-paint over an almost photographically precise background. They were a compelling and mature body of work for such a young artist and, inevitably, Andreiou wanted to explore, to exchange genres, to push the boundaries of his artistic vision. These towering metal agglomerates were born, like the scatological traces of a dinosaur age . . .

Everard's text runs to three full A4 pages. I do not have the attention span to get beyond the second paragraph today. Penelope can read it as she types it up and tell me if it says anything too untrue or ridiculous.

When I get back on the Thursday night after the weekend of Bryony's visit, the uniformly black eye of my answerphone is blinking red. I press 'play' and the automated voice says, 'You have *one* new *mess*age. Received *today* at *nineteen* thirty-*five hours.*'

'John?' It is a metallic, magnetic version of Nicola's lovely voice. 'John, I've been thinking about your idea and I'd really like to spend Christmas with you here. I'll go to my sister's between Christmas and New Year. Let's speak soon. Give me a ring over the weekend. You know the number. *Byee.'*

That is the happiest news that I have received for a

long, long time. I have a bottle of red to celebrate and two poached eggs with salmon and watch bad television until past midnight.

The phone rings just as I am climbing the stairs to bed. 'Eight-three-two-one-five-one?'

There is a whispering silence that speaks, as if the lines from a hundred, a thousand callers have been spliced together and they are all holding their breath, not knowing who should speak first.

'Hello? Nicola . . . ? Nicola . . . *Linda?'*

An incomparable void of static and suppressed voices. *Somebody* is there.

'Hello? Hello? STOP FUCKING RINGING ME UNLESS YOU'RE GOING TO SPEAK,' I shout before I can stop myself. The line goes dead again.

Chapter Thirteen

'Did you try to call me last night?' I ask Nicola tentatively when I ring her on Friday morning.

'Didn't you get my message?'

'Yes, I'm *really* pleased about it. It's great news. I mean later, though, around midnight.'

'No, that wasn't me,' she says. 'I was definitely fast asleep by then.'

'That's good,' I reply. 'I keep getting these blank phone calls where no one speaks. I shouted down the phone last night and whoever it was hung up.'

'Can't the phone company help?'

'I haven't tried them yet. I might have to, though. They're a bit strange, those calls.'

'Do you know anyone who might do that sort of thing to you as a prank?'

'I don't think so, but how would you know?' I reply.

'I guess you wouldn't,' she says.

'I'm looking forward to next week very much,' I change tack clumsily. 'Let's have Christmas Eve drinks up here. Let me know what you want me to bring on Christmas Day, apart from the drinks.'

'Just bring some good champagne and red wine, and yourself.'

'There's an excellent free-range butcher in Mayfair. They have huge turkeys in the window. Don't you think I should buy one there?'

'I can get all that locally. You're hardly going to want to carry a turkey home with you from Paddington, are you?'

'I'd be stuffed if the train was cancelled,' I joke.

'They don't get any better, do they?' She laughs.

'It's a date on the twenty-fourth, then?' I say.

'See you at yours at, what, around seven thirty?'

'That'll be perfect.'

The snow is back again. The bare branches of the trees in the wood between the Stone House and the Court House look as if they have been dampened and dipped in icing sugar. I walk in the woods much of the morning and into the frozen afternoon. I walk simply to keep moving. Linda and I used to have a game on our walks, to name each new species of tree that we passed. The English names, that is; the object was not to try to outdo each other with our non-existent Latin. We had other games, of course; easier to play but infinitely more hard to look back upon. Games that led to Bryony and games that led to nothing other than *having played*, having been a part of it all.

Oak, ash, sycamore, elm, beech, walnut, chestnut, horse chestnut, maple. All those that lose their leaves, all those that seem to die in winter. Some are natives, others brought here as the world opened up. You can tell their kind by their leaves, their stature, the shapes of their canopies, the texture of their bark, the fruits that they bear. Elms you can tell by their being dead in this wood, beyond winter; beyond all seasons.

I end up in a pub that I have never been to before in a village, or rather a cluster of houses around a single-track lane, beyond the woods. The barman is washing glasses and there are only two old men in the lounge bar, smoking woodbines and feeding crisps to the whiskery mongrel with them, as well as a man in his twenties who is leaning against the counter, covered in limestone dust and with his yellow hard-hat hooked to his belt. They all turn towards the door when I come in. The mongrel regurgitates a crisp as it growls; otherwise, I am greeted by silence.

I order a pint of cider and the barman nods at me, but continues the conversation he has begun with the builder about the progress of the local non-league football team in the FA Cup. Their talk about domestic football seems to act like some kind of talisman, an evil eye to ward off goblins or sprites or Americans. Perhaps they hear my accent and decide that I do not belong. They cannot know that I understand the offside rule. They mutter to each other in their thick Gloucestershire brogue. I retreat to the saloon bar. I understand the rules of the game.

There is a jukebox in the saloon bar. It holds quite a lot of Motown songs, as well as a good selection of early rock 'n' roll: Buddy Holly, Roy Orbison, Elvis Presley and the like. I ask the barman for change for a tenner and play songs back-to-back for about an hour, while I drink my cider and the second pint that I order from the stonily silent barman. The builder seems to have left. I swear that I hear one of the old men cough 'Bloody DJ' into his pint of stout.

The last week before Christmas is very busy in the gallery with the preparations for Jake's catalogue, which is going to the printers just after New Year. Whenever I think about Nicola, I find it very difficult to concentrate on what I am trying to do. I am like a hormonal teenager desperate for his first fuck.

Jake is unhappy with Charles Everard's text. He calls it in an email 'a pompous piece of crap that is more about him than me'. I tell him that it is too late to commission another piece from someone else, if the catalogue is to appear on time for the show; that he will just have to try to like it more. My email to him remains unanswered. The catalogue goes to the printers, with beautiful shots of the works by one of London's best photographers of sculptures – it is all in the lighting – and the text unchanged.

Penelope and I close the gallery on the evening of Thursday, 22 December. I know what I want to give Nicola for Christmas. I want to give her a painting, one that means something to me; something that I know about. The store-room at the gallery is small, but carpeted racks of framed paintings and works on paper run floor to ceiling. I had a show of Corinne Carr's work in the early nineties, before she left the gallery for a bigger, more famous one. At the time, she was painting beautifully delicate portraits in oil, or rather invented images of people that she conjured in her head. She said that her models did not move or need to take breaks for food or to relieve themselves. She asked me if she could paint me, however, and I said yes. She did it so that it looked nothing like me; a standing man in midnight blue, almost a silhouette with barely distinguishable features against a background of childlike trees in full leaf. She knew that they were my favourite thing, my emblem if you like. The painting is here somewhere. I want to give it to Nicola.

I spend all of the Saturday, Christmas Eve, trying to decide what to write in Nicola's card, and attempting to make the Stone House look more like a home inhabited by someone other than a lonely bachelor. I formulate a plan. One: light a fire in the stone-cold hearth. Two: empty the glass-recycling bin down in Stroud. Three: polish a pair of silver-handled knives and forks. Four: surprise her with supper. Cook it in time for when she arrives. Five: select music that is more about *us* than *me*. Six: do not drink before she arrives. *DO NOT* drink before she arrives.

There are gradients of familiarity and the path can be a slippery one. I cannot decide between 'Merry Christmas & a Happy New Year, love John' or 'Wishing you a very Happy Christmas & New Year, love John x' or 'To dear Nicola, wishing you a Happy Christmas, much love, John xx'. In the end, I choose the second one. It is not 'love' as in Linda, it is 'love' as in lust. But you cannot write that, can you?

Eight o'clock and she still has not come. I am on my third glass of red. A rack of lamb roasts in the oven like a slow-cook time-bomb. Where is she? The vegetables would be soup if I had put them on for when she said that she would arrive. I flick through Saturday-night television channels distractedly, half watching and half listening out for her.

Ten past eight and she is standing on the other side of the frosted-glass front door like a diffuse apparition.

'I'm sorry, I'm so late,' she says as I open the door. Her cheeks are slightly flushed from the cold and she is wearing a black or navy-blue knee-length coat. 'Taxis around here *never* come when they say they will.'

She hands me a bottle of red wine as she squeezes past me in the narrow hallway and kisses me quickly, almost shyly, on the lips. I take this as another sign that she does not feel that what has happened between us is a mistake. She smells of beautiful fresh air.

'I hope you haven't eaten,' I say. 'I've made us some supper.'

'I haven't even had lunch; I'm *starving*,' she replies. 'I spent the day in Cheltenham, being a dutiful great-niece in an old peoples' home there and then doing some last-minute Christmas shopping. I even got *you* something.'

'How exciting. Will you give me a little hint?'

'You'll just have to wait until tomorrow,' she replies.

I go into the kitchen to open a bottle of champagne and take Nicola a glass. She is standing at the sitting-room window with its open curtains, looking out onto the darkness of the valley. The fire seethes and cracks and stray sparks fly out of the grate onto the stone hearth. Here and there, the lights of houses or lonely cars penetrate the landscape saturated with blackness, like planets or shooting stars in the night sky. Otherwise, the valley is unpopulated by light.

Nicola smiles when I hand her the glass and I suddenly

realise that she is still wearing her coat. 'I'm so sorry; how rude of me,' I say. 'Too busy thinking about a drink for us.'

'I don't mind. I needed to warm up; it's freezing out there.'

'But still . . . my parents didn't pay all those school fees for nothing,' I joke.

'I was just admiring the view and the room again. They're lovely. It's just how a Cotswold cottage should be.'

'In some ways it is . . .' I trail off. 'It's very nice to see you. Do you want to eat in here near the fire?'

We are standing in the window together and I gently place my right hand in the small of her back, then lean in and kiss her on the lips. She turns towards me and does not break away or twist out of my clinch, making some kind apology, as I feared she might. Her mouth is so sweet and soft, so sweet and soft.

The conversation and the wine flow and we do not finish supper until after eleven. She spends the night with me, but we just hold each other. I stay wildly erect until I eventually fall asleep and we lie naked together like cupped spoons in a drawer; me holding her close and caressing her stomach, her breasts, her hair. She says that she wants to make love, but I have forgotten to buy protection. She says she has some at her house: at eighteen, I would have run there and back for the chance of sex, but it is too late for that. What a difference nearly thirty years makes.

That warmth beside me, that colonisation of the blank tomb of the right side of the bed. I cannot describe how it feels to have *life* there again.

I wake up from a deep sleep and Nicola is not there. I can hear sounds coming up from the kitchen. Christmas Day. Ice on the outside of the windowpanes. *Numb day, numb day, numb day. Two years, two years, two years.*

After coffee and porridge (I never usually *eat* breakfast), we walk down through the frozen wood hand-in-hand, me carrying a bag full of bottles in my left hand and Nicola holding her present, still wrapped, in her right. We do not see another soul all day; it is as if we are alone together in a new world, like Adam and Eve. I feel like a little boy holding her hand.

We prepare the turkey and vegetables together. The word '*stuffing*' gets me going, it really does. The *texture* of the word. The late Christmas lunch cooks on and in her large green Aga. The quick brown fox jumps over the lazy dog.

We open the first bottle of champagne at eleven and the presents soon afterwards. Well, present singular, as the only gift that I can see under the small Christmas tree, exquisitely decorated with miniature beeswax candles and gingerbread biscuits in the shapes of houses and snowmen with brightly coloured ribbons, is my one to Nicola.

'I *love* it. Who's it of?' she says as she pulls back the paper and the bubble-wrap. 'It's beautifully done.'

'It's not of anyone in particular,' I lie. 'One of my artists did it for me years ago and it means a lot to me. I wanted you to have it.'

'It reminds me of the woods here,' she says.

'That's why. I'm pleased you noticed the connection.'

'It's so sweet of you.' She kisses me slowly and takes a long slug of champagne. She is wearing her brown woollen knee-length dress and patent-leather dark-brown high heels from last night and her shoes are flecked with traces of mud from the walk.

'Give me five minutes,' she says. 'I'm just going to get you your present.'

She has shed her shoes at the bottom of the stairs. Her bare feet hardly make a sound as she climbs them. I finish my glass and pour myself another.

The sitting-room feels twilit, even though the Georgian

windows let on to a bright lawn and shrubberies still tinged with frost, irradiated by the low winter sun. Nicola has lit the candles on the tree and they give the room an atmosphere of warmth, of life, of family. They remind me of my childhood. They make the sitting-room feel like a church; the light that they cast is almost religious, the glow before an epiphany.

The sound of sharp heels on the stairs. My eyes nearly pop out of my head: she is wearing a velvet mini-dress the colour of fresh blood, with a white fur trim around the cuffs, hem and neckline. Her hair looks black in this light, like polished jet.

'I wanted to give you something special for Christmas,' she says and flashes her green eyes at me. 'Come here, Santa's little helper.'

My legs feel as if they are going to give way. It must be the champagne so early in the day. Nicola stands on the first step of the stairs and holds out a small turquoise leather jewellery box in both hands, smiling beautifully. Her skin has that rich, sweet smell of lily of the valley. I open the case that she is still holding in her warm hands; mine are shaking very slightly with tremens again. Inside is a pair of silver cufflinks with what look like small dark garnets cut in a cabochon.

'They're Edwardian,' she says. 'I bought them at a good jeweller's in Cheltenham. They're Birmingham assay apparently, 1908.'

'They're wonderful; they're far too generous of you, Nicola.'

'Nonsense; you deserve to have a nice Christmas again,' she says and kisses me long and full on the lips. I cannot believe my luck.

We sit on the sofa and drink champagne into the afternoon, waiting for the turkey to cook. By three o'clock it already feels like dusk and the candles are burning themselves down to stubs, the light that they give off ebbing and flickering on the walls.

Suddenly, as if something unnamed and unnameable has reached a critical mass between us, we are playing a version of spin-the-bottle without the bottle. We dare each other in turn, without saying a word, to remove our clothes. I forget to feel embarrassed by my pallor and lack of toning; seeing her body naked erases absolutely all thought from my mind. I am like a rabbit with myxomatosis caught in the most knock-me-down glorious headlights that I have ever seen. I look down at her and say, 'Have you been to Brazil lately?'

'That's a very personal question.' She smiles and blushes.

'It feels very personal,' I reply, reaching gently between her legs.

The television flickers in the corner. Our flesh flickers in and out on the Chesterfield. Images of a bright white and candy-pink neon-tube word-sculpture by the American artist Bruce Nauman flash on-off, on-off in my mind in throbbing capital letters. I am amazed that the Queen is able to keep her mind on her speech on the television:

'This yah, win thrits to world piss aind the laives of ordinry civilyins ah et en all-tam hah . . .'

>>RUN FROM FEAR/FUN FROM REAR<<

'. . . aind wut we tik as terrah firmah is shikkin by terrah, by bims aind man's capac'ty for villins . . .'

>>RUN FROM FEAR/FUN FROM REAR<<

'. . . we mist all rimimbah thet God moves in mistress ways . . .'

>>RUN FROM FEAR/FUN FROM REAR<<

'. . . *aind en and en and* OH *and en and* OOH *and en and en and* AH *and en and en . . .'*

When I come, I realise it is the first time inside a woman in more than two years. It is the release of so much *pressure*. All my Christmases have come at once. I feel guilty; I don't know why. It was Linda who left me.

I am writing this and it is already past midnight. Nicola is fast asleep under a blanket on the sofa. I have forgotten to call Bryony. *I have forgotten to call Bryony.*

Chapter Fourteen

January, that bleakest of months, passes in a blur like the landscape seen from a train window. Christmas has given way to the New Year; Saint Nicholas to Nicola. The sky is white-grey with cloud for the whole of the month. I do not remember seeing the sun once.

Nicola and I spend evenings, nights, together at least twice a week; either up here or down at the Court House. In the early days of an affair, or of love if you are lucky, familiarity makes the heart grow fonder. The absence only comes later.

My bank manager has a goitered neck like a vulture. The foreclosers are circling in. I have offered them five paintings as collateral on the loan and the bank has asked an independent valuer to visit the gallery and appraise them. I do not imagine that they will have heard of any of the artists, or know the true value of the works.

I do not want to tell Nicola that I am closing the gallery yet. I will just say a few words at Jake's opening, explaining that I have had enough of leading two lives between town and country and that I am going to carry on dealing from home. I will hardly be a loss to the London art world. I do not even register on the radar these days.

Bryony comes to visit on the third Friday in January and it is so good to see her again, to talk to her and tell her how much I love her and have missed her, after our month apart. Nicola rings on the Saturday morning to see if I want to do something in the evening. I cannot tell her about Bryony. I simply make the excuse that I have to go to see Tim and

Joanna in Wiltshire for the weekend again, and that we will have to do something nice together early next week instead. There will be no walking in the woods for Bryony and me this weekend.

I take her to Bristol Zoo on Sunday. The traffic on the M5 motorway is snarled up like the big cats in their concrete enclosures. I do not like zoos; all that natural, vital life contained in its manmade hell of pacing up and down, up and down with blank eyes and nervous tics like a convention of patients with Obsessive-Compulsive Disorder. Still, I thought that it might be good for Bryony to see these animals in their unnatural habitats, so that she can appreciate all the more how they *should* live. She wants to be a wildlife vet now.

'Dad, when Mum and Uncle Simon took me to Egypt we saw wild camels in the desert near the pyramids.'

'You don't *have* an Uncle Simon,' I say, my voice rising in pitch uncontrollably.

'Da-*ad*, you *know* who Simon is; he's Mum's – um – *friend*. He comes to stay sometimes.'

'I don't want you to mention his name again,' I say. One or two people turn and stare at me by the zebra enclosure when I say that. I did not mean to shout.

Bryony is very quiet in the car back to Stroud. I am worried that she does not enjoy staying with me any longer; things are too quiet for her here. She is becoming an urban teenager and I live out here in the sticks. My home is not her home any more.

'I saw humpback whales off the coast of Newfoundland on TV,' she whispers. 'I'd *really* love to see them in the wild.'

'I don't think wildlife vets operate on whales or marine mammals of that size, at least not in their natural habitat,' I say.

'Would you take me on holiday to see some whales one day?' she asks quietly.

'I'd really love to; that would be quite a treat.'

Nicola cooks me supper down at the Court House on the last Tuesday of the month. 'I've missed you since last week,' she says when she opens the door.

'I'm sorry about last weekend; one of those friendships from childhood. It's difficult to say no to Tim and family when they ask me over, and they do that often since I've been on my own.'

'And you can say no to me?'

'Not usually, it seems.' I smile and kiss her on the lips.

'So, what have you been up to?' she asks as we eat.

'Not much. That trip to Wiltshire and work, that's about it. The gallery's busy at the moment.'

'Selling a lot?'

'No, not *exactly* I'm afraid. We're preparing for that show I told you about.'

'*Jake* somebody?'

'Andreiou – it's Cypriot, apparently.'

There is a photograph of Nicola and her husband on the mantelpiece in the dining room where we are eating, taken at some smart event. She is wearing a sky-blue ball-dress, tasteful but slightly over-the-top; a touch of the late eighties insinuating itself into the mid-nineties when the photograph must, mathematically speaking to look at her then and now, have been taken. They look so young. He is, of course, wearing a dinner jacket and is quite handsome in the way of City types. He must have gone to public school; he has the jaw and that look in his eyes. I realise that I do not even know what his name was. He looks out of the photograph at us like a chaperone.

'What was your husband's name?' I ask, pointing at the photograph. 'He looks nice there; you both do, together and individually.'

'He *was* nice. His name was Jasper, like the stone.'

'That's a strong name. I've never met anyone with that

name before. There used to be that comedian on TV, didn't there? Don't West Country locals call wasps something similar?'

'I don't know; I've never heard them call them that. He was a WASP, though, through and through.'

'What d'you mean?'

'A White Anglo-Saxon Protestant: you Americans know a thing or two about them, I've heard.'

'Do we? I'm not sure. I've lived here for far too long. Never had any contact with the Church: religion strikes the fear of God into me.'

'Me too, particularly since he died. We used to call his tumour God's Gift. It was a glioma, one of the worst types you can get.'

'How the hell did you cope?' I ask. 'It must have been bloody hard looking after him.'

'It was a nightmarish eighteen months. I wanted him at home till the end, not in some grim hospital or hospice . . . You get through these things somehow.'

'I don't know how,' I say, 'I really don't.'

There is the sound of snapping twigs and branches in the undergrowth outside the dining-room windows. A young roe deer, not much larger than a greyhound, has come onto the lawn and is bathed for a moment in the light from the windows before it disappears into the night once more. Nicola looks out of the window and does not seem to see the trembling life that has made a momentary appearance beyond the glass. Perhaps she only sees her pale reflection or the aura of bright light from the room. She has gone very quiet, folded in on herself in the memory of grief.

'I'm sorry to bring up the subject of your husband like this. I didn't mean to pry,' I say to rouse her out of herself.

'You're not prying. I really don't mind talking about him. He's not a taboo subject. I don't have no-go areas like you seem to.'

'Still, I'm sorry if I upset you,' I say quietly, stroking her back softly, feeling her firm flesh and the stacked vertebrae of her spine through her silk blouse. 'I don't have no-go areas; I'm just not ready to talk about some things. They still hurt too much.'

'I understand,' she says. 'I'd never push you to talk about things that make you uncomfortable. I'm a good listener: that comes with my job, but I can't hear what you don't say.'

'I promise you'll be the first to hear if I have something to say about those things,' I echo her words. 'You're one of the only people I *could* talk to about them. Tim tries to listen but doesn't really understand. His marriage is fine and he's got two happy children. He's never lost anyone important from his life.'

'Lucky him,' she says. 'Lucky him. I'd like to meet him and his perfect family sometime.'

'Then we'll have to go to Wiltshire together one weekend and visit them. I'd like them to meet you too,' I reply.

She thinks that I go there far more often than I do. I cannot see her path through life ever crossing with Tim's. I could never let that happen.

Chapter Fifteen

Jake is getting anxious about how the critics will receive his new body of work, his metal men. I am worried that he will be lucky if any of them actually bother to visit the gallery. Ten years ago, most of the major papers and art journals sent someone along to review the shows that I put on. That brought the public in and the sales of works flowed naturally. It is so much easier to find buyers when they come to you. Today, I am lucky if one or two papers include a review: perhaps *The Mayfair Gazette* or the *St James's Times* might send someone junior along and give my show a short write-up as a local-interest story beneath an advert for an organic butcher or a bespoke tailor.

The installation takes two days. The men that I have hired to transport the eleven sculptures from Jake's studio to the gallery on a large truck have to take the skylight out from the roof above the gallery's main viewing area and crane the largest of the sculptures in that way. The landlord insists on being present throughout much of this operation and his attitude of suspicious scrutiny makes my resolution to close the gallery after Jake's show all the more certain. I do not tell him that, however.

They are all standing to attention now, Jake's motley army of agglomerate soldiers.

They look like the walking wounded after a particularly vicious campaign. They are shrapnel-men, blasted apart and put back together again by a blind God. I do not know what people will make of them. They will not look like art, I imagine, to those people who have an idea that art can only be art if it is of the pleasing blob-on-canvas or splash-on-paper kind. They look like the results of an accident in a welding shop. I think that I have become rather fond of them.

It is a rainy early February evening in St James's. I would not call it a *big* crowd, but there must be fifty or sixty people in the gallery. The metal golems of Jake's larger sculptures now seem to be striding across the wooden floor, to be mobile, mobilised. The smaller ones are positioned on simple white plinths, to be scrutinised at eye-level by the viewer. The roseate Charles Everard is here, glass in hand, trying to engage an openly hostile Jake in conversation about his latest works. Jake waves a bottle of beer at him as he tries to escape into the safety of his audience.

It is time. I tap my wineglass with my ring. I have not been able to take it off yet. 'Um, ladies and gentlemen,' I begin, glancing at Nicola who is dressed in a lovely *eau de nil* dress that matches her eyes. She winks at me and smiles. 'Ladies and gentlemen, thank you so much for coming tonight. As many of you know, I've had this gallery for nearly fifteen years now and Jake had his first exhibition here – can it really be? – almost ten years ago. It was a show of paintings then, making his name almost straight out of art school, and as you can see it is found-metal sculpture now. These sculptures are enigmatic ciphers of their age, to my mind extremely powerful statements of a new direction in Jake's work. I would like to welcome you to the show, which – without wanting to steal Jake's thunder – I'm very sad to say will be my last one here. But what a high note to go out on.'

I find myself saying these words and meaning every one of them. There are murmurs of genuine praise and feigned or, at least, puzzled consternation in equal parts from my audience.

'I think it'll probably come as a surprise to nearly all of

you, but I'm closing the gallery in March after the end of this show. I'm a country boy through and through and I've had enough of the commute into London and the current state of the gallery scene here. I think art dealing's a young man's game these days. I'm going to continue nurturing talent, trying to find young artists from art schools around the country to support alongside the more established artists on my books who, I hope, will stay with me as I deal by appointment from my old Cotswold house in Gloucestershire. Please enjoy Jake's show.'

There is a smattering of applause like a box of damp squibs going off. 'Hear, hear,' Charles Everard says halfheartedly. I cannot tell if he is being sarcastic. You would think my ear might be attuned to that peculiarly English trick of saying something without meaning it after all this time. Penelope is looking sad behind her raised glass of red. Jake raises a quizzical eyebrow or two and turns to an art dealer next to him, who has come along like a seagull hovering behind a trawler, and mutters something into his ear.

'You didn't tell me your plan,' Nicola says. 'How nice to have you all to myself in Glos seven days a week.'

'It'll take some getting used to; the not commuting or being in London, I mean.'

'I don't imagine you'll miss London,' she smiles. 'Except the gallery itself, of course. How amazing to have had one at all. It's a nice place. Are you going to sell it on as a going concern?'

'Afraid not; it's closing for good.'

'I'm pleased to have seen it,' she says.

'I'm glad you have done. This is what I've been doing for a living for most of my adult life. I'll miss it, despite the hassles.'

'I'm sure I can find ways to divert you,' she strokes my arm.

'I'm looking forward to that. I'd take pleasure before business any day of the week.'

'John, you're a dark horse, aren't you?' Jake says, coming over with a glass of red for me as Nicola goes to take a closer look at his behemoths. It must be my fourth or fifth glass; I am beginning to lose count. 'Why didn't you tell me your news – we've known each other for a long enough time by now through the ups and downs, haven't we? You're a bit like a young dad to me, if you don't mind me saying that.'

'I'd prefer *older brother*. I didn't want to worry you. Not with the show coming up. I thought that Penny would've said something. It's mostly a lifestyle decision. You can understand that, can't you? That bit about sticking with me, I said that for the audience. If you get an offer of better representation on the back of this show, bloody well grab it.'

'No offence, mate, but I'll have to. Don't know how my work would go down in your neck of the woods, nice as it must be.' He laughs.

'Hirst has his studio down the road. We're hardly the Outer Hebrides.'

'Quite so,' he says. 'I'm a city boy, though, you know that. My audience is still fairly young: the nouveau-affluent mostly, not weekending wigged barristers and stockbrokers.'

'There's actually an art-loving middle-class crowd who *live* there full-time, you know?' I say.

'Is there now? Like a good Beryl Cook or two, do they?' he grins. 'It's good to see some people here. You and Penny did a good job on that. I wish that drunken tosser would leave me alone, though. He really is an unmitigated prat.'

'An unmitigated *influential* prat, I think you mean. He can help you, Jake, don't forget that.'

'Yeah, maybe. The trouble is, his way of helping involves a tube of KY Jelly and elephant-strength rubber-jonnies,' he says and laughs uproariously.

* * *

As I am searching for Nicola's coat at the end of the evening, I find Penelope crying in the back office. I feel that I have badly let her down somehow.

'I'm sorry; I haven't handled all of this closing business very well, have I?' I say. 'What luck've you been having finding something else, Penny?'

'It's not about finding a job,' she says, wiping at her eyes with the back of her hand. 'I've had one or two other offers lately and Jake has asked me to move in with him. I'm sad for *you*. I know how bloody tough everything has been over the past few years. I'm worried about you: being lonely, stuck out there at home every day all day.'

'I've got Nicola now. I'll be okay. It's so sweet of you to worry, though. I couldn't have managed without you, I really couldn't.'

'I really hope you *will* be okay,' she says, smiling with her eyes still brimming with tears. 'I want that so much for you. We've been a good little team, haven't we?'

'We bloody have,' I say. 'Just a run of losses lately, that's all.' I give her a kind of awkward, tight bear-hug and suddenly my own tears flow and flow. It must be the wine. I am beginning to feel very drunk. I am suddenly punch-drunk, although we are drinking red wine.

Valentine's Day and the snows have come back again. I do not know how I should feel today. Guilt at what was occludes the pleasure at what is like low winter clouds before the sun. Nicola is taking me back to Il Trovatore again to celebrate the day. I hope that our Italian waiter with a West Country accent is having another night off tonight.

My Valentine has me hypnotised in her spell. She has green eyes like the deep waters of the Nile; she is my raven-haired Cleopatra. Better beware the asp. My Valentine has eyes that could charm snakes. Beware the asp. She has a dead husband, a dead husband who will be our chaperone tonight.

Chapter Sixteen

I first met Linda in the Junior Common Room at King's when we were both nineteen-year-old undergraduates in our first year. I would not say that it was love at first sight, but I certainly thought that she was a very attractive girl. She was tall and dark blonde, with a fine-featured, very open face. Who would not be drawn to someone like her? I do not know what she made of me the first time that we met.

She was not a student at King's, but at the London School of Economics, which even in the late seventies was a superior institution. She was far brighter than I was: there is no question about it. She was straight As, as her daughter will be. I was awash with Cs.

She was playing darts with a very odd, almost underarm, throwing action. She was totally unaffected like that and simply did not care what other people might think of her. She laughed at herself without any embarrassment as one dart after another missed its target or bounced off the board. The group of friends around her seemed to see her as someone to look up to, a kind of unselfconscious and self-deprecating leader who managed to inspire others to try to be better people even while not taking herself too seriously. She had that effect on me: I tried and failed and look how I have ended up.

We did not talk much about where we both came from or what our lives had been like when we were first getting to know each other. I just knew that she had been to some grammar school up north and had always been considered as one of the brightest girls in her year. When she had come up to the London School of Economics she had been shocked to find that everyone else seemed just as bright, if not brighter, and that she had real competition for the first time in her life. She was interested that my father worked for Washington, because of the politics side of her degree. She had a real depth that I found intriguing; she was not religious, she did not even believe in God, but had her feet firmly on the ground and balanced my character so prone to its flights of imagination and excess.

It was not all a meeting of very different minds. I wanted to sleep with her, but for some reason seemed to find the idea of getting to know her in the flesh, as it were, almost sacrilegious, as if the act would taint something pure between us. It was not that I was particularly unconfident in that arena in my late teens and very early twenties. There had been a few others whose haloes had been tarnished by the grease of my loins. I am an American, after all: sex is one of our great national sports. It was that I saw her differently from the other women who I found attractive; I knew that she was more special than they were. Perhaps I realised even then she would be the love of my life.

We did not become an item for a long time, until almost the end of my third year. I was reading English with a subsidiary in French and Linda was studying her politics with philosophy. My degree engaged the ear and mouth, hers the higher faculties. She was a short walk away up Southampton Row from my campus on the Strand, but there were one or two other girls I was interested in for the first couple of years of university and I only saw Linda when we met, often apparently by chance, through our extended social group of college friends. She was a close childhood friend of one of my roommates, with whom I have now lost touch completely. He obviously thought that Linda was too good for me. He was jealous of the attention that she gave me whenever we all met up: you could see it in the way he constantly tried to position himself by her side when a group of us was out; you could hear it in the way he always told everyone stories about their childhood together, to show how far back they went. It wasn't that he wanted her as a lover for himself; he liked men, not women. But he kept on trying to warn her off me. She went with her heart, not his head, in the end. He only ever spoke to me again briefly once or twice when he used to ring our home, many years later, to talk to Linda.

It was at a house party in Notting Hill in the spring of 1980, three months before we graduated, that I had drunk down enough Dutch courage to try it on with her. I was genuinely surprised when she reciprocated; perhaps her judgement was impaired by the impending liberation from the hard academic labour that we all faced that year, and by harder liquor. What was Linda like as a lover? She was very tender, she *felt* everything very intensely. Nicola has sex almost as if she has become detached from her body, as if she is being watched by a panel of judges ('It's a *six point nine* from the Swedish judge . . .') and trying to convince a particularly embittered Eastern European audience that she is natural World Championship gymnastics material, despite being English. Linda never seemed more alive, more in the essence of herself, than when we were making love.

Linda's other friends seemed to like me more than my former roommate did. I think that they thought I was somehow more streetwise than they were, with their provincial English backgrounds. Little did they know that, far from Washington and the sheer scale and shine of the US, the only place where I felt happy was the English countryside, walking the woods and fields with someone beside me, or alone.

We were practically inseparable until she left that Christmas Day. We moved in together in the autumn after university, into a one-bedroom apartment in Shoreditch before it became fashionable and was more about degeneration than regeneration. At first, I viewed our living together, our *being* together, with ironic detachment, as if it was happening to someone else. It meant more and more to me, I *meant* it more and more, as the weeks and months, the years went by.

Things were hard financially in our twenties, but we both fought to find our way at a time when work, careers, *success* seemed to have become a new kind of competitive sport. Mobile telephones cost as much as televisions do today and were the size and weight of breezeblocks, reminiscent of field telephones from the Second World War. There was a plague of grey slip-on shoes throughout the City, and indeed the whole country. There seemed to be a great deal of bouffant hair going around. A tide of Estuary English flooded the land. An efflorescence of cash saw the art world begin to boom.

Linda tried her hand at journalism on several local London papers and I, with the benefit of some name-dropping of contacts in diplomatic circles and the promise of a cash-rich list of potential clients, scraped and bowed my way into a second-rate commercial gallery near Piccadilly. I did not know much about art at that stage, but knew that I liked the cut-and-thrust, the drama, the intrigue of the world that swirled around it like a money-sucking cyclone.

The problem was that I drank too much even then. What else has the problem ever been? I got drunk at our gallery openings. I was a wallflower who became so plastered in order to talk up the god-awful nineteenth-century still-lives, landscapes and nudes that the gallery sold that I would not, could not, do my job of actually *selling* on the night. Usually, I was a good salesman on a one-to-one basis during the day. You do not have to believe in what you are selling to sell it well, just as you do not need to believe in what you are saying in order to lie convincingly. You can train yourself to pass the lie-detector test. The problem was that the gallery's sales reached their zenith, their apotheosis, their giddy heights, at the monthly *vernissages*, when into the two large viewing rooms were crowded perhaps one hundred and fifty of the most cash-laden and taste-bereft collectors in London. Those monthly events, multiplied by twelve, accounted for fifty percent of the gallery's takings each year. It was these crowds of philistines that made me need to drink to get through those opening nights. I could not change. Linda liked me for it in some ways then; she thought that I was just a little bohemian and out-of-kilter with the everyday. That first gallery asked me to leave after a couple of years.

I repeated the same mistake, with minor variations in the details, throughout my twenties, but the art market was glowing white-hot and it was not difficult to find a job in those days in the slightly less than blue-chip galleries. You made connections, contacts. I moved forward in time, from the nineteenth century into contemporary art and somehow knew that this was my *métier*, my subject-matter, my meat-and-bones, my intellectual manor. I got fired again and my parents offered to give me my small inheritance early as a lifetime gift. As their only child, the Stone House would come to me eventually in any case. On my thirtieth birthday they gave me enough money from their retirement fund to pay for the rental of my own gallery space for a couple of years, and for me to employ an assistant or to live on the rest for a short while.

Linda and I got married that same year, in a simple ceremony at Marylebone Register Office. Both of our sets of parents and Linda's sister were there, of course, and an unmarried Tim was my cheaply suited best man. That day must have been the highpoint of my life, that and the day Bryony was born.

We were happy and in love in those first London years and having Bryony later on, just before we moved down here to the Stone House with my parents' blessing, only made it even better for a while. Aren't all of our lives built out of other peoples' clichés? I don't think that we ever stopped loving each other. I know that I never stopped believing Linda was more special than other women, although I certainly did stop making her happy when I look back at myself now in the sober light of day. She stayed with me because she loved me, not because she necessarily liked me. The loving keeps you in a marriage; the liking makes it work. Leaving was not a choice for her until she found the strength to go in the ice and snow that day. Her going was just meant to be a warning, a lesson, a shot across the bows for me. I know that she would have come back to me if she could, I just know it in the deepest recesses of my heart.

Chapter Seventeen

March is a month of notices: of a surprising number of good reviews for Jake's show and of eviction orders. I have informed the landlords that I am vacating the premises at the end of the month, but have not paid the rent since the turn of the New Year. They can keep my deposit. They want that money, however, for potential delapidations and are playing hardball.

I lock up the gallery for the last time in the middle of the month, as soon as Jake's show has come to a close. Eight out of the eleven metal men have sold. My commission on them will help me to survive, to hang on financially, for a while. Turning the gallery's mortise lock into place for the last time dislodges something in me.

I take Penelope and Jake out for a drink in the pub on Duke Street and then on for supper in a St James's restaurant as a kind of farewell. It is obvious that Jake is trying not to appear too happy about the reviews on my account, because he thinks that I am perhaps sadder than I actually am about closing the gallery. I am grateful to him for his thoughtfulness. I know from Penelope that he has also had one or two approaches from other galleries, although he has the tact not to bring that up right now either. Penelope is in love with him, I am sure of that. You can see it in the way she touches his arm or hand when she talks about something that relates to them both.

'I still can't believe it,' she says. 'It's been such a big part of my life for the past seven years.'

'You've got to see this change as something positive,' I reply. 'We're moving on in new directions, aren't we? Jake with his sculpture and this new buzz about his work–' *touch, touch* goes her soft right hand on his strong left arm '–and you'll be swamped with job offers, Penny, I just know it. I'm obviously sad that it's come to an end, but I've learnt a lot about life, if nothing else, building up the gallery and the business, if you can call what I've done building it up. I found Jake, didn't I? And I discovered Corinne Carr and Max Jones: just a couple of my successes. I'm looking forward to doing something different; to dealing from home.'

'Won't you miss London?' Jake asks.

'You know, I don't think so. I *thought* I would when I first considered closing down, but I don't think I will now.'

'I can't imagine life without this city,' he says.

'You're still pretty young, Jake. What are you, thirty-two? I promise, even *you* will long to be somewhere else one day. There's a big world out there.'

'Yes, thirty-two: well remembered. It may be a big world out there, but it's full of crap art,' he says, '– except New York, Tokyo and Berlin, of course.'

'Won't you be *lonely?*' Penelope asks. 'I know you're strong from how you've coped, God knows how, for the last two years, but don't you worry you won't have *people* around?'

'I've got Nicola now. She's more than enough company for me.' I laugh. 'And I've got Bryony to think about.'

'John, please,' Penelope says, 'please see someone. Talk to them about what you've been through, what you're going through. Please look after yourself for me.'

The waiter is clearing away our plates as she says these words and he glances over at me from behind Penelope's right shoulder. Jake is looking down at the empty place that his plate has vacated: he seems embarrassed somehow, lost in thought, as if he is unwilling or unable to involve himself in this conversation that is not about art.

* * *

The gallery's stock arrives at the Stone House in a small lorry perhaps one week later, towards the end of the month. I think that it is a Friday, although the days are already beginning to roll into one another, to elide together, now that I no longer have to commute or to keep regular hours. I can work until two a.m. on gallery business, sending out emails to old clients telling them of my move and drinking down a bottle of red, and then sleep until noon if I wish. The answerphone is my new assistant.

Bryony will have to sleep in the small spare bedroom when she comes to stay. Her room is stacked wall-to-wall with framed paintings and works on paper now, with a narrow corridor running the depth of the room between the stacks. I own my surname in works of art.

The valuer appointed by my bank could not make it to the gallery in time, the two miles across the city from his place of work. Instead, he trundles on the push-me-pull-you train into Stroud station on the rainy Monday morning after the stock has arrived and I collect him from there and drive him back to the house. His name is Brian Renfrew and he works for the insurance company that covers my bank's business-loan arm. He looks like a child mathematics prodigy grown middle-aged and talks with the monotone, unmusical voice of someone who studied accountancy at night school or some regional polytechnic.

'How long will this whole thing take?' I ask.

'I suppose until I've found eighteen thousand pounds worth of pictures,' he intones.

'There's a roomful upstairs,' I reply. 'Is contemporary art your bag?'

'My what?' he asks, pushing his glasses up the bridge of his nose with a thin index finger.

'Your thing: your specialist area?'

'I don't understand why people make such a fuss about it,' he says moronically. 'I always think my kids could make the things by contemporary artists that I've seen. I can easily get independent prices on your artists for my valuation, if there are any of those available, from information on the Net. All I need are the artists' names.'

'Very well then,' I reply between tight lips. 'I'll show you upstairs and leave you to it.'

I take him up to the room and let him get on with his robotic quantity surveying of the fruits of my hard graft and the friendships that I have forged with their creators over the last fifteen years of my life. He will understand nothing of their quality. Who does he think he is, invading my home and denigrating my career like this? While I am drafting emails on my laptop in the sitting-room, tap-tap-tapping out my anger on the keyboard, I can hear his footsteps on the floorboards above me as he moves the pictures from one stack to another. His glasses can freeze over before I will offer to help him.

Every few minutes his muffled voice filters downstairs, speaking in bursts of no more than twenty seconds. At first, I think that he must be talking to himself, that I have an involuntary garbler on my hands, as well as having to endure his presence in my home. '*Click* . . . car . . . landscape in oils . . . image seven . . . one to one-five . . . *click*,' he announces. He is committing his wants to Dicta-phone.

'Would you like a coffee?' I ask at eleven thirty.

'Milk and two sugars, please,' he sends back down in his drone.

Milk, two sugars and a good dose of ex-lax, I say to myself as I search the medicine cupboard in the kitchen for the plastic bottle whose contents I sometimes needed when I was taking Valium. It will not do him any harm, this liquor for loosening the bowels, but will make this day one that he will not forget for a long time. *Welcome to the Cotswolds, Home of Diarrhoea.*

By one o'clock, he is asking where the bathroom is. He seems to be in there an awfully long time. I hear a stifled groan at one point. As he returns to the stacks of pictures, an almost imperceptible scent of cow-byres wafts down the stairs.

'Would you like a bite of lunch?' I shout up.

'N-no thanks,' he says. 'Could I just have a glass of water?'

'No problem,' I reply.

The pitter-patter of tiny feet on the floorboards above continues into the afternoon. Brian works in half-hourly cycles of lifting, moving, Dictaphone work then bathroom. He appears at around three with an ashen face and a faint sheen of sweat on his upper lip.

'I think I've got what I needed,' he says. 'Is there any chance of a lift back down to the station?'

'That would be my pleasure.'

'Not feeling too good,' he says. 'Think it must've been the pasty I ate on the train on the way down here.'

'I hope you've learnt something new about contemporary art at least,' I reply with the faintest of smiles.

Nicola and I go away to Cornwall for a long weekend at the end of March. I drive us to Padstow in the Volvo and we stay at the austerely grand, granite-coloured hotel up on the headland above the harbour. I have enough money at the moment from the commission on Jake's sales, but if I continue living like this I don't think that it will last me too long.

I have been here twice before. My parents brought me to Padstow once when I was in my teens, as a part of their 'doing England' campaign. Back then it was an unspoilt small fishing port and there was even talk of an old witch who lived in one of the more distinctive houses on the left of the harbour, with a covered stone balcony like a pulpit for the insane where she stood and babbled on warmer days. I even saw the old crone once, standing in her stone portico and talking to the swirling waters of the harbour in language as indecipherable as the patterns of the waves. I came back once again with Linda and Bryony, when she was less than a year old. The witch, if she really ever had been one, was long dead. Today, my Volvo is not alone and crowds shop at the local delicatessens and stock up on bouillabaisse before heading off back to the nearest motorway.

We have the very first argument of our relationship, more a minor disagreement, the evening that we arrive. It starts with me wanting to drink and her wanting to eat.

'I've just driven for four and a half hours to get here,' I say. 'Give a guy a *break*. I just want a couple of pints in the local.'

'You know I don't like pubs,' she answers. 'They're so exactly that: *local*; parochial. I thought we were going out for dinner.' Nicola has spent half an hour dressing and putting on her makeup, even though her skin at thirty-six looks just as good without it.

'Indulge me just this once,' I say. 'I'm tired from the drive. We'll have supper afterwards.'

'Indulge you? I do nothing but, on many fronts.' She pouts for England and goes out onto the balcony for a cigarette, then another.

In the pub, Nicola makes me order her one Pimm's and lemonade after another, while I drink two or three pints of the local beer. I do not think that the barman has had a request for Pimm's before. When I order the first one he asks, 'D'you want a dash of lime with that?' The bottle still has its top sealed. He twists it off with a flourish as if he is about to pour a much more exotic cocktail.

The pub is heaving with the local Saturday-night crowd and Nicola acts like a threshing-flail on all of the men. If they are the eager stalks of corn in a cornfield, she flattens them in crop-circles around her with her flailing beauty. One local, a dark-haired man of about thirty, good-looking in a feral kind of way, keeps staring at her. He has dark eyes like polished flints, the eyes of a magpie. He looks like he would steal the shit off a dung-beetle.

'I don't think you'd want the sort of attention he'd like to give you,' I whisper in her ear.

'How d'you know? I might.' She pouts sulkily and adjusts her sparkly low-cut top.

'Put yourself away and let's go,' I say, already slurring slightly. 'I don't think it meant *soliciting* when the Law Society qualified you to practise.'

'You cheeky git,' she says and laughs for the first time tonight. 'You give me more attention one-to-one, then, over dinner and I'll forgive you for bringing me to this dive. What's it called anyway, the Fuck 'n' Firkin?'

'I've no idea; I didn't notice the sign when we came in. Too busy looking at you.'

Our sex that night is particularly good. We are getting to know each other's bodies well now; to lick, feel, find what makes us tick, tick, tick like little time-bombs, tighten and release like the coiled springs of an alarm-clock. An 'I love you' escapes her lips as she climaxes. I assume that it is just a slip-of-the-tongue of pleasure. I am not her man of stone.

Chapter Eighteen

I am an April fool: a pinch and a punch for the first of the month. Not even Bryony has sent me a card. The only one that I receive is from Tim and family. I used to get teased at school for having a birthday on 1 April, but the good thing was that each year they all forgot about this reason for teasing me after only a week or two.

Forty-six and all I have are the television and a bottle of wine for company. I did not want to tell Nicola in case it embarrassed her that she did not know it was my birthday. But then again, how could she have known that if I have not told her?

Penelope sends me an email, asking how I am and saying that she misses my silences the first thing in the morning when I arrived at the gallery with my need for a caffeine fix before I regained the use of speech. I take it as a birthday greeting, even though she does not specifically mention the day in her message.

The clients that I thought were loyal to the gallery must check their emails and their answerphones only rarely. I have not sold a picture in two weeks. Translating from the actual to the virtual when selling works of art is not easy; people want to see, hold, and touch what they are buying, to look for the aura of originality in it as if discovering it for themselves. You can sell posters, multiple prints, anything, it seems, other than one-off pieces of fine art from a website without the public wanting to view them first-hand before they actually part with their money.

The aura of the original: I could go out and purchase a pot of house-paint tomorrow and a fat horse-hair brush and paint my mark on old bits of board, on prepared canvasses, on my walls like a fresco. The individuality of my hand would not make this an original expression. All over the world, people go crazy and smear their faeces on their walls. It does not make them artists. That is the problem with people: they do not know whether they are looking at shit or genius. They have to be told.

The bank has sent me a list of twenty-five works that they are taking as collateral on my defaulted loan. That makes an average retail value of just over seven hundred pounds per picture. Brian Renfrew might have been generous with his bowels, but he was terribly tight with his prices. I send back the list to the bank, carefully annotated.

~~Jake Andreiou, 'Shut Eye', oil on canvas, 1994, £1,200~~
  sold
Jake Andreiou, 'Life's a Gas', oil on board, 1995, £1,000
Corinne Carr, 'Portrait X', oil on board, 1998, £900
Corinne Carr, 'What shall we do with the drunken
  Sailor?', watercolour, £500
~~Sandra Langdon, 'Untitled', oil on canvas, 1993, £900~~
  sold
Sandra Langdon, 'Untitled II', ' ', 1993, £900
Max Jones, 'Fluffer (Pornography Series)', cibachrome
  print, £500 . . .

The list goes on. In all, I mark seven as sold and add in a B-team set of replacements, selecting the worst pictures from my stock of more than one hundred and fifty works and giving them values so that they total the shortfall. They will all be packed when the shipper comes to collect my debt.

I am not feeling well and my brain is rebelling more forcefully than it usually does. It seems that the drinking fuels

147

these intrusive thoughts that I have; drinking and all of this time that I spend alone. My brain has become convinced, on very slender circumstantial evidence, that Nicola did something bad to her husband. I cannot get these thoughts out of my head. I am not sure what my mind thinks about all of this yet, what my heart feels about these biochemical suggestions that my synapses fire out, telling me outlandish stories. It is difficult to feel comfortable seeing her, being with her, when I am like this. I am worried that these thoughts might pounce out, escape over the high walls that I build around them, and attack her.

I have been looking up gliomas on the Internet, the type of tumour that Nicola says her man of stone had. There seem to be so many different types, all of them fatal: oligodendrogliomas, astrocytomas, ependymomas, oligoastrocytomas. There is very little mention of what the end-stage of the illness is like, although words such as 'coma', 'feeding-tube' and 'fits' all appear like spectres at the feast of my search results.

I cannot believe that Nicola had her husband at home until the end and looked after him on her own. That does not seem possible to me at all. I think that she is not telling me the truth for some reason. I do not know why. I sometimes wonder what is going on beneath her beautiful exterior. I cannot stop thinking about it today. Nicola is so difficult to read; she would make a perfect poker player. I am sure that she makes an excellent lawyer.

The ploughed fields to the north side of the Stone House are covered in a light dusting of late snow. A flock of birds starts up like the notes shaken from a sheet of music. I have to get out, out into the open. I am like one of those animals in their cages at the zoo: a mangy brown bear, perhaps, rubbing itself endlessly against the steel cage of its mind, or a flea-bitten hyena or jackal, picking over the dead flesh of old thoughts.

Nicola and I have an unspoken rule not to see each other

during weekdays – I never drive down into Cheltenham to see her at lunchtime, for instance – but only on week-nights when possible and at weekends. She often only gets back to the Court House from the office quite late into the evening and sometimes has to travel to see clients in other towns throughout the South West. She probably thinks that I am working hard at my newly configured business, not suspecting even for the time it takes for a single pulse of thought to pass from one neuron to another that I am researching the disease that she says killed her husband.

There is a fierce north-easterly wind. The fine powder of snow is whipped into my face as I walk. I reach that dark tunnel of trees again on the shorter road route into Stroud, the green light filtering down through the dense frost-laden foliage at this spot as if to the bottom of a lake. My nerves jangle like sheared steel on steel whenever I come near to this place. I do all that I can not to come here, but my body forces me to walk out to this section of road as if on a terrible pilgrimage whenever the urge takes it. There is always utter silence here. Cars only drive past every three or four minutes. Perhaps half an hour passes before I even realise that I have stopped walking, that my feet have glued themselves to the thin layer of icy leaf-mould at the edge of the road.

Things make their indelible imprint on this world; events leave behind their mark on places long after we are gone: they echo on down through the generations. Perhaps their muffled cries leaked out of the wreckage that day and could be heard still in this silence if only one listened closely enough. I was not there to hear them until it was far too late. I am still trying to make sense of it all. I am still trying to find some meaning. I feel as if my soul has been sucked out and coming here only empties me even further until all that is left is flesh and bones.

My feet unstick themselves at last and I am off again like a fugitive up the country lanes to the top of the Cotswold escarpment. The scattered villages up here have a feeling of otherworldly remoteness, of isolation. If the snows were any heavier, you would not be able to drive in or out of them. Unlike the position of the Stone House, there is no view down from up here. The villages punctuate a flat plateau of arable land, of one farm after another with dry-stone walls dividing each field from the other. The houses are built from the same Cotswold stone as the walls, which turns lichen-grey after decades and centuries of exposure to the harsh unbroken winds and the changing elements.

We looked at a two-bedroom cottage in Far Oakridge, one of the quaintest villages around here, just for fun when we decided to move down to Gloucestershire full-time. I sit on a bench on the village green there, with its old-fashioned cast-iron red telephone box and the Victorian post-box with its 'VR' insignia. My breath plumes in the frozen air like a smokescreen. It is the middle of the Easter holidays and I watch the cottage that Linda and I looked at in the village, to see how life there is now.

There is a light on above the front door. It is nearly noon and someone must have forgotten to switch it off. Nothing happens at first. A few cars pass. One or two pensioners hobble carefully along the road with their indistinguishable small brown dogs, whiskers discoloured by an endless diet of cheap dog food.

You see people like the family that emerges from the house if you order what you wear from clothing catalogues. They look like they are on their way *en famille* to a round of golf and wear pastel shades. In the catalogues they have thousand-yard stares, but in real life they look adoringly at one another as, suddenly extinguishing the exterior light and appearing through the wooden front door of the cottage, they make their way to a grey Mercedes estate car. They are intact. They are, or at least appear to be, a nuclear family rather than post-apocalyptically fractured and broken beyond repair. He is about forty, with a full head of nut-brown hair. She is mumsily attractive and slightly younger. Their two children, a girl and a boy both under ten, look like the sort of children you would write round-robin Christmas letters about. They glance over at me, sitting only twenty or thirty yards from their front door, with the unoccluded eyes of childhood. They probably think that I am a country tramp, taking the spring air.

I take Nicola out to supper on Saturday night, not down into Stroud but on the fifteen-mile drive into Cheltenham. I am still finding it difficult not to look at her with the eyes of a detective. I still find it difficult not to look at her with the eyes of lust.

Cheltenham feels like the big city after my sequestration in a small hamlet for more than a month. The light from shop windows and the beams of car lights gleam on the tarmac wet with melted snow.

'What was it like growing up around here then?' I ask.

'It was nice, safe. Pretty but boring, I suppose,' she says.

'What did you do as a teenager to keep yourself out of mischief?'

'Mostly nag our parents for lifts into town. We lived a couple of miles out in the countryside towards Evesham. My sister and I went to the cinema, the pubs and clubs when we were a bit older, shopping. What do most girls do when they're teenagers?'

'Chase boys?'

'There was a bit of that. More them chasing me, actually,' she says with a laugh.

'Did they catch you often?'

'That would be telling,' she says.

The Georgian and Regency façades are filled with up-market boutique shops, mobile-phone stores, restaurants and pubs. The spa waters that made the town famous have been channelled to a solitary unsupped tap at the Pitville Pump Rooms.

We drive out before supper to the house where Nicola grew up. At first, she does not seem keen to go there, but I insist and she gives in. I wonder if she is somehow ashamed of where she comes from, or simply uninterested in revisiting her past. The countryside is pitch-black and I cannot see much on the way there, only the heavily-inked outlines of trees and occasional buildings against an almost indigo sky.

'It's round this next corner on the left-hand side,' Nicola says after we have driven for about fifteen minutes from the centre of the town.

'It's so dark I can't see much,' I say, concentrating on the winding road ahead, illuminated by the converging beams of the headlights.

'Pull in here,' she says suddenly.

I stop the car in the mouth of a single-track, metalled driveway that appears to peter out into blackness. There is a thin moon in the cloudless sky, but you could get quickly lost in this darkness.

'Follow me,' Nicola leans over and whispers in my ear, before opening the door and getting out of the car. 'I know where I'm going,' she adds quietly, then shuts the car door behind her. I switch off the ignition and the lights and follow her down the driveway. I am using my mobile phone as a torch, but it gives off only a very weak, silvery light. The track curves gently downhill for perhaps two hundred yards between what seem to be two large fields of grass. We turn a bend about halfway down the driveway and Nicola takes my hand in hers. Suddenly, lit up like a cruise ship, a beautiful seventeenth- or eighteenth-century manor house emerges from the bottom of the small valley, the sort of house that local millionaire merchants in the wool trade had built for themselves back then.

'Bloody hell, that's rather grand, isn't it?'

'This is where I grew up,' she says simply. 'I was very happy here as a child.'

'I can see why. It's beautiful. Was all of this land yours as well? All the glossy magazines would salivate over a house like this.'

'It was our home, John,' she replies quietly, linking her arm in mine and leaning her head on my shoulder. 'I loved this place. My parents eventually lost Broadstones after Black Wednesday. My father invested quite heavily in Lloyds and came out with nothing. It killed him.'

'Not literally, I hope.'

'I mean it,' she says. 'He never recovered. Their marriage began to unwind and his health suffered badly. He had a quadruple heart bypass at sixty-three and was dead two years later,' she says with a twist of vehemence in her voice that I have not heard before.

'I'm so sorry,' is all I can reply.

The following night back at the Stone House, the telephone calls begin again. The usual static and terrible silence. The first call cuts out after a few seconds, but the phone rings again five minutes later.

'John, I'm sorry I didn't say anything before.'

'Who *is* this?' I ask, my vocal cords suddenly tightening so that my voice comes out hoarse.

'You know who I am,' the female voice says.

'No, I don't. NO, I DON'T,' I shout. 'Please stop ringing me. *Please.*'

'John, we need to talk,' she says. 'We need to talk about what happened.'

For a moment I think that it is Linda. Something tears inside me. It cannot be her. This time it is me who cuts the line. She does not try to call back again during the long dark hours of the night.

Christ rose again at Easter. That is what the Bible stories say. He rose again and saved mankind from sin. I never believed those stories as a child; they seemed too illogical to me. They were no truer than the fairy tales that my mother read to me, sitting on the edge of my bed, before lights-out.

This Easter everyone is on their way to DIY superstores. The True Cross is cut-price in the timber yards. It is made of MDF. I used to hide little chocolate Easter eggs around the garden for Bryony to find. I had to remember not to hide them too high up, not to place them out of her reach on the branches of trees or in the small cracks in the walls of our house. I could hide the eggs a little farther up each year that she grew, as her field of vision took in ever greater horizons.

I have sent Bryony an Easter card with a little yellow woollen chick inside. I hope that she does not think that it is too infantile or babyish. I hope that my message of love from father to daughter reminds her that I am here thinking of her, and that I feel alone. I am jealous of her mother's possession of her daughter. I am not seeing her again until next weekend.

The winter weather has gone and the green shoots of spring are everywhere. No one is buying my pictures, my business is becalmed. I am stranded on an island of my own making. It is a green and fertile island, but an island all the same.

Chapter Nineteen

I cannot stopper these thoughts that are effervescing in my brain that Nicola has a secret, that she is hiding something terrible, that what you see is not what you get with her. The thoughts are building up pressure, they want to uncork themselves. It is easy to be blinded by how kind she is to me. I cannot let her meet Bryony: I think that would be very awkward for everyone concerned. I need to know that Nicola is long-term before I introduce my daughter into the equation.

Nicola is the regular one in all of this, despite her being so much more attractive than I am and able, I am sure, to do a lot better than me. She rings at least once a day to ask me how I am and what I am up to. I am more of a twice-a-week man. I have had enough of telephones.

I do not know why she needs to lie about her man of stone; why she tells me that she looked after him at home without any help until the end, apart from daily visits from a Macmillan cancer nurse with shots of morphine for the patient. The Court House is not a hospital or a hospice; it is not equipped with what you would need to tend to a man in the terminal stages of a disease. The cancer eating away at his brain would have rendered him inert, unable to eat or drink, to relieve himself voluntarily, for the last weeks or days of his life. Perhaps Nicola is ashamed that she could not look after him; that she had to surrender him to the healthcare system in the end. That, or he died from something else or in another way entirely and she is not telling me.

* * *

In the last week of April, I have my first sale since the closure of the gallery. The man leaves a message on my answerphone, having got the new number from the gallery website, and introduces himself as 'Mr Vicks'. Never trust a man who introduces himself as 'Mr': he will always be a cantankerous idiot or an illiterate cretin. Think of Mr President, George W. Bush, or the Mr Men.

I ring Mr Vicks back and make a joke about him being the heir to the VapoRub fortune. It misses him by a country mile.

'Now look here,' he says, 'saw your website and want to buy something for the wife. It's her sixtieth, see.'

'I do indeed,' I reply. I suspect that he might be Welsh. 'How can I help?'

'She likes trees,' he says.

'So do I; they're one of my favourite things.'

'How much is it then?'

'How much is what?' I ask.

'The one with the trees, see,' he snaps back.

'D'you mean the one with the man standing in front of some trees, by Corinne Carr?'

'*Finally* we're getting somewhere,' he says with the voice of a father talking to his slow child.

'It's sold, I'm afraid. I must've forgotten to take it off the website.' Balloons and pins to his self-inflated rudeness.

'Anyone would think you don't want to do business with me,' he says. 'I've made millions in fruit 'n' veg. I own a chain of greengrocers that stretches from Mold to Llandrindod Wells.'

'Good for you, literally,' I joke. 'I do have another painting of trees.'

'Is it on your website?' he asks peremptorily.

'No.'

'Why not? Isn't it any good?'

'Quite the opposite,' I reply firmly, 'it's really rather good. It's by Max Jones, one of my gallery artists. It's an oil

156

painting called 'Forest Fare'. I'm asking three thousand for it.'

'Can you send me an image?' he asks.

'D'you have an email address I can send a digital one to?'

'It's bigjohn2001@hotmail.com, all lower case,' he answers.

'Please let me know that you get my email.'

'I'll be in touch if I want to take it further,' he says and hangs up.

Three days later he rings back. 'Mr Vicks here again,' he says.

'Ah, hello there. Any thoughts?'

'My wife likes it. I'm not so sure. I'll offer you two for it.'

'This is not some sort of bazaar,' I reply. 'It's a gallery.'

'You bargain in business, see.'

'You don't go into Waitrose, Tesco, Asda, wherever you go, and haggle over the price of a turkey,' I say with a strained laugh.

'I do exactly that if I think I can get it cheaper.'

'Your life must be pretty stressful, then. Two-eight.'

'Two-two.'

'Two-six and it's a deal,' I reply. I will hang up if he tries it on once more. He is silent for about as long as it takes to swallow a mouthful of tea.

'Okay, I'll come on Friday and pick it up with a cheque,' he says. 'Who do I make it out to?'

'John Stack, as in hay.'

'Two Johns,' he says with a laugh.

'Where are you coming from?'

'Just north of Birmingham: give me your postcode and I'll be with you before midday. I have sat nav, see,' he says.

Bigjohn2001 arrives on Friday and must be one of the shortest men I have ever seen. As the car pulls onto the gravel by the side of the house, I think for a split second that it is driving itself. He is less bluff in person. I am over six foot and he must be under five. I offer him a cup of coffee, but he declines. He ums and ahs over the painting, looking inexpertly for flaws in the canvas surface as if he knows what he is talking about, then hands me an envelope with the cheque in it.

'It's been nice doing business with you,' he says.

'Don't you want the painting wrapped?' I ask.

'No bother. It'll be fine in the boot as it is.'

When he has gone, I open the envelope. The cheque is made out for two thousand, five hundred pounds.

That voice on the telephone echoes in my head, sometimes loudly, sometimes in a whisper. I lied. I have lied to myself. I knew who it was straight away, the first time that she finally spoke. It was Linda's younger sister, Bryony's aunt. What does she want from me after almost two and a half years? I just want her to leave me alone. I have nothing to say to her or her family. There is nothing that I can say. I will never forgive them for accusing me of having driven my family away, of having destroyed their lives because of who I am, by being me.

Nicola has to go away for a week or so to her sister's in Oxfordshire, as her sister, despite being only in her early thirties, has had a cancer scare with a lump in her breast and her husband cannot get out of his business trip to the States.

Bryony arrives on Friday night and it is as if the Stone House switches from 1920s black-and-white silent film format to bright Technicolor. She brings the spring with her. The first thing that I make her do is to call her mother and get her to say that she is being taken on a surprise road-trip for a few days into next week as an early birthday present, and that she will not be at school on Monday or

158

Tuesday. She goes into the sitting-room to make the call and I do not hear all the words of her conversation. I guess that Linda will be angry about Bryony missing school. She does not like me disrupting the routine and she will have to come to Stroud station on Tuesday evening rather than on Monday morning to collect her daughter now. Bryony comes into the kitchen looking happy about the trip, but a little drained by having had to persuade her mother to let her go and have time off school.

I want to take Bryony to the seaside. I have not been there with her for a long time. After I moved over here full-time as a child, my parents took me to the north Norfolk coast two or three times. It is a magical landscape. You still see hares leaping in the fields and deer grazing in the shadow of the hedgerows. I want to take Bryony there.

I used to masturbate to mental images of some of the few girls at our school, to snapshots of women culled from TV and imprinted onto the retina of my mind's eye, even sometimes to thoughts of Tim's mother, who at one time used to be an airline hostess, when I was about fourteen or fifteen. My mother caught me once in the bathroom of the house my parents had rented for the vacation in Wells-next-the-Sea. She was from Ohio and was not amused. It was one of the most humiliating experiences of my life.

I wonder if the nascent bud of Bryony's sexuality is beginning to unfurl itself as she approaches her thirteenth birthday, now that spring and new life is in the air. I want her to remain a child forever; I cannot comprehend the idea of her being caught up in the squalid exchanges of physical love, in the leaking surfaces between hope and fact. I want her to remain a child, innocent of all that. It is important to me.

The Saturday morning is bright and clear. I drive eastwards avoiding motorways, first on the road to Cirencester, then off towards Oxford and through Bicester, Buckingham, Milton Keynes, Bedford, Cambridge and on north-east. Bryony listens to her Walkman, humming occasionally, looking out of the window at the countryside, the towns speeding past, talking to me over-loudly when the mood takes her. I am concentrating on the road, only the road. I am so tired and it is beginning to hypnotise me. After three hours and already somewhere out in the Fens, I turn off the road and pull into a garage with a café attached.

Bryony needs the bathroom and there is one at the back of the large room strewn with dark-green plastic chairs and tables like those you would find in a garden. I walk through to the back with her and show her the unisex lavatory. I lock the main bathroom door behind us and she slides the bolt on the cubicle, while I use the urinal with its fine plastic mesh of unspeakable caught detritus.

'Are you okay? You're very quiet,' I say when I have finished and am splashing my face and hands with water.

Silence. '*Bryony?*'

'Shhh,' she replies. 'I'm listening to music.'

'Hurry up; we've got to get going again.'

I unlock the main door and wait in the corridor that leads from the café into a courtyard at the back of the building, stacked with milk crates and baker's pallets.

She is taking her time. 'Come on, Bee. Let's go,' I shout through the door. An unshaven yokel of about thirty-five, *genus* woodsman, lorry driver or pederast, comes out of the café and glances at me strangely as he puts his hand on the bathroom door.

'My daughter's in there,' I say. 'She won't be long.'

'She's not using the urinal, is she?' He laughs and barges his way in.

'Bryony, we're going *now*,' I shout again. 'Come out of there.'

After half a minute, the yokel comes back out and stares at me. I could swear that he mutters 'bloody weirdo' under his breath as he makes his way back into the café. Bryony emerges nonchalantly a minute or so later, clutching her pink Walkman in her hands. We escape to the car through the back door of the building.

The North Sea is slate-grey when we first catch sight of it. We see it from a distance, cupped like a pool of indolent mercury between low hills. As I drive us closer, we can see the small waves breaking on the sandy beach, heaving and subsiding almost imperceptibly like an anaesthetised patient.

I park the car in the empty car park and Bryony jumps out of the passenger seat, then races down the grass-covered sand-dune path to the water's edge. The air takes your breath away. It blows in from the North Sea having crossed the flat lands of northern Europe from the Urals or Siberia. For a moment, it erases all thought, all pain. I take in deep gulps of the air over and over again, until I feel faint.

Bryony takes off her shoes and socks and paddles in the shallow waves, rolling her jeans up above her knees. The water must be freezing. When I was a child, I used to love playing in the sea. There is no ocean near Ohio, my mother's home state; she always used to wring her hands with worry, in case I drowned. I trust Bryony not to disappear under the waves on me.

I have booked a twin room in a B & B in Wells, in the back streets behind the road with its whelk-stalls and cargo-hoists that runs beside the estuary. I take the luggage up to the rather Spartan room, while Bryony sits on the low wall by the estuary, eating a frozen ice cream.

The guesthouse is only about three hundred yards away from the house that we rented when I was in my teens. Not much has changed here since; thirty years may have passed, but this corner of Norfolk still seems to be caught in the seventies. Perhaps it is just that I have been here before and that I am seeing the town with the eyes of the teenager that I was then.

Bryony has finished her ice cream when I find her again. The offshore wind has picked up and the large gulls are struggling to hold their positions in the air above the few picnickers, wrapped up thickly in wind-cheaters and scarves, on the narrow strip of paving between the road and the harbour wall, dropping down to the estuary waters below.

'Dad, can we go on that train over there?'

'I don't know where it goes, Bee,' I reply.

It is a small electric train, with a locomotive modelled on that of a steam train and five open-sided carriages that seat only four or five passengers each. We discover when we are on it that it trundles only a mile or so along the estuary, further out to sea and the out-of-season car parks. We get off at the end of the line and walk along the banked breakwater, looking at the rocks, the tall coastal grasses, the wheeling gulls, and the wading birds whose names I do not know.

'Still want to be a wildlife vet, in this cold wind?' I ask.

'Not here,' she replies, pushing stray strands of her long hair out of her face. 'In Africa, I think. I love big cats, Dad. I want to work with lions, leopards and cheetahs in Africa.'

'What about tigers?'

'*Da-ad*,' she says. 'You know they don't live in Africa.'

We walk back to Wells along the breakwater and I take Bryony to a quiet pub on the front. While she sips her Coke and watches the television up in a corner of the main bar, I have a couple of pints of the local real ale. It is the liquid equivalent of stabilisers on a wobbly bike. I am a Raleigh racer with a few pints inside me.

We have an early supper of a shared large basket of

scampi and chips. It is all so English and out-of-season. I think that the barman assumes I am a tourist from the States who has got his months wrong.

'Your lot don't normally start coming here until the weather heats up a bit in June,' he says as he pours me another pint. He makes no mention of children not being allowed in his pub.

I take Bryony back to the guesthouse around eight o'clock and make her have a quick bath, then tuck her up in her bed. While she reads before lights-out, I lie on the nylon eiderdown covering my bed and flick through the channels on the small television perched on its shelf on a moveable arm jutting out from the wall. All that mechanical ingenuity and there is crap-all on.

I leave Bryony, once she has promised to turn out the light by nine thirty at the latest, and go back to the pub. I order myself a mediocre bottle of red wine and drink it while watching the television and flicking through one or two tabloid newspapers, the kind that Linda used to say were the literate man's toilet paper.

The drinkers in here are all men. They look like maritime types, although that could just be my imagination; they look like they come from generations of seafarers, lobster-potters, creel-netters, sail-menders. They have salt-bitten hands and coarse-grained accents. They ignore me as if I am a ghost in the room or a fly on the wall.

I finish off the evening with another pint of the local bitter and by closing time I am so drunk that for a moment I forget where the bed and breakfast is. Standing outside its door at a quarter to midnight I fumble in my coat and trouser pockets for the door-key on its wooden fob, like a magician whose prestige trick has gone terribly wrong.

Bryony is breathing quietly and I do not turn on the light. I need to be sick. My stomach is as disobedient as my hands. I get to the cramped en suite bathroom and kick the door shut behind me, then crouch down at the mouth of the toilet bowl and vomit over and over again. My body cries out like a beaten and abandoned child.

Bryony is now with her mother again. May Day has been and gone. *M'aider, m'aider, m'aider.*

Chapter Twenty

There is a message on the answering machine when I get back to the Stone House. It is a tinned version of Nicola's calm, controlled voice.

'Where are you, John? I've been trying to reach you over the last few days. Please ring me. I'm at home again now.'

I have not seen her for ten days. It feels as if we have agreed to spend some time apart, but nothing has been said. We have just had places to go and people to see that have taken us away from each other for a while. The fermentation in my head, the fomenting of my thoughts, would have kept us apart even if it had only been the woods that were separating us during those days. The fizzing juices of my mind are slowly going flat like half-drunk glasses of champagne turning tepid in the heat of a room. It would not take much to shake them up again; to invigorate them with the old sparkle of suspicion.

'Hello, Nicola, how's your sister doing?' I ask when she picks up the phone.

'John – thanks for finding the time to call me back at last,' she says with a slightly bitter twist to her laugh. 'It was a false alarm, thank God. Don't think I could've coped with watching someone else I loved dying from cancer.'

'That's a big relief,' I say. 'It would've been just too much for you to bear.' In truth, her phrase 'someone else' does not ring quite true to me somehow.

'Where did you get to?' she asks.

'Oh, I just went on a short trip to the coast: didn't want to spend the long weekend here on my own.'

'I was worried when I couldn't get hold of you,' she says.

'Everything's fine; no need to worry about me. It's good to hear your voice again, though.'

Nicola comes over to the Stone House the next evening. It stays light until almost eight o'clock and we sit out in the garden on clap-down wooden chairs that I have found in the shed, sharing a bottle of rosé.

'You know, I took quite a risk getting involved with someone again,' she says suddenly. 'Emotionally, I mean.'

'The same goes for me: I'd been on my own quite a long time, as you know.'

'It's just that sometimes you don't seem very *present*, to use psychobabble,' she replies. 'You often seem like you're somewhere else in your thoughts when we're together.'

'You're the one who's been away gallivanting in Oxfordshire,' I joke. I cannot make her laugh tonight.

'Come on, we're both *adults*,' she says. 'I was hardly gallivanting. Why won't you talk to me about this?'

'I'm only too aware of being an adult,' I reply.

'Let's try to have an adult conversation then.'

'Don't you want some supper first? Let's talk about all of this in the morning when we're both a little less tired,' I say, trying to evince willingness to tackle the issue of my mental absences while stalling for time, hoping that she will forget the topic after a night of sex or sleep.

'Okay, but I'm not going to suddenly forget about all of this. My worries aren't going to evaporate,' she replies, 'not unless you actually do something about them that is.'

We make adult conversation of a different kind that night. We are more fluent, far more honest, in the language of the flesh, in the nuances and idioms of mouth on mouth and skin on skin, in the slow building of every sentence to a pitched question, only to answer in the next breath with another question, than we are in the language of the mind, of mere words.

I still do not know what Nicola sees in me, why she puts up with my unexplained regular absences when Bryony comes to stay; my sometimes being elsewhere in my head when we spend time together. I think that she could have any man that she wanted. Perhaps her confidence in her relationships with men is lower than one would believe to look at her, to know what she does for a living. I think that she had isolated herself since her husband died, that she had been alone in her ideal home in the woods. I cannot understand why she did that to herself, why she made herself so alone that she needed someone like me of all people. Perhaps it really was because of a grief that she had not been able to move beyond until we met. Perhaps it is just that she sees something of herself in me. Perhaps she recognises in me something of her isolation, her loss, her enforced self-reliance. Perhaps she thinks that we are kindred spirits, two of a kind against the world of people with perfect family lives: couples with two-point-five children and a dog or a car called Rover that is full of life rather than shit that never quite makes it to the dumping stage.

I have never asked her who the man was – slightly bursting at the seams – who was with her when we met that time at the gallery in Stroud near the station. She has never mentioned any other man in her life since her semi-precious husband Jasper died, apart from the odd date before we got together. Stone to stone, ashes to ashes, dust to dust. Perhaps the man was just a friend; perhaps he was her accountant, her lawyer, her financial adviser, her therapist. Perhaps he was her lover after all. I do not want to ask her and it does not matter, yet.

'John,' she says in the morning, 'we didn't get very far with our conversation last night, did we? Don't you think you should go and see someone, a doctor, about things? I've been worrying about you while I've been away, about your drinking.'

'I'm fine,' I say. 'There's nothing a doctor can tell me that I don't already know myself. There's really no need for you to worry.'

'Doctors are there to help,' she replies. 'That's their job; fixing things.'

'I don't need to be fixed. I'm not broken or defective.'

'Anyone could understand why you need to drink. It just goes from being a crutch to being a yoke, that's all,' she says. 'I've seen it happen before.'

'It's no yoke.' I laugh dryly.

'Why d'you always use humour as a defence?' she asks gently, kissing me on the cheek.

'I don't; I'm just a naturally funny guy,' I reply.

'Funny weird or funny ha-ha?'

'A bit of both, I guess. What d'you think?'

'The jury's still out.' She laughs her silver-bell laugh.

'Talking of juries, where I'm from they still have the death sentence,' I say.

'I've never believed in capital punishment,' she replies. 'Mind you, a bit of gentle *corporal* punishment can liven things up in the bedroom, or so I've heard,' she adds quietly.

'D'you mean whips 'n' chains and things? I've no idea; I've never been with anyone who liked that sort of stuff. My wife was more missionary than corporal, if you know what I mean.'

'What about before – *during* – her?' she asks.

'There was no one else while I was married,' I reply, my voice sharpening to an edge that I did not mean to give it. 'Before, I only ever had a thing for nice English girls.'

'I'm a nice English girl.' She laughs again.

When I get back from a long walk the next day, there is a note rolled up and pushed through the letterbox, like before.

THE COURT HOUSE, FOLLY LANE, NR. STROUD, GLOS.
I just came up to say hello, but you were out. I wanted
to give you the number for the GP's surgery in Stroud,
in case you're not registered. I know what men &
doctors are like. I'll come with you, if you want me to,
just give me a call. Love, Nx.

She must carry her headed notepaper around with her
in her handbag, unless she somehow already knew that I
was out before she came up to the Stone House. I will go
to the doctor, but not for the malady that she sees in me.
I want to ask him something, something that might tell me
what I need to know about Nicola.

May is superheating itself. The sun beats down on the
landscape and the birds are all a-twitter with excitement in
the hedgerows. It is mad, unseasonable weather. The sun
bakes your head. You could go mad in this weather. The
leaves on the trees in the wood are already beginning to
turn brown in the heat. The air is thick and humid down
here and flies drone in the undergrowth. There is a heady
smell of rotting plant-life. The wood exhales its alcoholic
breath.

This is the last place that we came to as a family. That
weekend before Christmas, we walked down to the
woods and I remember Bryony, aged ten, playing like a
little balancing gymnast on a fallen tree-trunk. Her mother
looked on, smiling her gentle smile, and she seemed
happy, or at least as happy as any adult in the twenty-first
century can be. I had no idea that things would change
forever five days later; that she would not come back to
me. The weather was icy then and hoarfrost clung to the
fallen leaves and the trunks of the trees. Now May is superheating itself and we are all going to hell.

I have an audience of trees. I lie down on a soft bed
of leaves and moss laid over harder earth and look up at
the canopy of branches high above me. They look like a

web of arteries, veins, capillaries. They would bleed if you cut them. I would bleed if I cut them. I have not got the strength; I am not brave enough to end it. Life must endure; I must endure life. I cannot cut it. I have never been good enough. Linda knew that and that is why she is gone. Nicola will realise her mistake with me before too long.

Tim is in the area and wants to come over. He is the last person that I need to see at the moment, with his Stay-Press confidence and bleached-white cheeriness when I am feeling so down. He insists on coming up to the Stone House for lunch between meetings in Malmesbury and Bristol. I would sooner not eat, or eat alone.

'How've you been keeping, Jack?' he asks when I open the front door. 'You forgotten what a phone is or something?'

'These last few months have just been a bit busy, that's all,' I reply. 'I've been seeing quite a bit of Nicola.'

'I bet you have,' he says with a porcine snort of a laugh.

'And I moved out of the gallery.'

'You did what?' he says, as if his ears have just turned deaf on him.

'I told you about it months and months ago, what I was planning to do. I shut the gallery in March and moved all the stock here.'

'Why on earth d'you do that?' he asks, an incredulous undertone creeping into his voice.

'Because I was getting fed up with the commute and not being at the top of my game any more,' I reply.

'Were you *ever* at the top of your game, matey?' he asks. That word 'matey' again. I cannot stand it. It is a Trojan Horse of a word. It insinuates itself into his language and does not speak its mind.

'For the size of the gallery, I was one of the most

influential in the mid-nineties,' I reply. 'A number of artists that I first showed have gone on to great things.'

'You talk like a PR man,' he jokes. 'I'm proud of you. It's a real pity you closed the gallery, though. Why didn't you tell me before you made the decision so we could talk it over a little?'

'I've just told you: I actually *did* mention it to you before; you must've not heard me back then,' I reply.

'How the hell're you planning to survive financially?' He suddenly sounds like the older brother I never had. I am not in the mood for his casual concerns about my finances. He suddenly sounds as if he means what he is saying.

'The joys of mortgage-free living; you should try it sometime,' I reply, patting him on the back.

'I don't come from Washington aristocracy,' he says. 'And you've still got to find money for food, bills, Council Tax, Nicola, haven't you?'

'I don't come from Washington aristocracy either. American meritocracy, that's all. My father worked hard for what he got. The US government liked him because of his record in Korea: they like a good war veteran in high office, they do. It's a hang-on from the Civil War I think.'

'My father also worked hard for what he got. He got angina,' he laughs.

'Don't give me the poor-boy spiel,' I say. 'He was well-off enough to send you away to school.'

'More's the pity.'

'What d'you mean? You *loved* it. You were a natural St Botolphian, made for it like a little toy soldier. You were Head of House, remember?'

'It was all such a long time ago,' he replies.

'You seem to go all misty-eyed whenever we mention Botolph's. I sometimes think you must sleep in your First-XI pullover.'

'Shut up,' he says, trying to punch me on the arm and only brushing my shirtsleeve as I laugh and jump out of the way.

'Stop it, Timmy. It's time for prep, I mean lunch,' I say as I go into the kitchen to prepare some food.

It is almost midnight when the telephone rings. When does a telephone ringing at the dead of night ever bring good news? It might be your lover calling to whisper that she loves you before she goes to sleep some place far away, but it isn't. It might be an excited American academic telephoning to tell you, his esteemed colleague, that he has been asked by the Swedish Academy to break the news in a barely audible whisper that you have won worldwide recognition with the Nobel Prize, but it won't be. Your wife is gone and you have never done anything good in your life. It is that narrative voice again, that ghost in the machine telling you endless bad things about yourself.

'John,' Linda's sister's voice says in a whisper, speaking like dust on the wind, 'John, I'm sorry to be calling so late.'

'It's been more than two years,' I reply.

'I'm sorry about all those other calls . . . I couldn't speak . . . I couldn't find the words . . .' she trails off.

'I don't know what you want from me after all this time,' I reply.

'. . . I didn't know what to say.'

'There is nothing to say.'

'I'm so very sorry for how we were to you afterwards; my family, I mean,' Linda's sister whispers.

'SORRY ISN'T FUCKING GOOD ENOUGH,' I shout down the line without being able to stop myself. 'It isn't enough after all this time.' The line goes dead.

It is only mid-May and you could wring the humidity out of the air. This weather has got to break soon. Vivid yellow fields of oilseed rape seem to be taking over the landscape;

perhaps farmers around here cannot make a living these days from arable crops and pastureland. The oilseed rape is turned into high-grade machine lubricant to fuel the industrial revolution in Asia. I do not remember bright yellow fields when I was a child. They are an unstable Van Gogh yellow, an E-number yellow, a yellow coloured in by man's unnatural hand.

Bryony is waiting on her usual bench at Stroud railway station on Friday evening. It is as light as a mid-winter midday at five o'clock. She is paler than usual; I hope that she is not sickening for something. She is not reading for once, but has her headphones on and her Walkman on her lap. She does not hear me at first when I call her name. She seems to have grown up a little more, to have blossomed more beautifully, each time that I see her, but she is still my little girl, my only child. I do not want her to fade from my life, for her mother to win by keeping her away from me as she grows up. I would give up drinking if she were to come to live with me for good one day.

'Dad, where d'you come from?' she asks when she sees me.

'I just parked the car out front and came in through there,' I reply, pointing over towards the entrance arch.

'No, I mean where did you live before you came to England? Why haven't I ever been there to see it?'

'You have been to America; you just don't remember because you were very little. We went with Mum to Washington when you were two or three, just before your grandparents died. We even took you down to Florida and Disney World. You went a bit green on one of the rides.'

'I'd like to go there with you again and visit where you grew up.'

'I grew up here mostly. Washington's a nasty place, Bee, some areas are no-go. That means there're too many gangs and guns. It's much better here.'

'Sounds cool,' she says.

'It's really not; it's baking hot in summer and the mosquitoes are the size of horseflies.'

'*Da-ad*,' she says. 'You know what I mean. Promise me you'll take me there one day.'

'I promise I'll think about it.'

'*Ple-ease*, Dad,' she says, looking up at me with her most soulful and sad eyes.

'Let's go – to the car,' I tickle her in the ribs and she tries to squirm away from me.

I wake up with a pulsating headache on Saturday morning. That central heating again: it magnifies the hangover to the size of an asteroid, a galaxy, a whole universe of pain. The drinker's equation: two bottles of claret plus central heating over too little water equals a morning of tremens and dry heaving.

Bryony waits patiently downstairs, reading or watching television, until I emerge towards midday.

'Are you alright, Dad?' she asks, looking at my drained face.

'I've got a bit of a tummy upset today, that's all. We'll go out soon,' I reply.

Bryony was quiet last night and I wonder whether she is sad about having lost her bedroom to my stock and having to sleep in the small spare room now. If so, she has not said anything to me about it. She looks worried today; I guess it is because of my drinking last night and I feel bad about that. I drank at the kitchen table while she was watching television in the sitting-room, and then in the sitting-room in front of a parade of ever more desperate television programming when she had gone to bed. She is not fooled, though; she knows what I am doing and not being able to stop me with her presence, with her love, must hurt her. It must make her feel like nothing.

* * *

I lied to Nicola. I told her that I was going to visit Tim and family again this weekend. I do not want her coming up here unannounced when Bryony is around. She cannot share this part of my life with me.

Bryony and I do not get far this weekend, only for a walk on Saturday up to the top of the escarpment and through the fields full of new life. She says that she likes the sickly-sweet smell of oilseed rape. Bees make honey from its pollen. It seems strange that they feast on the nectar of plants that we use for machine lubricant and that we then eat the thick, crystalline honey that they produce from the plants as if it were manna from heaven.

Chapter Twenty-One

The end of May has brought rain with it. The earth drinks it in and drinks it in until, when the rains stop, the earth looks dry again. It is a little like a newborn child's need for its mother's milk, for love.

Nicola needs love, or attention. She has left me two new messages, asking why I have not called her. There is a hint of anxiety in her voice now. I think that I have her snared. An absence of reciprocation makes the heart grow fonder. I want to give her physical attention: I have the energy for that. I do not want to love her, to give that part of myself to her. Linda will not let me go that easily.

'How are you?' I ask when I call her back.

'John, what d'you think?' she says, with an unpleasant edge to her voice.

'That you're probably angry with me for neglecting you.'

'I'm angry with you for doing another of your disappearing acts,' she replies. 'It isn't hard to let me know what you're up to; if you're okay. Is it so hard to ask me how *I* am now and then?'

'I just asked you how you were.'

'Are you really interested?'

'Of course I am; I've just had a lot on, that's all.'

'You can't keep doing this to me, disappearing under full radio silence. It's not fair on me.'

'My aerial's up now,' I say to try to make her laugh.

'Is it really?' she says with a sudden smile in her voice.

'It's transmitting a good signal. Can you hear what it's saying?'

'Is it on *short* wave?' she laughs.

'It's saying in a very tiny voice: I want to see you, I want to see you, I want to see you.'

'What are you doing tonight?'

'Nothing: staring at the elongating shadows as the sun sets, listening to foxes mating in the wood. Fancy coming over for a sun-downer and a listen?'

'Aural sex: it does sound magical,' she says, 'but you've really upset me this time. You've got to stop disappearing like that; you've got to stop ignoring me. No man's ever treated me like this before. We'll have to forget all of this otherwise.'

'Come on, please don't be like that. I'm sorry for how I've been lately, distant and things. I've just got a lot on my mind. I think, I mean I hope, you'd kind of miss me if I wasn't around, in your life.'

'I would – I do: that's the problem. God knows why. It's not difficult for you to sort this out; you've just got to want to. I don't have much free time: I'm sure there're plenty of men who'd be only too happy to fill it for me if I was interested.'

'I'll fill it for you. Come on, come up and we'll have a nice evening together.'

'You promise?'

'Of course I do.'

'Okay, we'll give it a try. I'll bring the gin and see you about seven.'

Nicola is looking as lush as green grass when she comes over. The rain has stopped and the sun is breaking through the clouds. It all smells so fresh; there is a pornography of damp earth smells, of teeming phototropic life, on the air. She is wearing a jade-green summer dress that makes her dark hair and pale skin shine with an astonishing lustre. She is like some being from a glossy higher plane beamed down to this earthly Paradise. It is hard to believe that she might have been capable of killing someone. There would have been no blood on her hands, that is for sure. She is too clever by far to have let that happen. That is the lawyer in her.

When I imagine that something untoward might have happened to her husband, I do not see her doing it to him herself. I picture an unknown lover of hers harming him; someone sneaking into the Court House in the middle of the night while she is conveniently away on business and smothering her husband as he lies sleeping in their bed, that sort of thing. I will find out what happened to her man of stone. I have made that promise to myself. It somehow excites me to think that Nicola might have had her husband done away with. I do not know why. Perhaps it is all just a ridiculous fantasy; nonsense born of alcohol whispering its mad ideas to me at night.

My garden has lost its sense of boundaries. It is going back to nature and I am going with it; to seed, to pot, my brains to mulch, my career out to grass. Nicola is not much of a gardener; she does not look after me. I will not let her.

I pour us two large glasses of her gin and top them off with tonic, lemon and ice, then carry them out to the paved terrace area by the back door, where Nicola is sitting on one of the two damp-looking deckchairs. I should have put them away when it rained.

'Don't you have a gardener?' Nicola asks.

'No need. I used to do it myself,' I reply. 'I've sort of given up on it in recent years. I wanted it to find its own voice.'

'It looks like it wants to be a hillside meadow.'

'Perhaps I should get a couple of sheep or a goat. That would keep the grass down.'

'Don't you have lawnmowers in the States?'

'They have lawnmowers the size of your tractors there, mostly driven by illegal Mexicans and Latinos. Grass bandits, as it were.'

'You should look after your garden,' she says. 'Gardening's a state of mind. I was pruning the first time we met properly, if I remember correctly.'

'I was worried what you might do with those pruning shears.'

'I was worried what you might do with those hands.'

'Nothing, other than nervously clutch the drink that you gave me.'

'Why were you *nervous?*' she asks, laughing.

'I wasn't used to being so close to a beautiful woman. It'd been a while.'

'I could tell,' she says. 'Your hands were shaking.'

'That wasn't nerves or embarrassment. I get that sometimes: it's a physical thing. It goes with my headaches in the mornings.'

'And there was me thinking it was my womanly charms.' She laughs awkwardly.

'Those made me a little tongue-tied; still do,' I reply.

'Don't try to make me feel better,' she says.

'I mean it. You'd make any man weak at the knees. I'm sure you know that.'

'Maybe I used to know that; I'm not sure any more. The only effect I seem to have on you is to make you want to disappear,' she replies quietly.

'You know that has *nothing* to do with you. I just have other things I need to do.'

'Such as what?'

'You know; business things. Seeing people we – Linda and I – used to know, and so on.'

'I thought I was meant to be saving you from being lonely,' she says as if suddenly realising the redundancy of her role.

'I don't want to be some mercy fuck of yours,' I reply.

'Some *what?* You're hardly that, whatever that is.' She laughs. I am not quite sure how to take that laughter.

'What I mean is I don't want you to be with me because you feel sorry for me. Are you saying I'm no good in the sex department either?'

'You'll do,' she reaches over and pinches my cheek

gently, then takes another sip of her gin. 'That's the bit you're not bad at.'

'Your talk that time of whips 'n' chains and things made me kind of nervous.'

'Don't be silly, I was only winding you up. I'm not really into that stuff,' she says and giggles like a teenage girl.

'That's a relief; I don't think I'd look very appealing on a sex swing.'

'Oh, I don't know,' she laughs again and winks at me.

'Mind you, the English do say try anything once, except incest and Morris dancing.'

'I thought those were two of England's favourite pastimes. Perhaps that's just in the villages around here,' she replies.

'I have visions of a large Morris-dancing family of yokels mating amongst their bells and sticks,' I say.

'I'd keep those visions to yourself, if I were you,' she says and laughs.

I go into the kitchen to make us two more gin and tonics and just as I am about to walk into the garden again, the telephone starts ringing. For a second I cannot decide whether to go into the sitting-room and answer it or to let it ring until the answerphone kicks in. I decide to let it ring and it sounds out loudly like a tocsin across the valley in the utter silence of the evening.

'Didn't you want to get that?' Nicola asks.

'No one I want to speak to ever rings me.'

'Except for me, of course.'

'That goes without saying,' I reply.

'You don't answer the phone very often, do you though?'

'I think I've become allergic to telephones. They always seem to bring nothing but problems.'

The voice on the answerphone is Linda's sister's voice. Why is she calling me again so soon, why is she ringing so early in the evening? What does she want from me after all this time? I just want her to leave me alone.

'. . . *I need to speak to you . . . please call me back . . . I've been looking at your old letters again, there's so much pain in them . . .'* Her voice goes on and on in its static haze.

'Who the hell's that?' Nicola asks.

'Just someone I used to know,' I reply.

'It sounds like you still know her if you're writing letters to her. What's the pain about? Has it got something to do with your wife and daughter?'

'No – and I'm not still writing them. That was a couple of years ago. She's living in the past.'

'Well, as long as you're not sending her *French* letters . . .'

'No, only the kind that tried to tell her and her family the truth about things.'

'What's that, then?'

'It doesn't matter any more. I've realised even the truth has its sell-by date.'

It is almost nine o'clock and darkness is falling on the valley like a moth-eaten blackout curtain. The stars are beginning to emerge through its fabric, shimmering and pulsing light years away.

'Let's go inside. It's getting cold,' I say. A breeze has picked up and all the birds in the garden and further away in the woods have fallen silent, as if they are expecting trouble.

The answerphone's red eye is blinking at me when we go into the sitting-room and I press 'delete messages' without listening to the rest of what Linda's sister has to say. I make a fire and Nicola watches as I screw up sheets of newspaper into balls, then place kindling carefully on top of them and finally add two or three small logs.

'Were you ever a Scout?' she asks.

'Do I seem like the kind of man who was ever a Boy Scout?'

'Oh, I don't know. You're good at tying knots, at least in what you say. You know how to light fires of various kinds. Isn't it a bit strange to be having one in late May?'

'Isn't it strange that it's still so cold at night?'

'Good point,' she replies. 'Perhaps we've already had our summer: summer in spring, spring in winter. Something weird's going on with the weather in this country.'

'Haven't you heard the news? The earth's heating up.'

'Don't you think that's just climatologists being hypochondriacs about the planet?'

'I bet that's the first time those two words have ever been used in the same sentence,' I reply.

'Well, I did do Law at university.'

'When Gloucestershire becomes a landscape of giant sand dunes, with the warm waters of the North Atlantic lapping against the pebbly beaches of Cheltenham's high street, we'll know they were telling the truth.'

'I think we'll be long dead by then.'

'I hope so. I rather like green fields and woods.'

'I rather like sandy beaches and the sea,' she laughs.

'What are you doing still living around here, then?'

'Jasper fell in love with the place. We were on a walk around here when we were visiting my parents and saw the house. He went back without me knowing and made an offer that the old lady living there couldn't refuse. He bought it for himself initially: we weren't that serious by then; it was very early days.'

'How did you meet?'

'What, me and Jasper? He was actually one of the good guys working for Lloyds of London when my father lost his money. He tried to help him. In the end, there was nothing he could do.'

'Wasn't it a bit difficult for your father?'

'I told you: I believe it killed him.'

'I mean your being with a man on the side of Lloyds.'

'He didn't know him for very long. We didn't really get together properly until quite a bit later, after Dad had died. Dad only knew him as an underwriter who was trying to help sort out the nightmare that Lloyds had left its Names in.'

'Still, it must've been like sleeping with the enemy.'

'No, not really,' she replies and goes very quiet.

The flames devour the logs, which hiss quietly because they are damp, and the embers glow red-hot and fall upon themselves. I put two more logs on the fire and Nicola asks for another large gin.

'How could you say that to me?' she asks suddenly.

'What d'you mean?'

'What you just said about Jasper being the enemy. He was my *husband*, John.'

'I didn't mean it, I'm sorry. I think I must've made the gins too strong.'

'Jasper's *dead*, John. You of all people should know how to talk to someone who has experienced hurt and loss in their lives.'

'What d'you want me to say? All I can say is that I'm sorry.'

Nicola sits in her chair and looks into the fire. Its light is reflected in her eyes, which seem to have a layer of moisture on their surface that was not there before.

'I'm tired and going up to bed,' she says.

'But we haven't eaten anything.'

'It's too late; I'm not hungry any more,' she replies.

Why do I always have to open my big mouth? Why do I always have to say what I am thinking? It is so un-English. The fire seethes and steams as I put more logs on it. I sit in front of it with a half-drunk bottle of red from the other night and some cold food from the fridge.

It is pitch-black outside and cold, but when the fire has burnt itself out long past midnight I take my glass and sit in a deckchair, listening for sounds of life in the garden. It is unusually quiet. At first I can see nothing, but gradually the shapes of trees and hedges reveal themselves as my eyes become used to the darkness. This making-sense of the world: we are better at it physically than emotionally. You rarely see people bumping into each other on the street or walking into lampposts. At the same time as they negotiate the physical world with the precision of swifts darting from one eaves to another, their minds are elsewhere, stumbling into terrible trouble, falling down manholes of doubt and desire, being sucked into quagmires where they slowly drown.

There is the sudden sound of something large and half-blind moving through the undergrowth. I sit still, hardly breathing. It comes nearer, but I can see nothing. It rustles and snuffles, unafraid of the noise it makes. Suddenly it is on the lawn, only ten feet away from where I am sitting. It is a large badger, perhaps a male, with its black-and-white head raised to scent the air. It looks in my direction, but does not seem to see me. It is probably searching for beetles or grubs, earthworms or roots, whatever it can find to sustain its voracious and omnivorous appetite. Perhaps it is searching for the truth.

I go up to bed at around two o'clock and Nicola is sleeping deeply. I climb in beside her and lie on my back, looking up at the ceiling and waiting for sleep to come. We are like two marble effigies on top of a tomb tonight.

In the morning, I wake up to find an empty space in bed beside me. Nicola is standing in the sitting-room, looking out of the window at the valley and cupping a mug of coffee in both hands. I walk up behind her and clasp my arms around her waist, pulling her body into mine.

'I'm really sorry about last night. It was a stupid thing to say.'

'It was pretty unforgivable, John,' she replies. 'I wish you hadn't said that. More than anything, it was bloody unfair on Jasper. You'd understand that if you'd known him. He felt so bad for my father for what Lloyds had done to him.'

'All I can say is I'm really sorry, about what I said and

about your father. What d'you want me to do to prove how sorry I am?'

'You don't have to do anything. Just grow up a little; not everything's as black and white as you seem to think it is,' she replies.

'I think it's having been an only child. It made me a little selfish. I want you all to myself, rather than sharing you with your memories. I think I'm just a little jealous of Jasper,' I say simply to try to appease her.

'I could say the same for you. I can understand why you live in the past a lot of the time, but it's really not healthy. I sometimes wonder whether you're thinking about Linda when we, you know, do it.'

'That's ridiculous. Have you seen how goddamn beautiful your face is? I don't even want to shut my eyes when we're making love, let alone think about doing it with someone else, past or present.'

'There's one thing you *can* do for me,' she says.

'What? I'll do anything within reason.'

'You can go to the doctor. I want you to get help for your drinking,' she says. 'And to learn how to let go of things that are gone.'

'I will, I promise,' I reply. 'I'll go to the doctor first thing on Monday.' Nicola would not like to hear the conversation that I am going to have with him.

Chapter Twenty-Two

June lovely June now
Beautifies the ground
The sound of the Cuckoo
Through the green woods resounds

I have an unquenchable thirst. The more I drink, the thirstier I become. The sun's burning eye watches me and will not let me stop.

My business account manager has written to say that the twenty-five works appraised by Egg Slacks will be consigned by the bank to public auction this July. He adds that any shortfall between the net results of the sale and my gallery loan will be pursued vigorously through the courts. Good luck to them with the auction: I am the dealer, or former dealer, of these artists and I am unable to sell a single piece by any of them at the moment. If only I had held onto more works by the now better-known amongst them. I am down to my last few thousand pounds in my personal account; I need another hit soon.

I must find a way of attracting new buyers for my stock online. I need someone to help me make my gallery website easier to chance upon on the Internet; the happenstance of words entered into search engines must be tamed to favour finding my site somehow. Otherwise, no one knows that I am here now that most of my old London buyers are no longer responding to my emails. I have no other way of earning money than through selling off the remnants of my stock over the coming years. These works are meant to be my nest-egg, my bolt-hole, my financial salvation. It is no good if the artists who made them have fallen completely out of fashion.

I think that Nicola secretly believes that I have got money stashed away somewhere. She could not be further from the truth. I have debts squirreled away like rotting tubers, black holes waiting to suck me in.

Penelope has sent me an email, saying that I should go to the graduation shows at all the art colleges in London and the south-west nearer to home; that I still have the eye to spot young talent. I reply that Nicola is the best young talent that I have found for a long time. I do not have the energy for cheap-wine-fuelled art-school parties any more. I am losing my appetite for contemporary art as my taste for alcohol grows, but I do not tell her that.

The doctor's surgery in Stroud is a red-brick monolith towering above the lower part of the town, a cruise ship for the sick and the infirm. It is a long time since I last saw a doctor; there is nothing they can tell me about myself that I want to hear. The two receptionists are as bovine as the cows in the fields on Plawhatch Farm down the valley from the Stone House. They chew the cud of their bubble-gum or chewing-gum, only interrupting the repetitive movement of their mouths to answer questions from the patients in the waiting-room with the dead-eyed, confrontational stares of complete disinterest.

'My name's John Stack. I've got an appointment with Dr Ward at eleven thirty,' I say to the tops of the receptionists' imperfectly-peroxided heads as they bend to lip read their magazines. At first, they do not look up but carry on reading. I can hear the smacking of their lips as they digest the words with the juices of their gum.

'Yor?' one says suddenly.

'I'm sorry?'

'What's yer name, luv?' the fatter one asks in her thick brogue.

'I just told you. John Stack, as in hay.'

'Loike a bawks full o' tender-stecks,' the thinner one laughs.

'No, not "stick", "*Stack*",' I say more loudly. 'The Stone House, Folly Lane: I'm on your system; I made the appointment by phone on Saturday morning.'

'Take a seat, luv,' the fatter one says.

The Stroud show has come to town, the parade has found its way here. The waiting-room is full of coughers, chokers, gaspers, gurners, limpers, no-hopers. They are not like me; my disease is something other than theirs. It is only when I come to places like this that I remember that I am not from around here, that I do not really belong.

The flow of patients through the double doors to the doctors' surgeries is glacial. Someone's name is called out by the receptionists, still with their heads bent, every fifteen or twenty minutes. It is after twelve by the time John Stick's name interrupts the syncopated coughing.

Dr Ward's room is the first door on the right through the double doors, if I have understood the fatter one correctly. I have the urge to walk straight in, as if I am going to chance upon him doing something untoward to or with one of his patients, but I force myself to knock first. There is a muffled 'Come in' and I open the door to his office. Although he is seated, I can tell that he is a short man. He wears a garish bowtie with peach polka dots on an azure ground, perhaps to compensate for his lack of height impact. He swivels his chair with a flourish to greet me.

'I don't think we've ever met before. I'm Dr Ward,' he says, reaching out his small, dry hand and giving mine a low-impact shake. His undulating Scottish accent goes up and down like the Highlands.

'I gathered that from your doorplate,' I joke.

'Och, I think we have a Canadian wit on our hands,' he

says, grinning, and raises his eyes to the wall somewhere above my left shoulder with the universally recognised expression on his face that suggests your interlocutor is seeking reaction to your wisecracking from some imagined third party. I can tell that he likes to be the solo star of his little show. He talks with a slightly forced jollity, rolling his curdled Scottish Rs and raising his eyebrows to punctuate the inflection of certain words. He sounds almost as if he is Scandinavian.

'I'm actually American – and I'm not so sure about my wits these days, I'm afraid.' I laugh hollowly. The chromed stethoscope hanging around his neck glares back at me in the sunlight slanting through the blinds.

'So how can I be of help today? How long's it been since you last came to visit us, Mr Stack?' he asks, suddenly becoming serious. He glances at the computerised records on the screen in front of him.

'It's been about two and a half years now,' I reply. 'I've actually come about a friend of mine, though, not about myself.'

'If only I had a pound for every time I've heard that line when people have something awkward they want to talk about. I see from your notes that you were prescribed Valium back then after some un-noted trauma or crisis. How are things for you now?'

'My girlfriend thinks I drink too much,' I reply.

'And do you?'

'What's too much? I often feel it isn't really enough.'

'Regularly more than twenty-one units a week for a healthy adult male is too much. Why d'you feel you drink too much, or rather sometimes not enough?'

'You mean the reasons, or the facts?'

'Whichever you feel most comfortable talking about.'

'I just like red wine, and sometimes real ale. I was never into smoking, but I've drunk alcohol since I was fourteen or fifteen. It's the British national pastime, drinking, isn't it?'

'It does seem to be, yes. We Scots are particularly good at it. It's an expensive pastime, though, as far as the Health Service is concerned,' he replies. 'D'you know what the prolonged overuse of alcohol can do to your body?'

'Make it live longer by stopping you from killing yourself?' I reply, completely deadpan.

'Actually, exactly the opposite: it's a form of slow suicide,' he replies. 'The liver cells gradually deteriorate and become fatty or cirrhosed; your brain cells die off more quickly and your memory can become seriously impaired. In the most extreme cases, it can result in liver failure.'

'I'd better try and cut down then, if I can.'

'It'd be a good idea. You're getting to an age when it starts to become a problem. You can get away with these things when you're younger,' he says. 'Have you noticed lately that the whites of your eyes are very slightly jaundiced? I'll need to arrange for our nurse to take some blood for a liver function test and we might need to refer you for a liver biopsy, depending on what the test shows.'

'I feel like I need a drink,' I joke and Dr Ward smiles dryly.

'You just might. Try to stick to far fewer than twenty-one units a week from now on because of how long this seems to have been going on. Ideally, I'd recommend you stop drinking alcohol altogether, but we can decide on the best course of action when we have the results of your tests.'

I look at him and something in his eyes tells me that he knows full well I will not heed his advice.

'A friend of mine has a brain tumour,' I break the short silence punctuated by the hollow ticking of the clock mounted on the wall above Dr Ward's desk. 'All I know is that it's a particularly aggressive type and that he's had a terminal prognosis. His wife has promised to nurse him at home until the end. Would that be possible – I mean, looking after him at home right to the end?'

'Have you ever seen the end stages of cancer, or more

particularly of a brain tumour?' Dr Ward answers my question with a question, a dark smile curling his Calvinist's lips.

'No, I haven't had that pleasure,' I reply matter-of-factly.

'It's a terrible disease. You wouldn't ask that question if you knew more about it. Brain-tumour patients often go into a coma in their last days. They would have to be cared for in a hospice or hospital.'

'So her promise to look after him at home until the end isn't possible?'

'I don't think so, not unless she's a modern-day Florence Nightingale with all the equipment of an Intensive Care unit and a team of doctors on standby – but you must bear in mind that I don't know the specifics of this chap's diagnosis or treatment and couldn't comment any more coherently if I did, because of patient confidentiality.'

'I wouldn't think his wife knows the first thing about doctors and nurses. She did Law at university, as far as I know,' I add redundantly.

'I'm going to give you some leaflets on local Alcoholics Anonymous groups, if I may. It might be good for you to go along and at least listen,' he says, looking straight into my eyes again as if he can see something in them that should not be there.

'I went once before. All that Twelve Step malarkey reminded me of teetotal Brownshirts.'

'It's up to you in the end,' he replies, raising his eyes to just above my left shoulder again. 'You're an adult in control of your own life: we're just here to diagnose and advise.'

As I leave the two fat lady Bingo callers for the sick behind their Formica counter, still chewing their gum with relish, I follow a man who has just left one of the other doctor's rooms, his jacket folded over his right arm. He turns as he holds the door open for me and I know instantly that I have seen his face before. At first I cannot think where.

His car is parked two cars away from mine and we open our drivers' doors in a moment of almost balletic synchrony.

'Nice weather for a check-up,' I call over to him.

'Indeed,' he says and laughs. 'This sunshine can be very curative.'

'I trust the good doctor didn't find anything wrong with you?'

'I wasn't actually there for a check-up – I *am* one of the good doctors, or so my qualifications say.'

'Ah, I thought I'd seen your face somewhere before,' I reply as he gets into his silver-coloured Mercedes, first hanging his jacket up on the hook in the rear driver's-side door arch.

'Me too,' he smiles disinterestedly without looking at me as he starts the car and shuts the door with an abrupt and finely engineered slam.

Back at the Stone House I cannot stop thinking about him. I have only been to the doctor's surgery in Stroud three or four times since I first moved here with Linda full-time. I am somehow certain that I have never seen him in that context before.

I throw the Alcoholics Anonymous leaflets from Dr Ward into the outside dustbin and open a mediocre bottle of burgundy. The high June sun is blazing down today and I take the bottle and my glass into the garden to sit in one of the deckchairs, just to watch for signs of life for a while. After the rain in late May and the immolating weeks of sunshine in June, you can almost see the plant life growing before your eyes. There is the rich smell of water evaporating from deep down in the soil up through the thick grass. I am a totalitarian dictator silently orating to ten thousand, a hundred thousand, limitless blades of grass and leaves gradually turning brown in the boredom of silence and endless heat.

I could have gone back into the surgery and asked the gargoyles which doctor had just left, but the sclerosis of their self-absorption would mean that they probably had not noticed, or else would not understand my question. Even if they told me his name, it might mean nothing to me; it might not put his face and the context in which I have seen it before together.

I still do not know what to do with all of these countless days of freedom; how someone occupies so much empty time. Linda and Bryony, the commute and my gallery dominated my life for so long that I had no need to think, just act. Action after action after action, like a rip-off Action Man made of inferior materials. See him select a pair of underpants! See him pour his daughter's breakfast cereal! See him get a seat on the 7.45 to Paddington! See him sign his business cheques at work! See him drink most of a bottle of wine when he gets home from work! On and on and no space in which to think. The problems come when that space opens up before us like a void.

How do you avoid a void? You fill it with drink; you animate it with repetitive thoughts going round and round like mangy dogs chasing their tails. It is never really filled, though; finding vices or virtues to occupy your days is no more than laying a floor of ice unsupported over a canyon or a chasm. Sooner or later you will plummet to your inevitable breakthrough.

I wake up in the middle of the night, although that seems to be a misnomer as the dawn light is already creeping over the horizon just after four a.m. What synapses have fired or connected in my short sleep? I suddenly know where I have seen him before: those amoeba-like paintings, the humiliation of looking at them alone amongst a crowd of worthy couples, all dressed up for a night out at their local gallery. He was the man who took Nicola away from me the first time that I met her properly, the first time that we spoke.

You could not write it. I first met the woman who lost her husband to a terminal disease on a date with a doctor. He must have been a very useful ally to have in her crisis. I would be very interested to know who signed the man of stone's death certificate.

That night I walk down to the Court House for supper with Nicola. We sit on a rug on the large lawn behind the house, the grass perfectly striped by the mower with the precision of a grass tennis court. I decide that a nonchalant reference to my encounter is the best approach.

'I met someone you know yesterday,' is my opening gambit.

'Who was that then, John?' she asks, the lily of the valley on her skin hypnotising me.

'A doctor at the surgery in Stroud. The one who you were with when we met at the gallery in Stroud that time.'

'Oh, you mean Philip Howard,' she says with a laugh, although she seems to stiffen very slightly at his name.

'That was a strange place for a date.'

'We were categorically *not* on a date. He's not my type at all.'

'Does he collect art or something?'

'Not as far as I know,' she replies. 'Nothing that you'd call art anyway.'

She is giving nothing away. It is like talking to a witness who has been intimidated into silence. Either I am asking the wrong questions or else she does not want to tell me the answers. She serves out a tabouleh salad, some succulent-looking cold chicken and hunks of still-warm brown bread. I pour us two large glasses of dry white wine. A jackdaw is calling in its see-sawing voice in the woods behind us.

'If you weren't on a date and he doesn't collect art, what on earth were you doing together at the gallery?' I ask, emphasising each word quietly as if talking to a child who is being deliberately evasive.

'Do I detect a hint of jealousy, John?' she says and kisses me softly on the cheek.

'Not at all, no. He's not my type.' She laughs again, loudly.

'He's not much of a looker, but he's well off, I can tell you that.'

'I saw his silver Mercedes and his capped white teeth,' I reply.

'You should see his house. It makes mine look like a cottage.'

'So, what were you doing with him at the gallery then?' I ask again.

'D'you mean, "How d'you know him and were you sleeping with him?" You're being like a teenager in a school playground.'

'I'm asking because I want to know.'

'Perhaps I'm not telling you because I don't want you to know. The truth is . . .' she trails off and suddenly looks very sad.

'The truth is what?'

'The truth is that each year, on the anniversary of Jasper's death, his friends meet up in his favourite pub over in Woodchester to celebrate his life. It's a real local's pub and I hate going to pubs, as you know. I go because I'm his widow. It's mostly his old school friends and people he got to know around here. Philip Howard was at school with Jasper's oldest brother, who's about fifty now.'

'It's a strange coincidence that he's a doctor in Stroud of all places.'

'Isn't it?' she replies. 'He was very kind during the illness. Someone to help us understand what was going to happen.'

'So, there was nothing going on between you then?'

'What? For God's sake: no. What's the matter with you? We met at the station because my car was in the garage that day and we were too early to go over to Woodchester. He's happily married. When we saw people drinking beer outside the gallery, we just went in to investigate.'

'I'm very glad you did. I don't think I'd ever have had the courage to come down here and say hello if we hadn't bumped into each other there first,' I reply.

'Well, if you're so glad, stop asking me all of these ridiculous questions. Surely me being with you, *caring* about you, is enough?'

'Of course it is; I'm sorry. I'm just feeling a little paranoid at the moment, I guess,' I lie.

'Well don't, *please*. How did your visit to the doctor go?'

'What, Philip's colleague? He had a jolly Scottish accent and a strange bedside manner.'

'What did he say about your drinking?' she asks, not looking me in the eyes.

'What could he say? He gave me the usual spiel and leaflets. He wants me to have some tests. I put the leaflets straight in the bin when I got home.'

'Why d'you always have to do everything the hard way, John? I wanted to give you your life back,' she says, looking suddenly very hurt.

'I'm so sorry; I'll try, I promise. Let's just have one more glass of wine, just one more.'

The sun has fallen behind the wood and the long shadows of night are crawling out of the undergrowth and over the lawn.

Chapter Twenty-Three

Where do the days go, where do they go? It is almost the end of June already. I need to decide what to do about Nicola.

She calls me at least once a day and we are now seeing each other every other night again, as well as at the weekends when Bryony is not around, just like we did in the first months of our relationship. I think that she is becoming more attached. I am worried that I will run out of semen; out of things to say. Perhaps I could ask her for more details about her man of stone's disease by way of conversation, about what his last days were like. We would see how long the relationship lasted then before the iron curtain of her silence came down.

She wants to go away with me again; I suggested Scotland, as I have so little money at the moment. She said that we would go Dutch and split the costs, that she wants to travel somewhere much further away than Scotland, somewhere where she has never been before.

We have agreed to go for five days to D.C. Call me sentimental, but I would like to see my first home again, my elementary school. I want to see where my parents ended up for their last years; to visit their graves again. I have not been back to the city since their funerals more than a decade ago. They died within six months of each other; my father first, of colon cancer, and my mother of a broken heart. I want to take Nicola to Capitol Hill and the White House; to show the city off to her, show her off to the city of my fathers.

We are going at the end of the second week of July. I

wish that we could take Bryony, but I am not ready for Nicola to meet her. I have a lot to do before we leave; a lot to learn about Nicola. I have made an appointment to see Dr Howard on Monday, three weeks to the day since I last visited the surgery. He will not need to practise his diagnostic arts on me. I will try out my investigative skills on him.

When I pick up Bryony on Friday evening, she seems to be keeping a secret that threatens to explode through the pores of her skin in her blushes, to burst out of her mouth in her rosy-lipped, half-concealed smiles. It takes me until Saturday lunchtime to tease her secret out of her.

'It's a boy,' she says suddenly, chewing her sandwich with open-mouthed excitement in a wholefood café in Stroud.

'Don't speak, I mean *eat*, with your mouth open,' I say.

She giggles and continues her chewing, then takes a sip of organic orangeade.

'He's in Year Nine. He told Nadine who told me he likes me. He's lush. He's called Jason Frognall.'

'So what are this Mr Frogspawn's prospects?'

'Frog-*nall*, Dad,' she replies.

'And where are you getting words like "lush" from? It's very unlike you.'

'Nadine,' she giggles again.

'I'd rather you used "nice" or "cool". I thought almost-teenagers weren't meant to talk to their dads about this sort of thing.'

'You're different; you're not really like my dad,' she says and smiles sweetly.

I do not know how to reply to that. I sip my tea, heavily fortified with sugar, and let the pain of her unintended comment slowly dissolve in my bloodstream until all I feel is numbness.

'I was your dad full-time until you were ten, Bee. I didn't

want you to go away. Seeing you only twice a month leaves a big hole in my heart.'

'I think that there's a hole in Mum's heart as well. Her and Uncle Simon have been shouting at each other a lot lately,' Bryony replies.

'I've told you before never to *mention* his name.' My hand shakes with the sudden thickening in my blood as I reach for the salt to make this bland food more palatable. One or two patrons of the lentil and the bean-sprout glance over at me as I knock over the bottle of organic ketchup on our table. Bryony blushes hard and stares into her tomato and basil soup.

'Sorry, Dad,' she says.

'Have you told your friend Nadine that you like this boy?' I ask, after we have sat in silence for a minute or two, Bryony still stirring auguries in her soup and me staring at Xeroxed posters for holistic medical practices and the Alexander Technique.

'Er, no!' she replies. 'Nadine would think I was a little kid. She's already *thirteen*.'

'Keep this Frogman swimming in the dark; boys like a chase. Mind you, if I ever hear that he even tries to hold hands with you, I'll drive down to Bristol and give him a talking to.'

'*Da-ad*,' Bryony says. 'You're embarrassing me.'

'That's what fathers are for.'

Stroud surgery is the spitting image of itself. The same two ruminants, the same coughers, identical crisp- and cola-fuelled, yellow-toothed children, and those ubiquitous septuagenarians and octogenarians who clack their teeth and probably only come to the doctor's surgery for some company and a quiet sit-down.

The delay is even longer this time. My appointment is for half past two and I do not get in to see Dr Howard until nearly twenty past three. Roly and Poly do not answer the telephone with a polite 'Stroud surgery', a friendly upbeat on the surge of 'surgery', but instead eructate a *basso profondo* 'Allo?' each time, as if the caller is disturbing their chewing.

It is like a limping Olympics. I have never seen so many one-legged, rickety-limbed, bow-legged, club-footed people gathered in one place. It is as if all the patients lining the walls of the waiting room, their backsides spilling over the inadequate chairs, have inhaled every feather on a poultry farm. They cough out the effluvia of pneumonia, the common cold, tuberculosis, influenza, lung cancer, who knows, SARS. I am just about to get up and leave when 'Mr Stick, room three' is grunted out.

Dr Howard has dark-brown sunglasses stuffed into his shirt pocket and looks as if he has just stepped off a yacht. He wears cream-coloured chinos with pastel-blue deck-shoes and has a pullover draped over his shoulders. He carries his slight excess weight well; even his double chin and full cheeks are expensively shaved and pampered, with that buffed sheen that only the well-heeled seem to have on their skins.

I wonder if any of his friends or neighbours might have noticed any change in his lifestyle some time after the death of the man of stone. He would have had to carry on working full-time as a General Practitioner, so as not to raise any suspicions after he had faked the cause of death on Jasper's death certificate. I wonder what he might have told his wife to explain the sudden slight improvement in their living standards after the small windfall of his share of Nicola's dead husband's life-insurance policy blew into his bank account. Perhaps he told her that he had secretly been doing some consultancy work on Harley Street one day a week, saving up a nest-egg with which to surprise her like an expensive gift at Easter. Perhaps she was in on the whole thing as well.

'Hello, I'm Dr Howard,' he says, shaking my hand firmly with his overripe fist of carefully manicured fingers.

'We met briefly in the car park here a few weeks ago,' I reply.

'Oh, I'm sorry. I just see so many people in this job; you know how it is.' He smiles and swivels on his chair to face his desk, then taps a key on the computer keyboard so that my details flash up on the screen.

'I haven't seen you as a patient before though, have I?'

'I've only been to the surgery a few times over the years. I never really get ill, touch wood,' I reply.

'That's good to hear,' he says. 'Are you worried about something in particular that's brought you here today?'

'We met each other once before as well, last autumn at the gallery by the station. You were with my near-neighbour, Nicola Fenshawe,' I reply without answering his question. He does not flinch, but smiles warmly.

'How is she? We're close family friends,' he says. He is damn good; he must have trained himself to betray no surprise, no alarm in his eyes or on his skin since his involvement in the man of stone's death. He would definitely pass the lie-detector test.

'She's well. I was sad to hear about the death of her husband a few years ago.'

'It was an absolute tragedy. His brother and I know each other well. He was only in his forties.'

'I didn't know Mrs Fenshawe then, but she says she looked after her husband at home until the end. Surely that isn't possible?'

'I'm afraid that I can't discuss any details with you. I wasn't Mr Fenshawe's doctor and we've got a duty to patient confidentiality in any case, as you'll understand,' he replies firmly. The steel shutters are already down behind his eyes. He will give nothing away. 'Mr Stack,' he continues after an embarrassing silence, 'I see that my colleague discussed your concerns about your drinking with you. D'you think you've made any progress since then?'

'I'm not sure how I'd define *progress*,' I reply.

'I'd like you to have a couple of blood tests,' he says, flashing his penlight into my eyes, one after the other. 'We could wait for a nurse to be free one morning, but that could be in a week or so. I think we need to get them done sooner than that. If you don't mind, I'll take the blood myself right now. I'm a bit out of practice, but I should have no trouble finding a vein.'

'N-no, I don't have a problem with that as such. I just don't think you'll discover anything sinister.'

'Let me worry about that,' he says. 'You might be at risk of your liver having difficulties because it is trying to cope with breaking down the alcohol. This can lead to problems with such things as brain function. Have you noticed any muddled thoughts or memory loss at all lately?'

'Not that I can recall, no. I feel that I'm thinking particularly clearly at the moment, in fact. The benefit of living a quiet life in the countryside,' I reply.

He opens a sterile syringe packet and asks me to roll up my right shirt sleeve well above the elbow. The syringe's needle has a large bore; it is almost the type of thing you would see one of Bryony's vets inject a horse with. He examines my arm for veins closely, taps it just below my elbow several times to raise them and swabs the area where he will send the horse-needle deep beneath my skin.

'You'll feel a slight scratch,' he says as he slides the needle into my arm.

'Ow!' I squawk like a minah bird or a parrot. As nuclear holocaust is to Civil War skirmish, so his introduction of the needle into my arm is to 'slight scratch'. It feels as if he has embedded an apple-corer into the soft part of my flesh.

'I'm sorry, did that hurt?' he says, with a sharp look in his eyes. 'The vein was a little harder to reach than I thought.'

I wonder whether he made it as painful as possible on

purpose, as retribution for my asking about Nicola's man of stone.

My deep crimson blood, my claret, my ruby-red fills one plastic phial at the back end of the syringe, which he then unplugs from the needle unit to replace with another, itself soon filling up with the force of the beating of my heart. He snaps the cap shut on the second phial and places a plaster over the red mark already gently growing beneath the skin on the inside of my elbow, where a network of blue veins spreads like a river delta.

The bruise inside my elbow slowly expands like a conurbation and turns dark blue in the days after my visit to Dr Howard. That is the price I had to pay for asking awkward questions. My mind has been endlessly buzzing with possibilities for answers to these questions for days and nights now. How did Nicola and Dr Howard do what my mind says they might have done when the man of stone's brother was on the scene? That is a possibility that I had not factored into the equation: that he had a brother. My solipsistic way of thinking as an only child did not allow for that. Surely his brother cannot have been involved as well: this is no Cain and Abel story. I have no answer to this question and it keeps me awake at night.

Chapter Twenty-Four

Nicola and I arrive at Heathrow for our flight to D.C. at midday on 14 July. This small country is so full of people; even finding a space for my Volvo in the long-stay car park has taken nearly forty minutes. The check-in queues in Terminal Four stretch like hissing fuses right around the huge hall.

Our flight is at three o'clock and, once we have checked in, Nicola having spent the long wait sitting on the lip of our luggage trolley as we crept forward in the queue, we drink bad coffee in Departures. I watch her as she looks at the crowds of passers-by, this conveyor-belt of humanity. I have her under surveillance at the closest possible quarters. She has such an open expression; it is hard to look at her and see beneath her skin to the secrets that might lie buried there. It is so hard to look at her without falling for her every time, without being seduced by her face's tricks, her body's treats. It is like staring at the sun; it leaves a dark imprint on your retina that grows the more you look at it.

I usually try to sleep for much of the time on a transatlantic flight, but the temptations of the free trolley bar and Nicola keep me awake this time. Drinking the contents of a miniature bottle of Scotch on the rocks does not really seem like drinking at all. I have a neat row of the bottles, empty and brilliant, on my clap-down tray before we have even edged out over the western cusp of Ireland above the great blue void of ocean.

I did not call the surgery for the results of my blood tests before we left. I do not really want to know what they have to say. That news can wait until we get back home from

D.C., like an unwanted homecoming gift. 'Home' is such a hollow word. It echoes around your mouth like an empty metaphor that lost its meaning long ago, vaporises on your tongue like seventy-percent-proof alcohol.

We are taking a northerly course. By the time that we have reached the southern tip of Greenland, Nicola has watched two films on the in-flight entertainment system and I have rallied a small army of shiny glass soldiers. We are flying in Economy and the miniature television screen embedded in the seat in front of Nicola is so close to her face that she threatens to become absorbed into the drama that she is watching. The man in the seat in front of me has reclined it so far back that he is almost lying in my lap. We always used to fly in First Class when my parents and I were shuttling across the Atlantic for the government. I do not think that they would be comfortable at all with all of this tight proximity to their fellow passengers.

Nicola leans against my left shoulder to sleep for the second half of the flight and I look out at the fractured continents of clouds and the continuous early evening light for hours. This is the closest that we will ever get to time travel. Nicola is deeply asleep and does not make a sound; her breathing is slow and regular, her breath warm against my neck. Her intimacy, her closeness, her seeming trust in me, is this called love? Many people would give it that name. Nicola does not use such language in the daytime, but I think that she is slowly falling. Whatever happened to him, I think that she has been lonely since her man of stone's death. What we have feels so far from what Linda and I had together. I cannot forgive Linda; I have tried to do so for so long. I cannot love Nicola for what she did.

We land at Dulles International airport towards seven in the evening local time. Nothing seems to have changed much in the last ten years, although everyone is now carrying electronic hardware, handhelds, palm-pilots, cellular phones. They are all plugged into networks, wired into one another's brains. This terrorism of cells: I have never wanted a mobile phone. Linda's sister would only try to get through to me, somehow.

The rush down the slope towards Immigration is like a Western buffalo stampede. Nicola and I are soon separated by passports, by country of birth, by nationhood. Her queue for foreign nationals is far slower than the line for us Americans and I have already collected our luggage from the carousel, that merry-go-round of plastic leather and fake Louis Vuitton, by the time that she comes through to find me in the hall, looking weary from the grilling that the Immigration officials always give to foreign visitors who simply want to spend some time in their chosen land. She hangs on to my arm as we go through Customs together to find a taxi rank outside Arrivals.

The Arrivals lounge is thronging with disembarked passengers, slowly unfurling themselves after long flights like green buds in spring. There is a taxi rank and there is a queue that rivals the one at Heathrow. It is almost forty-five minutes before we are in a cab heading the twenty-five miles eastwards into downtown D.C. as the sun sets behind us. I did not grow up here, but rather in Georgetown where many of D.C.'s leading lights in politics and the media and its captains of industry live to escape the random violence and traffic of downtown. They would probably call Georgetown upper-bracket, with its distinguished university and its quaint old stone buildings on M Street.

It is a queasy homecoming, if you can call it that. I have a headache the size of a Yorkshire moor and the low-slung suspension of the cab sends us bumping over potholes and drain covers as we approach the city. It does look beautiful, I will give D.C. that much. It has been raining here earlier today and the lights of the city reflect themselves in the streets slick with water. Everything here – the buildings, the avenues wide like rivers, the men and women hurrying by wrapped up in raincoats – is on such a huge scale. The US has a taste for grand statements: it sells itself big, it sells itself brash, it sells itself bold. One of its seats of government is the Senate and D.C. believes that it is the new Rome, but there is an albino ape in the White House. We are living in an age of simian degeneracy.

Nicola and I are staying in a small boutique hotel in Georgetown and we take a detour there first to drop off the luggage and so that she can freshen up. She is very quiet and sits far over on her side of the cab's wide back seat, her elbow on the window-ledge, looking out at the red and white lights of the traffic and the warm yellow lights coming on in buildings across the city ahead of us.

'Are you okay?' I ask.

'I always find long-haul flights tiring,' she says. 'John, we agreed to go on holiday together. I didn't know there'd be three of us.'

'Who's the third?' I ask.

'He's called Jack or Daniel or Jameson, I don't bloody know. He's not joining us for the week. I just want us to have a happy holiday.'

'We will. Why're you exaggerating something that isn't a problem?'

'If there's no problem, why did Philip want you to have blood tests so urgently?'

'Perhaps because he likes putting large needles into peoples' arms.'

'He's not a cruel man; he's actually very kind,' she says. 'I know you don't – *can't* – see that for some strange reason.'

'But he was over-emphasising the risks. I don't drink nearly enough to have done myself any permanent harm.'

'Why're you punishing yourself like this? What's *wrong* with looking after yourself better? You know I care about you, God knows why. You owe it to your daughter and to Linda, if not to me, to look after yourself.'

'*Punishing* myself? It's a bloody pleasurable form of punishment, if that's what it is. I owe Linda absolutely nothing at all,' I reply.

The hotel is a brownstone townhouse and the staff seem to have been brainwashed into speaking like characters from a long-lost America of two-tone spats and pillbox-hatted bellhops bringing you the first edition of the *Wall Street Journal* on a silver salver. They are wearing nylon or polyester uniforms, but speak in fawning illiterate anachronisms. 'Would m'lady like us to send up a foot *massooss* after your long flight?' is the concierge's first question to Nicola, whom he has just addressed as Mrs Stack.

We eat supper that night in a smart downtown restaurant. When I ask the sommelier to suggest a bottle of red to go with the lamb that we have both chosen, he asks whether we want Californian or French. I look at him as if his slack lips have just shot spittle into my eye and he comes back with a very good bottle of claret cultivated on the rich loam of French soil. Nicola and I have ordered the same courses from starter through to pudding, like gastronomic twins.

'So you don't mind if I have a glass or two with supper then?' I ask.

'As long as I'm keeping my eye on you,' Nicola says and smiles her beautiful smile. 'I don't think a couple of glasses of wine each night would make much of a difference, not now,' she adds.

I feel that she is watching every sip, every gulp, every slurp as I drink. I think that I will become teetotal when she is around. The taste of tannin, of grape, of ethyl alcohol, is sour tonight.

'I thought I'd get the cab to take us past Capitol Hill and

the White House on the way back,' I say, as we carefully move spoonfuls of cold gazpacho between the shallow bowls and our mouths like robots low on battery power. Nicola yawns into her napkin as she dabs at a corner of her mouth; it is nearly one o'clock in the morning in England.

'Does this feel like coming home?' she asks.

'God no,' I reply. 'It probably feels almost as alien to me as it does to you. I just know where things are, how to get around.'

'Are you going to show me where you grew up then?' she asks.

'I guess I did most of my growing up in England. I'll show you the house where I was born though; there's no blue plaque there, mind you.'

On our second full day in D.C., we take a taxi out to Arlington National Cemetery so that I can show Nicola my parents' graves. The cemetery is so large that, if you are standing at its centre, you cannot see its edges. It is a city of white marble tombstones, of occasional spectral angels and polished raised sarcophagi.

It was raining both times that I came back to bury my parents. Alpha and Omega, father and mother, matter to matter, dust to dust. The black-clad watchers around the grave were more numerous for my father, who was given a full military burial because of his service in Korea.

It takes us nearly an hour to find the graves, which lie side by side in one quiet suburb of the cemetery beneath a cypress tree. The map that we were given at the gate, its 'You Are Here' only for the eyes of the living, has an inked X marking the spot of my family treasures. I gave the concierge for the dead my parents' names at the gate and he went into his office to consult the cemetery's computer records for some minutes, coming back out to make his mark on our map seemingly as randomly as if a tourist had asked you for directions to St Paul's and you had pointed out the Tower of London on a London street plan.

I cannot feel anything when we eventually find them, lying silently there together. It has been so long. Loss does not stop with the death of your parents: it keeps on coming at you until you too are gone.

'Are you alright?' Nicola asks, putting her arm around my waist and resting her head on my shoulder.

'I'm glad I came and that you're with me. I don't know how often I'll be able to come back again,' I reply.

Our hotel is only a few streets away from my childhood home, a large Victorian townhouse just off M Street, and we go to stand outside its impenetrable walls two or three times during our five days in Georgetown. I point out where my bedroom was to Nicola, where I tripped down the gleaming front steps after our maid had just been polishing them and knocked out a milk tooth or two. Lyndon B. Johnson had not long been elected President and my father was not a happy man. He gave me a clip around the ears for falling. When I look at the house, now probably occupied by some banker or hedge-fund manager, it feels as if I never lived here; as if I am looking at someone else's past.

Is there anything of that falling boy left in me? I have drowned him out with alcohol. I have chased him away with self-pity and hard work. He has gone for a long walk to the hidden head of a secluded Gloucestershire valley where only the farmer and the livestock ever go, and will not be coming back again. That boy has abandoned me to myself. I cannot blame him for that, for what I have become, for walking away. He had such a comfortable start in life. He had all the material things that any boy could need. I would not recognise his face, always so eager to please his hero of a father, if I were to bump into him on the street.

* * *

Our five days together go quickly in a diorama of meals, walks around the safer areas of the city, trips to boutique shops for the perfect pair of heels for Nicola, and capital-city sex. There is the incessant static of car-horns, sirens, footfall, aeroplanes, and voices. The city refuses to silence itself for our sex. We jokingly consider going to hear a lecture in one of our subjects at the university and making out like teenagers in the dark recesses of the auditorium, until we realise that term is out. However close I get to Nicola, however often I penetrate her, get inside her skin, I am no nearer to knowing what really happened to her man of stone, to pinning down the truth. She probably thinks that she is my reality these days, with our having spent all of this sudden time together. I do not buy her reality: I am only interested in my version of events.

The night before we fly back to England, I go for one last look at where I lived until my father's posting to London, when we swapped brown brick for the striding white marble porticoes of Belgravia. I wish that seeing all of this could somehow touch me, could make me laugh or make me cry. All that I can see is my depleted bank account and the image on a loop in my mind of empty bottles dropping from the sky, each smashing into a thousand pieces one after another, without making a sound.

When I get back to our hotel room, I am just about to open the door when I hear Nicola's voice talking in a monologue that ebbs and flows with the rhythm of the person speaking on the other end of the line. 'He was asking about *Jasper*? . . . Why the hell . . . ? What did you *tell* him? . . . Good . . . I know,' then, after a long pause, 'I know; I know. Oh God, I'm *worried* . . . I think he might be having some sort of breakdown . . . What d'you mean,

"What about?" Isn't it on your bloody computer records? No? I'll tell you properly when I'm back . . . No, I just don't think it was such a good idea for him to come back here when he's in this state . . . Drinking? I've tried to make him cut down, to keep an eye on him . . . I know; I know . . . I'll get him to come back in to see you as *soon* as we're home . . .'

I tiptoe away from the door to our room and walk round and round the city block, not knowing what to do. I feel that I have been caught out somehow. When I go back about an hour later, Nicola hardly looks up from where she is lying on the bed as I open the door. I think that she has been crying. I lie down beside her and hold her close to me. The warmth of our bodies feels like betrayal.

Chapter Twenty-Five

Late July and the crickets are running riot in the grass. My business account manager has written to tell me that only fifteen of the twenty-five works sold at the auction; that I still owe the bank just over ten thousand pounds. I have no other choice than to borrow some money against the house to pay off my debt.

We got back from D.C. three or four days ago now and I have been on my own since we drove back to Stroud from Heathrow. Nicola still thinks that she is angry with me about my drinking in D.C.; I do not want to forget that overheard telephone conversation with the good Dr Howard, coroner and undertaker to the man of stone. I am going to take a sabbatical from seeing Nicola until I am ready to do so again later in August, when the grain dust from the crop harvests on the farms around here rises in the air like a storm in the desert.

The sun is beating down on the anvil of the earth. I was forged by fate; I am a hollow forgery of a man. The long grass in the garden has turned brittle and pale brown, like a distant race of etiolated natives waiting for colonisation by the whirring blades of history. I have decided to grow a beard or, rather, my hands have decided no longer to shave my face.

Nicola rings on the Friday after we return and I let the answerphone pick up this thin thread of human contact, as I will do for all calls from now on. There is a cool but conciliatory tone in her tinned voice: 'John, where are you? How are you? I want you to go back to see Philip; you really need to. I wanted to ask about what our plans are for this weekend. Give me a call.'

All these wants and needs. There is no 'us' or 'ours' any more. Those collective, possessive pronouns have been murdered and hidden in a shallow grave somewhere in the woods.

A letter drops through the door on Saturday morning, brought by the postman who whistles through the gap between his two front teeth. It is stamped 'Gloucestershire NHS Trust' and seems to be trying to frighten me. It is from the Gastroenterology Department at Cheltenham General Hospital:

23 July

Dear Mr Stack,

Stroud Surgery has sent us the results of your recent blood tests. We are writing to inform you that the levels of certain enzymes in your blood are significantly raised, leading us to suspect that there might be problems with your liver function.

We need to conduct further tests on your liver function and pathology. The tests will be conducted in the Outpatients Unit of our Gastroenterology Department at ten a.m. on 8 August. You will need to stay in Outpatients for the day and be collected from the Unit at four p.m., as the sedation necessary for liver biopsy will mean that you cannot drive or operate heavy machinery for twenty-four hours.

We would be grateful if you could call us at your earliest convenience to confirm this appointment.

Yours sincerely,

Ralph Prior
Consultant, Gastroenterology

I will not go to the appointment; there is nothing wrong with me. I would not be at all surprised if Philip Howard is behind the letter. It smacks of his hand. I wonder if Nicola already knows about this 'enzyme problem' as well. Perhaps that was what they were discussing on the phone: how to divert me from my enquiries into what really happened to the man of stone.

I must live at the Stone House as if I have gone away for a while, so that Nicola or Tim do not expect an answer when they come knocking at the door. I pull all the curtains upstairs and downstairs and take out the bulb in the automatic light above the front door. The empty bottles in the blue recycling box outside the back door would give me away as they mounted up; I will keep the box in the kitchen by the pedal bin from now on. I must leave any post to gather on the doormat, as I cannot appear to have been here to read it.

I have received an email from Penelope. She writes that she and Jake are getting married in the New Year and that I must give a reading at the wedding. She says that she misses the old days with me at the gallery and that I should come up to Town for lunch at some point soon. *How is dealing from home going? How is Nicola?*, she asks. She sends out a series of requests and questions, all of which would have negative responses if I chose to answer her message.

I think that I have reached a breakthrough with my drinking. If I drink only spirits, I get through far fewer bottles of alcohol each week and there are then a smaller number of empties to put in the recycling box. I have rediscovered the joys of bourbon, the poor down-home cousin of single-malt whisky whose lip-smacking elixir I first tasted on a trip home to D.C. aged about sixteen or seventeen, bought over the counter of a liquor store by a friend of a friend who looked twenty-one. We took it in turns to swig from the bottle, swaddled in its brown paper bag, on the long walk back to his parents' house.

It is terribly quiet up here. I last saw a car pass the house nearly twenty-four hours ago when I was getting into the Volvo to drive down into Stroud and fetch some provisions for the weekend. Very few dogs pull their masters up the dead-end lane that runs into the woodland past the Stone House; the odd farm vehicle rumbles past once or twice a week. Otherwise, I could be living in a different time, or after some unnameable catastrophe had wiped out my fellow humans from the earth.

I go for a long walk up to the top of the Cotswold escarpment, nipping at a small flask of bourbon as I go. The sun speaks a language of absolute power. Its rays banish all feeling as I walk, other than the heat on my skin and the warmth in my mouth from the bourbon.

The sky is so ineffably clear, with not a single cloud to give it a sense of scale, that it seems immense beyond belief, fading into a blue-white light like a wash of watercolour at the horizon. It is a weekday and the world is at work; only the occasional car or tractor passes me as I walk up the single-track metalled road that leads to the top of the ridge at France Lynch. My short beard is singing with sweat by the time that I reach the bench at the heart of the village, on a small area of green.

All of these rattling days stretching out ahead of me like an infinitely long goods train slowly travelling across a landscape, with wagon after wagon empty of its cargo of work, home, family, responsibility, of all the things that keep you here. All that I can do is to drink from the lips of my silvered pewter hip-flask and watch the world go by. The few witnesses to my being on this bench in the middle of a village far from anywhere but itself do not even give me a second glance as they pass at speed in their cars or walk past with dogs straining on their leads.

On my way home my legs walk themselves back to that

tunnel of trees again on the shorter road route from the Stone House into Stroud. They cannot help themselves; they cannot stop this dark migration. The ice of winter has been replaced with dust on the edges of the road, with a tidemark of fallen twigs and leaves desiccated in the heat that sends a sickness deep into the pit of my stomach. It all looks so untouched here, so innocent, so benign. Suddenly a car speeds past, braking late at the sharp bend in the road so that its tyres send rubber smoke out behind it drifting towards me, leaving two short parallel lines on the tarmac. The teenage driver and his ghost-white passenger look back at me and laugh silently through the glass before the car disappears around the bend. I fall to my knees in the dirt on the banked side of the road. I cannot stop trembling and shaking and crying.

Linda braked too late in the ice that Christmas Day when she left me. The police said that she might have been trying to avoid a sudden animal in the road. I heard the car's detonating impact with the trees all the way from the Stone House, where I was still standing in the frost on the lawn having watched the car disappear down Folly Lane, hoping that her anger would pass and that she would turn the car around somewhere, bringing Bryony home so that we could be a family again. I ran and ran when I heard that sound; knowing it was them, just knowing it was them.

All of this time alone has given me the space in which to think clearly for the first time in years. My mind has made itself up: I do not think that cancer killed Nicola's husband; I think that she did, or rather someone acting for her. I think that she killed him to avenge her father's loss of his money at Lloyds of London and his early death. I cannot be with her any more.

There is another message from her on the answerphone when I get back home. 'John, I don't know where you are;

I'm worried now. Please call me as soon as you get this. I came up to find you this morning, but you weren't in. I want to help you, be there for you, just so you know that. I think I love you, if that helps.'

What is a little lost love between two people who were once lovers? I am surprised to hear her using that word; it seems so out of place. It sounds like the sort of word that she would use to control me, to pacify me, to calm me down. Give it an opaque rubber teat and a plastic grip and shove it in my mouth. It is that sort of word: a pacifier. I will not be subdued by her; I will not be silenced by her body's conjuring of delights. I want nothing from her but the truth. Since that is the one thing that I will not get, I want nothing from her.

Where was the man of stone's brother in this cruel scenario that my mind lays out before me like a prosecutor putting forward his case before a judge? How could Nicola and Dr Howard have fooled him as well? Perhaps he lives abroad; perhaps he and the man of stone had not seen each other for many years. Perhaps there was a silence between them as impenetrable as basalt, marble, granite. Perhaps he had his reasons for believing that his brother died from natural causes, even if he went from being the picture of health one day to stone-cold dead the next. It does not add up. The details do not matter any longer.

There is always the taste of bourbon in my mouth like a bitter prayer, the last thing at night and the first thing in the morning. I am my own doctor; I dose myself until I can take no more, then wake up shaking as if I have slept the night in the middle of a forest in midwinter.

It is so quiet that I can almost hear the crops growing in the fields. My senses seem to be on overdrive; they have been honed by the grinding-wheel of isolation. I am a hare, a rabbit, a deer twitching at the faintest sound, the slightest movement. I cannot let my guard down even for a second.

Nicola came up to the Stone House today. I hid upstairs in the bathroom at the back of the house and heard her knock over and over again and call my name. There was a split second when I felt almost sorry for her, sniffing around my locked house like a sweet orphaned puppy looking for its parent, or a frightened child lost on a moor hoping for warmth inside an abandoned croft. I watched her for a few seconds through a small gap in the window-blind in the bathroom as she came round to the back of the house to peer into the kitchen window below me. If she had just looked up she might have seen me, or at least have seen my eyes watching her.

Once I had gone downstairs when I thought that it was safe to do so, I found another of her perfect notes pushed through the letterbox.

THE COURT HOUSE, FOLLY LANE, NR. STROUD, GLOS.
John, I'm so worried now. If you do not call me before
the end of the week, I'm going to contact the police.
Please, please ring me. Love, Nx

Leaving notes to a missing person, shoving messages through the letterbox of a shut-up house, must be the first sign of madness. Surely she cannot expect me to read her words if she thinks that I have disappeared or that some-thing worse has happened to me. She should be careful about getting the police involved: they might learn things from me about what happened to her late husband that I am sure they would be very interested to hear.

It is Bryony's thirteenth birthday next week and I must decide what to buy her to mark her coming into her teens. Each year that goes by, it is more difficult to think of the appropriate gift. I wonder whether she is going off the idea of becoming a vet. I am frightened that she will get bored of visiting me as she grows up.

Bryony is the only thing that I have left, the only person that I want to see. Everyone else just disappears when she is around, becomes unimportant. I forget the past; my worries seem to evaporate for as long as she is with me. She is like the most powerful antidepressant, the most wonderful tonic; it is as if she somehow reveals the secrets to immortality, to never-ending life. There is always a comedown to be suffered after taking any drugs; the symptoms of withdrawal kick in and you need more and more pills simply to stabilise you, to bring you back to where you can cope again. It is like that with Bryony: when she goes back to her mother all of the good that she does to me for as long as she is here dissolves and I am back to how I was before she came. It is a never-ending cycle of needing her here with me then being struck down when she has gone again.

The evenings are endless now. I have so much daylight to occupy, so many hours to populate with things to do. It is not getting dark until nearly ten o'clock at night and the wildlife hides itself in the woods and the margins of the garden until the sun has gone down. Even the badgers and the foxes do not give me any company as I drink on one of the deckchairs, just staring at the endless grass, staring at the endless grass.

There have been more silent phone calls eating up the answerphone tape. Two minutes of static is followed by the sudden death of silence as the tape spools out. It is funny that the tape can run static; it sounds like an oxymoron.

The weather broke last night. God or the Devil had been ratcheting up the humidity for days until it pooled in the air, lay over everything like a thick blanket. There was a solitary crack of thunder, the first volley of the air's battle against the earth, fired as a warning salvo, and then all hell broke loose. The sky lit up like bonfire night a few seconds after the thunder struck and the wood below the house was illuminated for the blink of an eye like a blackened stage set, the trees cut out sharply against the blinding light. Then syncopated explosions of thunder like shellfire shook the earth and the dead weight of rain came, pummelling the roof and the garden and the wood. In the morning, it was as if autumn had come early; pools of wet, sun-burnt leaves were eddying and swirling in the breeze along the lane and on the lawn in the garden.

The atmosphere is still fizzing with an electric charge; it might well storm again later today or tonight. My temples throb with bourbon and the energy in the air.

The thunder must have blocked out the sound of the answerphone late last night, or else the bourbon must have sent me into a deep sleep before I woke at first light on one of the two sofas. The machine's relentless red eye is blinking at me.

When you expect nothing you often get something. I was anticipating endless reams of static again, but hear instead that familiar voice, part Linda part stranger, from light years ago. *John, you've got to listen to me. You didn't do anything wrong. It wasn't your fault. I'm so sorry for how we were to you. Please answer my calls. I need so much to speak to you again.* Hearing Linda's sister's voice is like listening to her dark twin. There is nothing that she can tell me that I do not already know. There is nothing that she can say that would undo what her family did by blaming me for the accident.

Chapter Twenty-Six

I have planned Bryony's birthday party carefully. I have driven down into Stroud early this afternoon long before her train is due to arrive to buy an intricately-iced birthday cake with candles and a new pink dress for her.

I ask myself what would happen if she was not there when I got to the station; if Linda suddenly decided one day not to let me see Bryony any more, on a whim or because she had to move further away. I think that I would fold in on myself into the vacuum that she left behind like an origami lotus-flower collapsing in water. I could not survive her absence from my life.

I put the cake in the boot of the car, hoping that it will not begin to melt in the heat of late July, and lay out her new dress on the back seat. It is waiting to be animated, to be brought to life by her inhabiting of its shell-pink satin cloth. If she did not come, it would lie there dormant and helpless for eternity.

This town is the turning-point of my life and still I do not belong. It is somehow less than the sum of its parts. Its buildings, the rundown shops and offices near the station, hang together like the teenagers loitering around the peripheries of its scrubby park. They are bound together by accidental affinities, nothing more.

She is there; she is always there, sitting reading on the bench or looking into space, listening to her Walkman. Linda's legs are disappearing up the last few steps of the town side of the footbridge as I walk into the ticket office. I just know that they are hers from the perfect shape of them. I have not seen her for so many months and I feel sick at the sudden sight of what I have lost. I force myself from running after her. I am shaking when I give Bryony a kiss on the forehead.

'Are you alright, Dad?' she asks. 'You look scared.'

'I'm fine now you're here, Bee. I'm just a bit tired that's all,' I add to reassure her.

'You know what day it is tomorrow?' she asks as we are walking to the car, smiling her lovely smile.

'It's Saturday. You always come on a Friday and the day after Friday is always a Saturday.'

'*Da-ad*,' she says, making that pained expression that teenagers adopt like sudden grotesques.

'You don't *really* think that I'd forget your birthday, do you?' I ask, linking my arm in hers just before we get to the car. 'I promise I'll never forget it as long as I live.'

'I thought you might not remember exactly when it was. Dads are often bad at that sort of stuff. My friends at school say their mums even have to write "Love Dad" in their birthday cards for them sometimes.'

'Well, I'm not one of them, am I?' I reply. 'I mean, have I ever forgotten your birthday, even once?'

'I don't remember when I was really little,' Bryony says and smiles at me from the passenger seat. 'Maybe you did then.'

'Trust me, I didn't. I would remember if I had.'

I covered the pink dress with a rug that is on the back seat of the Volvo when I got to the station and Bryony has no idea that it is there, waiting for her. I hope that she is happy with it. A party dress seems fitting somehow. It is her birthday after all.

She is so full of life and I feel so dead. It is as if my brain-stem has been cauterised with bourbon or pain.

'Dad, why're you growing that beard?' she asks suddenly, glancing over at me as I drive.

'Don't you like it? I think it rather suits me.'

'It makes you look like someone else, like the prophet

Elijah, not like my dad at all.'

'So I *am* a wise man after all?' I joke.

'*Da-ad*,' she says again.

When we get back to the Stone House, I tell Bryony to take her small bag up to the spare bedroom, with its fold-up bed and its strata of discarded and unused possessions like an archaeology of the Stack family, so that I can take the cake out of the boot of the car and her dress off the back seat and hide them in the tall kitchen cupboard. When she comes back down, everything is hidden away.

'Dad, when can I have my old room back?' she asks.

'I've got nowhere else to store the pictures, Bee. Until I've sold them, you'll have to sleep in the spare room when you stay. That might take a few years. By then, you'll have grown up and probably be bored of visiting me. You're not upset about having to sleep in there, are you?'

'No, but I used to like looking at the garden from the window of my old room. I saw wildlife sometimes, foxes and badgers. I can't see the garden from the front.'

'You've got the whole valley to look at from the spare-room window,' I reply.

'It's not the same; everything's further away there,' she says.

'You can have my pair of opera glasses if you like; you'll be able to see more with them.'

'I don't know how they work.'

'You just put them up to your eyes like this,' I say, making goggles with my hands, 'there's nothing to it. Just hold them up to your eyes and look where you want to look. You'll be able to see all sorts of interesting things with them.'

I am not even going to try to hide the bottle of bourbon from Bryony while she is here. There is no point in pretending to be someone else; she knows the truth anyway. Children are good at that. They see right through you.

I pour myself the first long glass of the dirty brown liquid as I am cooking supper in the kitchen. Bryony is in her usual place on one of the two sofas, watching television. It sounds as if the programme is being broadcast backwards. I do not understand a word of what the hysterical presenters are saying. Bryony seems to find it very funny, however, and her lovely laughter warms up the house every minute or two. Friday-night television is to Bryony what bourbon is to me; a stimulant, an entertainment, a tranquiliser, a pacifier, a mind-rotter that makes your eyes sink into themselves, unseeing and oblivious to everything else. The new bottle is more than half empty before the evening is out. The television talks to itself incoherently long after Bryony has gone up to bed.

The day of her birthday dawns bright and clear. My head feels as if it has awoken in a very different season. Bryony will have cereal and milk for breakfast; I will have three Paracetamol tablets washed down with instant coffee and a dash of bourbon.

I want to take her somewhere special today. I have the perfect place in mind.

'Hello, sleepy head,' I say as she comes downstairs. I have been on one of the sofas all night and feel as stiff as if I had been folded up like old clothes in a suitcase.

'I couldn't sleep, I was too excited. I'm a *teenager*,' she says.

'You're still my little girl, though. You always will be.'

'When can I have my presents?' she asks.

'You haven't even had breakfast. Don't you think you should *eat* something first?'

'I'm not hungry. Can I have a coffee?'

'I think you're too young for coffee in the mornings. I need it, you don't. Your mother doesn't let you drink coffee, does she? You can have a cup of milky tea.'

'When we go out, Mum lets me drink coffee sometimes, on special occasions and things. Today's a special occasion.'

'I know it is, Bee, but I'm making you a tea,' I reply.

She takes her cup into the sitting-room and switches on the television again, while I sit at the kitchen table with my large cup of black coffee and the painkillers lined up in a little row. I take one after the other with a sip of coffee in between each one: white, black, white, black, white, black. I am worried that Bryony will not think of her dress as a present. Children want things that they can play with, listen to, watch; clothing is just a necessary, a given, a bore. Still, a pretty girl of thirteen should see how lovely this pink satin dress is. It is more than an item of clothing, it is a benediction.

I tell Bryony that she can have her present this evening and make her get dressed by ten. We are on the road in the Volvo by half past, my head thrumming with the rip of the tyres on the tarmac, echoing with pain to the sound of the engine. I glance in the rear-view mirror and see a white-faced man with dark-rimmed eyes and a darker beard. A profitless prophet. Elijah, as Bryony said. A prophet with sickness in his guts.

'I wish I could've just had a *peek* at my presents before we left, Dad,' she says.

'Where we're going is a kind of present in itself, Bee. Please don't keep going on about it.'

The truth is that I do not know where I want to take her. I have no idea where I am driving us to at all. I know the *kind* of place: a rocky seashore with high cliffs swept by the wind, gulls wheeling in the air and no one else but us to watch them.

The nearest sea is only an hour's drive away at Avon-mouth, but an afternoon spent watching the container ships come and go and the refineries pump out black smoke and bilge would not make Bryony's thirteenth birthday a day to remember. The nearest coastline that matches what is in my mind's eye is north Devon, three hours away. I will have to put my foot down if we are to get there by lunchtime.

The motorway is busy with holiday traffic heading south-west and it is nearly half past one before I pull off onto the A-road that takes us to the coast. Bryony has slept for much of the journey while I have been concentrating on the road ahead and she comes to with a series of yawns and stretches as the car slows.

'Dad, are we there yet? I really need a pee,' she says.

'Another ten minutes or so. I just need to find somewhere to buy things for our picnic. I'm sure the parking area will have a loo.'

'Where are we?' she asks.

'Devon,' I reply. 'D'you remember us coming here when you were about eight for that week, a little further down the coast?'

'When I went on that donkey ride on the beach and Mum said I rode like a jockey with my legs tucked up?'

'And we tried to go swimming and the sea was freezing cold even in June? Your skin turned blue and your teeth chattered.' We both laugh at these memories.

'Stop making me laugh; I really need to go now,' she says, giggling. 'I wish Mum was here,' she adds suddenly, as if a cloud has moved in front of the sun.

'I'm so sorry for everything, Bee. I can never tell you how sorry I am,' I reply. What she has just said makes me grab for my hipflask of bourbon in the driver's door compartment as I pull into the garage forecourt. I feel as if she has hit me in the guts and take a large gulp of the liquid when the car has come to a stop.

'There's a washroom over there. You go in and ask the man at the till for the key. I'll just get some petrol and food.'

'There's a seabird called a petrel,' she says sadly.

'There's a vegetable called a washroom,' I say to make her laugh again.

I find a secluded stretch of coastline for our picnic, on a part of the map where the lanes marked in white are so minor that they have no road numbers assigned to them.

At the end of one of these metalled tracks there is a small gravel parking area leading to a cliff-top path. Our car is the only one here. The crowds of tourists are all on the wide sandy beaches and in the resort towns further along this coast.

'This isn't where I had the donkey ride, is it?' Bryony asks.

'That was a few miles away from here. We're going for a walk along the cliffs and we'll eat our picnic up here then go down to the beach. It's a lovely day; you could even try swimming again.'

'Mum didn't pack my costume. I can paddle like before, can't I?'

Bryony walks ahead on the path and I sneak small sips from the hipflask every few yards. I choose a spot about twenty yards in from the cliff edge for our picnic, where the grass is thick and soft. All that we can see is the green sill of the cliffs giving out onto the hazy blue of the sea one hundred feet below us. Now and then, gulls catch the breeze and rise over the top of the cliff to watch us with their yellow eyes, hungry for our food. They cry out with the raised voices of an incident at an asylum.

We eat in silence just watching the view, devouring plastic-wrapped sandwiches, Scotch eggs, coleslaw using springy plastic forks, half-ripe tomatoes, crisps, sausage rolls and a chocolate mousse each for pudding.

'Happy birthday, Bee; I'm sorry about the long journey down here.'

'I'm really happy we're here. Last year it was stupid: I had a sore throat and spent my birthday in bed like a baby, with Mum bringing me up boiled eggs and soldiers. When we get back can I have my presents?'

'Didn't I promise you that earlier? Are you ready for a paddle and a walk along the beach?'

'I want to lie here in the sun for a little bit. I feel tired,' she says.

'We need to get going again by late afternoon, Bee. We don't want to get back to the Stone House too late.'

While she lies on the grass, surrounded by the detritus of our picnic and bathed in sunlight, I take my hipflask and walk carefully to the last few feet of grass before the cliff edge, then lie on my front and slide forward until my head is level with that place where air and land meet. I have never been afraid of heights and it is a false horizon in any case, with another lip of land jutting out from the cliff five or ten feet below. One or two wrong moves, however, and I would fall down to the rocks lining the land side of the beach like a sack of potatoes. This bourbon is making me forget which way is up now. It feels good not to know where you are in space. It makes you feel free.

'*DAD*,' there is a sudden shout behind me. '*Dad*, what are you *doing*? You're scaring me.'

'I'm just looking at the sea, Bee. It's very blue today,' I reply.

'*Please*, Dad,' she says. 'Can we go now? I want to go for my paddle.' It is a command rather than a question. I am suddenly the child and she the chastising adult. I crawl backwards from the void and walk with her down the cliff path to the shore.

The beach is wide and slopes very gently down towards the sea, which is a long way out. There is a concrete walkway in front of the rocks that line the cliff and a small building made of the same material that houses a male and female lavatory. Otherwise, there is nothing here but sand, sea and the flotsam and jetsam that it throws up. A group of bathers shimmers in the light a long way off at the other end of this immense stretch of sand, a family on a day out from Gloucester or Bristol or Plymouth, perhaps.

Bryony will not stop until she has reached the water. She walks across the sand, her sandals held loosely by their straps in her left hand and her jeans rolled up to just below the knees. She always loved the sea, even when she was very small. I think that she liked the way light flickered on its surface and was fascinated by how it moved. She used to call it breathing, what the sea did as it rose and fell.

I sit on a low sand dune at the top of the beach, clumps of stiff grass sprouting up here and there from its bald surface, and watch Bryony's dwindling shape as she moves towards the sea. She seems to be disappearing into the light. It is more and more difficult to see her through the hazy air and the glimmer reflecting off the water. I have the urge to run down the beach after her, to keep her in sight, not to let her paddle out too far. I suddenly remind myself of my dear departed mother. I must allow Bryony to be herself, to explore the world on her own terms. I have to let her go sometime. I have to let her go.

I do not drink any more bourbon for the three or four hours before the long journey home and down endless mouthfuls of garage-bought spring water from the plastic bottle in my picnic bag and sip lukewarm coffee from the thermos flask, so that I am fit to drive. We do not get back to Stroud until almost nine o'clock. I make Bryony sit quietly in the sitting-room without the crowding voices of the television in the corner, while I find a box of matches above the stove and light the thirteen candles on her birthday cake with its filigrees and flutings of pink icing sugar. I do my best to sing 'Happy Birthday' in my voice that is breaking with tiredness at this late hour as I walk into the room with the cake.

'Blow out the candles and make a wish,' I say as I put the cake down in front of her on the coffee table and her face lights up with the glow from the circle of candles. It is lovely to see her looking so happy.

I go back into the kitchen to fetch the dress from its hiding place, carefully folding it and tying it with a matching satin ribbon that I bought specially for the occasion. When I walk back into the sitting-room with the soft parcel, Bryony is just sitting staring into the flaming and guttering pools of wax that the candles have become. There are small rivulets of molten wax all over the top of the cake.

'God, the candles burnt down quickly. Bee, I told you to blow them out and make a wish. You've ruined the cake. What on earth were you doing?'

'I was waiting for you, Dad,' she replies in a quiet voice and suddenly looks sad. 'I was waiting for you. I wanted you to see me do it.'

'We'll have to cut the top of the cake off now when we eat it; it's *such* a waste.'

'Sorry Dad; I didn't know,' she says.

'Well it is your birthday; you can do whatever you like on your birthday, can't you?'

'Can I have a coffee then?' she asks with a smile.

'I've bought you a little present; I hope you'll like it. You remember what you said about dads being useless at birthdays? I tried to think of something you could wear to your party next week, now you're all grown up,' I say as I hold out the dress for her in both hands. She takes the parcel, quickly pulls aside the satin ribbon and lets the dress fall to its full length against her body.

'It's *beautiful*, Dad: thank you, thank you, thank you,' she says. She comes over and gives me a cuddle so tight that it is as if she never wants to let go. She smiles her lovely smile as she looks up into my face and seems happy again, so happy.

Sunday, the first day of August: the month when the earth turns to dust. I wake up late with a head full of pain and Bryony is still sleeping deeply, her door ajar, at ten thirty. Lazy bones catching no worms.

I somehow know that Nicola will come up to the Stone

House again this morning. I stand in my bedroom looking out of the window at the lane and the valley, just watching and waiting. All I can hear is the light breeze in the trees and Bryony beginning to stir.

Just after eleven I see Nicola's shape emerge from the woodland path about two hundred yards away and walk up the slight incline of the lane towards the house.

'Bee, come in here quickly. We've got to hide,' I call out to her.

'Why're we hiding, Dad?' she asks with anxiety creeping into her voice.

'Come in here and I'll show you.' Nicola has just reached the house. She is walking onto the gravel drive. I kneel down low and peek over the windowsill with Bryony crouching down beside me in her pink pyjamas.

'Who's *that*?' she asks, her eyes level with the window ledge.

'Oh, just someone I know. I'm hiding from her at the moment.'

Nicola bangs loudly with her fists on the front door. Bryony and I are both giggling uncontrollably. She hammers her fists on the frosted glass panes of the front door and we cower down on the floor beneath the bedroom window, trembling with laughter.

'*JOHN, John*, I know you're in there,' Nicola shouts over and over. '*I KNOW YOU'RE IN THERE . . .*'

I hear her sob several times and say 'Oh shit' to herself. 'Oh shit, oh shit,' she repeats in an ever more feeble voice. She bangs on the door again, but with less force and conviction this time, then her voice fades as she walks around to the back of the house. There is some staccato knocking on one of the windows giving onto the garden and the sound of her raised voice again, then absolute silence.

Bryony has stopped giggling and looks very pale, almost transparent with fright or shock. I suddenly feel more tired than I have ever felt in my life and lie down on top of my unmade bed covers. The bottle of bourbon stands unstoppered on the night-table within one short movement of my right hand. I am scared to shut my eyes in case I never want to open them again.

Bryony comes to lie beside me on the bed and looks into my eyes.

'Are you happy, Dad?' she asks, still looking pale.

'I'm only happy when you're here with me. I miss you and Mum so much still.'

'I wish we could be a family again.'

'So do I. Very, *very* much,' I reply. I cannot help my eyes filling with tears.

'Don't cry, Dad. Please don't cry.'

'I won't: I'm sorry,' I say.

I must have fallen asleep. When I open my eyes again, Bryony is not there. She must have gone downstairs. Why does her voice come out of my mouth? *Why does her voice come out of my mouth?*

Chapter Twenty-Seven

I do not take Bryony into Stroud on Monday morning. It is time now to go down to the Court House again. Linda can come up here herself to find Bryony if she wants her back. I am not going to play her games any longer; I am not going to do what she wants me to do any more.

Bryony and I walk down through the wood in the early morning and I hold her hand tightly so that she does not slip on the deep layer of dry leaves beneath the trees. When we are level with the roof of the Court House, I move along the contour of the steep slope perhaps one hundred yards from the outer edge of the wood until we can see the gates and the front of the house clearly.

It is nearly half past seven and the sun is already high in the sky, but its rays have not warmed the air yet. Bryony shivers slightly and huddles into me for warmth as we sit on the fallen tree-trunk that I have found, which gives a perfect vantage point over Nicola's car and front door, but is far enough away and in deep enough undergrowth to keep us hidden from sight.

'These are the opera glasses I was telling you about, Bee. Put them up to your eyes like this and you can see things that are far away much more clearly.'

'I can see a plant in a pot in that window on the middle floor and a light's just come on in the large room on the right,' she says after a minute or two of holding them up to her face with her pale hands. She looks as if she is enjoying our little adventure now.

'That's the woman who made all the noise at our house yesterday. She did something bad to her husband. I'm trying to find out exactly what happened to him,' I reply.

'How *exciting* – can I help?' she asks, her voice ringing out loudly in the utter silence of the woods

'Keep your voice down, Bee. She mustn't know we're here.'

Nicola usually leaves for work at about a quarter past eight. It is just a question of waiting until she drives up the track towards the main road. I have all the time in the world and enough bourbon to keep me warm until I get into her house. The woods are so quiet this morning. The birds are mute in the trees. The local fauna seems to have fled the scene.

I must have drifted off to sleep. I come to with a trail of saliva stretching from my itching beard to the top button of my shirt. Bryony is dozing with her head cradled in my lap. There is the sound of a car engine receding through the trees. The gravel forecourt of the house is empty. It is almost nine o'clock. She must have left late for work this morning, or have a meeting somewhere away from the office.

'Bee, *Bee*, wake up. We've got to go,' I say, shaking her gently awake.

'Wha–?' she says and sits bolt upright. 'I wasn't asleep. I was just resting my head; I'm bored. Can we go now?'

'We're going into this lady's house. She's gone out to work and she always leaves a set of keys under some stones near the front door. I've seen her do it before.'

'Isn't that called *burglary*, Dad?' she asks, looking worried again.

'I know her very well. I'm just visiting her as a friend. I don't want to take anything from her. I just want to look at some things in her house.'

'What things?'

'I don't know until I find them,' I reply.

The keys are underneath the edge of a Cotswold-stone

slab supporting the water-butt where they always are, with woodlice milling around them. I fumble for a few seconds with the two identical-looking keys in the pair of Yale locks, as I confuse them at first, then we are in through the front door into the large hall. I keep thinking that I can hear the sound of a car engine coming down the long drive.

'Bee, push that chair over to the window, sit there quietly and keep a look-out up the drive. I won't be long.'

'Can't I come with you? I'm scared.'

'*Please do what I say for once*,' I snap back. 'I'm doing this for you as well.'

'DON'T SHOUT AT ME,' she says with tears welling up in her eyes.

'If you see anything at all, run upstairs to find me straight away.'

'Okay,' she replies quietly without looking up at me. She is even more beautiful when she is frightened.

'I'm sorry I shouted at you; I didn't mean to,' I reply as I walk up the wide wooden staircase. 'Just keep your eyes peeled for a car or anyone coming up to the house.'

I do not know where to begin. The Court House is so large and Nicola could come back at any moment. Perhaps she is having a day off work today and has just gone shopping in Stroud for an hour or two. Perhaps she is working from home and has gone out quickly for some groceries. Perhaps she is planning to drop by the house later this morning on her way back to the office after an early meeting in Bristol or Gloucester, as she sometimes does. I climb the second flight of stairs to her bedroom as quickly as my legs will carry me. I feel like crawling into her bed before I have even begun to search through her belongings for some evidence of what really happened to her man of stone. The rocket fuel of my bourbon suddenly seems to be propelling me towards the cradling void of sleep and I am finding it very hard to resist its power.

The room spins on its axis and I need to vomit in the

pristine toilet bowl in her en suite bathroom. It takes me several minutes to wipe away all the traces of my sudden nausea. I must get some solids inside me soon; I cannot keep on drinking like this on an empty stomach. It is like swallowing battery acid.

The bedroom is perfectly arranged. The counterpane on Nicola's queensize bed looks as if it has been ironed into place. There are hardly any of her possessions, her personal effects, her *things* on show. It is a study in morning light on polished wooden surfaces and burnished metal.

I open her chest of drawers and see the tangled delights of knickers and bras, the turn-off of woollen socks and what appear to be neatly folded long-johns or supportive stockings. I am looking at her life from the inside out. It is all washed so spotless, so white. I can see no incriminating stains on any of it. No blood from the man of stone. He is clean gone, erased from the fabric of this house. Her toothbrush in the bathroom, her hairbrush, her flannel, her towel: they only hold traces of her DNA. His half of the pairing of these items is no longer there.

Her study is lined with books, although I have never seen her reading. What am I looking for as evidence more than three years after the man of stone's death? *Written* things; a scrap of paper with an incriminating phrase scribbled in pencil on it, a letter from Dr Howard to Nicola confessing his undying admiration for her, something in one of her diaries. I do not know any longer what I expect to find. I hope that Bryony is keeping a sharp-eyed look-out up the drive. Does she know how much I am relying on her? *Does she know how much I am relying on her?*

There is a writing-table and a chair in the study. I just cannot see her ever sitting at it; she would read through any legal documents that she had to work on at home in the sitting-room, I am sure of it. Perhaps it was the place where the man of stone came for solitude, to escape the demands of work, life, the commute, Nicola. Perhaps it is simply a showroom for knowledge that has remained mute, untapped, unmined. Perhaps this is where he died.

I would like to have seen Linda's face when she arrived at Stroud station an hour or so ago to find that Bryony was not there. It would have given me such joy to see her suffer like I suffered when she left; to see her lovely face again. She must be standing outside the Stone House now, calling her daughter's name like I called for her after they had gone. She must be ringing and ringing my telephone, hearing it echoing in the silence of an empty house. She will try Bryony on her mobile and Bryony will tell her how to get down here, how to find the Court House.

I go back down the two flights of stairs to check on Bryony and she is still sitting on the chair, looking out of the window at the gravel forecourt and the drive. She has fished her pink Walkman out of her coat pocket and is humming quietly to herself, oblivious to everything around her.

'Bee, BEE: are you keeping a good look-out?' I ask. She does not answer. I walk up behind her and tickle her neck. She jumps up from her chair and lets out a shriek.

'Dad, you *really* frightened me.'

'Don't move; I've almost finished,' I reply.

I have found a cache of Nicola's diaries in the study, shelved side by side in a neat row all in black, running from 1996 to 2005. I sit at the table with my hipflask of bourbon and flick backwards through their pages, time-travelling through the days, weeks and months of the last decade. So much is blank. I am looking for ciphers, signs, *anything*.

All of these endless printed days and there is just a sporadic, broken stream of consciousness of times and places and names in her precise handwriting. I thumb through 2005, 2004 and it is all so meaningless to me. Of course I recognise places: London, Stroud and Cheltenham appear over and over. I see her sister's name and other first names whose possessors I do not know. It is like going to a class reunion for a school you never attended. It feels like trespass. I take a nip of bourbon every other month or so. It washes away the taste of bile and hits my gullet with its afterglow.

I am about to give up on this endless trawling-through of dates and times when a line written in such precise handwriting that I think at first that it is some sort of printed religious quotation catches my eye. It is on the half-page for New Year's Eve, 2003: *It broke my heart to see him suffer like that.*

I flip back through the previous pages and it is written at least once against the lower margin of each day, over and over again like a litany:

It broke my heart to see him suffer like that.
It broke my heart to see him suffer like that.
It broke my heart to see him suffer like that . . .

The phrase starts when he stopped, early in 2003. She must have done something about his suffering. This is the only proof that I need.

'Bryony, let's go,' I call down the top flight of stairs. I am answered by the front door slamming a few seconds later and the sound of high-heeled feet in the hall that suddenly stop moving.

'*HELLO?*' Nicola's voice calls out loudly, the sound echoing around the void of the hall. 'Hello,' she shouts up again and I freeze.

I do not think that she can have heard my voice from all the way up here where she is two flights below; it would have been drowned out by her opening and closing the front door. I think that she wants to know why the door was unlocked when she came back to her empty house. I can hear the sharp heels of her shoes on the first flight of wooden stairs. I do not know where to put myself. Her huge bed is a divan. There is no space under it where I can hide. Where is Bryony? *Where the hell is Bryony?*

'Hello,' she calls out again. Her chiming voice is much nearer now, probably on the first-floor landing. I am looking around for somewhere to hide and in this stripped-down bedroom the only place that I can see is the wide built-in wardrobe with its double sliding doors. I tiptoe over to it on the thick carpet, slide back the left-hand door carefully and step into the recesses of the half-light, gliding the door shut in front of my face and staring into complete darkness. The residue of light on my retinas projects dancing kaleidoscopes of reds and oranges onto the inside of the door.

I can hear nothing at all except a steady thumping that gets faster and faster the more anxious that I become that Nicola has now reached the bedroom and it is her making this muffled banging noise, until I realise that it is just the beating of my heart in my ears: *thump thump the-thump thump* thump like the rhythm of a Northern marching band. Perhaps she has stopped her ascent. Perhaps she has decided that she must have forgotten to lock the front door after all. I put the keys back beneath the stone where I found them: I am a good Boy Scout. I am trying to keep my breathing shallow and regular and my heartbeat slows down to a walking pace again. The wardrobe is filling up with bourbon fumes. Where is the hip-flask? Where the hell is my hip-flask?

There is one last muffled 'Hello' from somewhere in the house and then an endless silence. She is probably circling around my hipflask, that shining evidence of an intruder in her study, not daring to touch it for fear of leaving another set of fingerprints on its incriminating polished surfaces.

Her delicious clothes caress me. Her silk dresses, her fur coat, her woollen trouser-suits press against my back, my legs, the sides of my arms. I can hardly breathe in this scented, clinging embrace. I need to get out of here.

She could be standing right outside the wardrobe door.

Perhaps she took off her shoes and tiptoed up the second flight of stairs, across the top-floor landing and into the bedroom. We could be virtually face-to-face. Perhaps she is even looking at herself in the floor-to-ceiling wardrobe mirror, turning and admiring herself over her shoulder; gazing at her arched back, her delicate shoulders, her exquisite backside, her brown hair tumbling over one shoulder. How would I know? Vanity is soundless. It is the ugly people who make all the noise. They shout and scream about the unfairness of it all.

I can still hear absolutely nothing but the pulsing of blood in my ears. I slide the door back millimetre by millimetre and the morning light creeps into my priest-hole. She is not in the bedroom.

I reach the landing without making a sound as I walk over the thick carpet and peer around the frame of the study door. She is not in there either. My flask is sitting where I left it on the desk and I put it in my jacket pocket then begin the slow descent down to the first floor. I take off my shoes and hold them as I climb down the stairs, as their heels would clatter on the hard wooden surface of each step and give me away.

I get to the first-floor landing without any sign of Nicola. Perhaps she is in the kitchen making coffee or working in the garden on this August day, perhaps she has gone for a walk up to the Stone House to look for me again, like a recidivist or an obsessive-compulsive who cannot wash her hands of it all.

I decide to make a run for it. I can see the front door through the balustrade of the landing. Bryony's chair is no longer by the window overlooking the drive, but in its original place against the wall again. She must have put it back there when she saw Nicola's car coming down the drive. She must be hiding somewhere here in the house as well, or else have escaped by the back door to the garden and on into the wood.

I reach the bottom step of the stairs to the ground floor and tiptoe towards the front door, turning the handle as quietly as I can. The door opens towards me and I walk through the aperture that its opening creates. I am free. It feels miraculous, like a hostage release.

The mistake that I make is to crouch down without shutting the door properly behind me so that I can slip my shoes back on before I walk across the gravel. Just as I have finished and I am standing up again, her voice rings out in the hall behind me.

'*JOHN*,' she says with a flush of anger rising in her throat, 'what the hell are you doing here like this?' She looks like she has just seen a ghost. 'Where the hell have you been for the last week?'

'I-I,' I stammer. It is just like our first meeting down here. 'I-I've come to see you, to say sorry. I thought I'd surprise you.'

'Well you've certainly done that. I *am surprised*,' she snaps back. 'You look god-awful. What's that mess on your face?'

She comes closer to me and stands in the opening of the door, which she pushes further closed as she reaches it, half separating us by a barrier of wood and glass. She seems about to reach out her hand towards my beard through the gap, to point it out to me perhaps or to caress my face, then pulls it back quickly again.

'You *stink* of booze. What've you been doing to yourself?' she says angrily. She looks almost embarrassed for me, or frightened.

'I've been busy,' I reply. 'I want to talk to you.'

'I have nothing to say to you while you're like this,' she replies. She looks at me as if I have just taken a shit on her doorstep. 'The door was unlocked when I came back from Cheltenham. That had nothing to do with you, did it?'

'I-I've only just got here. I wanted to talk to you.'

'Come back when you're sober,' she replies.

'I'm not drunk. I can't get drunk. I've tried as hard as I can.'

'I don't want to talk to you at the moment.'

'*WHERE'S BRYONY?*' I shout. I cannot help myself. '*WHAT DID YOU DO TO YOUR HUSBAND?*'

There is fear shining in her eyes now. She tries to slam the door in my face but I step forward and block it with my foot, pushing it so hard that she stumbles backwards into the hall. She is shouting and crying, 'Get out, get out, get out.' She will not stop. She will not answer my questions.

I get into the hall and she backs away from me towards the kitchen. I can hear sentences coming out of my mouth that make no sense to me at all. I am spitting words and saliva like a cobra.

'*JOHN,*' she screams, '*STOP THIS. Stop. Please stop.* Please don't do this to us,' she trails off almost to a whisper.

She is fumbling with her mobile phone trying to find a number, but her hands are shaking so much that she cannot control her fingers. She keeps backing away from me and puts both of her arms out in front of her as if to push me away. I can hear the distant sound of her mobile calling and calling someone who is not answering their telephone.

'PUT THAT DOWN,' I shout.

'JOHN, STOP!' she screams.

A disembodied male voice comes through the ether from the speaker of her mobile phone, 'Hello, hello, hello . . . ?' it says distantly. She glances at her left hand holding out the mobile in front of her and I turn to run down the passageway towards the kitchen to see if Bryony is in there somewhere so that we can escape together by the back door.

I am suddenly falling into space. I am going. I am gone.

Chapter Twenty-Eight

There is a muffled moaning sound. My eyes open on a damp brick wall in half-light. I must have knocked myself out. I do not know how long I have been lying here like this. I try to move my arms, to explore with my hands. I seem to be trapped under some sort of mountain of cardboard boxes. This place smells of mould and damp. I cannot see anyone else here. I realise that the moaning sound is coming out of my own mouth. The pain in my back and in my head hits me like an avalanche now. I have bitten my tongue.

I am in some sort of cellar with no steps that I can see, just sheer brick walls. The darkness is punctured by a rectangular patch of daylight almost directly above me and some thinner light coming from over in the corner. My back hurts so much that I think that I must have broken it. I can taste blood in my mouth. Nicola's face is hovering over the hole of light through the fog in front of my eyes. She is looking down at me and talking into her mobile phone. 'Philip, call me back, please call me back, *please call me back* . . . It's John, *you need to help me*,' I hear her say.

She sounds as if she is weeping in between her panicked words. I try to stand up and fall back into the crush of rubbish again. The space spins. I taste of something rotten. I put my hand up to my head and a wet patch of hair slicks my fingers almost black in this gloom when I look down at them. This must be where Nicola throws her old boxes and other recyclable garbage. The mound of cardboard seems to have partly broken my fall.

I am remembering it now: I thought that what just

happened was gone, but it has somehow stayed in the recesses of my memory and re-emerged. Why didn't she warn me; why didn't she shout out something as I was turning? This cellar must be about twenty feet wide with an even flagstone floor where the rubbish has not yet accumulated. It is the place where Nicola keeps all of the dirty secrets of her perfect home.

I feel helpless, sprawling like a newborn baby delivered into the mire of the world. I am stranded on my back like an upturned beetle, my legs kicking out uselessly with no control from my head. I need to turn over onto my front, to push myself up with my arms. My bed of litter absorbs my efforts, crumpling and shifting beneath my weight, and it is some minutes before I can get myself into a sitting position, my back protesting viciously and my head wound pulsing.

It takes me an enormous effort to lever myself up to vertical by pushing my arms against the cold wall. The ceiling of the cellar is high above me. I can stand. I can stand up. I am *Homo erectus*. The open hatch is far too high for me to reach. I stretch out my arms above my head and the rectangle of light is four or five hands above the tips of my fingers. Why is she not passing me down a ladder? She must have one somewhere in the house. I stand under the opening and shout and shout up, but she seems to have gone away from the hall again.

There is a grille in the far corner letting some daylight in. I stumble over to it: I am punch-drunk. I can see green grass outside. It must be the large lawn behind the house. My eyes are somewhere near turf level. Where is Bryony? Where has she gone? She cannot be far away. I know that she would have waited for me somewhere near the house. She must be wondering what has happened to me. I do not want her to be afraid.

Some time after Nicola first spoke I hear her voice again. She sounds more and more hysterical: 'Yes, ambulance . . .

The Court House, Folly Lane, near Stroud . . . Yes, it's GL5 0PR . . . Yes, of course he's breathing, he's been calling out. He's fallen into my cellar . . . I can't see him very well,' she says shrilly. 'Please make sure they know this is a real emergency. I can't get into the cellar to help him and I'm worried that he's getting worse.'

Perhaps Nicola does not know where the ladder is for some reason: that must be it. Perhaps she really cannot get down here without jumping. If she did that we would both be stuck. The old gardener must have put the ladder somewhere where she cannot find it, probably in one of the outhouses. Where is he when we need him?

'WHERE'S MY DAUGHTER?' I shout up into the light. Nicola does not answer. The wetness from my head is running thickly into my left eye. I wipe it away with my sleeve but it keeps coming back again and blurs my vision. I am worried that I am losing blood.

I go back over to the grille and try to rattle it. It will not move. It is set in solid stone. I can smell beautiful fresh air coming through it from outside. I can see sunlight above the trees on the edge of the wood. It is slanting through the foliage, a brilliant golden light dappled with green. There is a spider's web stretching across the top right corner of the grille and catching the light. A big black spider is just sitting there, fixing me with its eyes like polished beads. My back feels as if it is being sawn in two by two inept sawyers or journeyman carpenters ill-suited to their trade.

I feel like a prisoner in an oubliette. I feel like a condemned man awaiting his execution. I cannot help thinking that all of this was somehow a part of Nicola's plan; that she did not warn me because she wanted me to fall. If I looked carefully enough, perhaps I would find her husband's bones down here somewhere. Perhaps his grave is beneath these flagstones.

Why won't she help me? 'WHERE'S BRYONY?' I shout up again. Nicola still has not come back to the opening. I cannot see her face. I can hear her hard heels walking quickly over the stone floor above me.

I am looking around for something to stand on, but the damp cardboard boxes that have remained uncrushed by my falling weight are all sagging and empty. There are a couple of galvanised buckets, a trunk coated in grit and dust, a mop fixed into place by ancient cobwebs in the corner opposite the grille. There is nothing that I can use to raise myself up and give me purchase on the frame of the opening. It is at least ten feet above the floor. I try to jump and almost manage to reach my hand into the void of light; I feel sick and things hurt badly when I do. The horizons shift and tilt.

'*HELP ME*,' I shout up as loudly as I can. 'Get me out of here.' My sleeve is wet from wiping at the stinging wound in my scalp. Why won't she help me?

'WHERE IS BRYONY?' I shout out angrily again. I am trying to make Nicola hear me, to get her to understand, to come back from wherever she has gone and listen to me.

Suddenly her face is looking down into the opening again. 'The ambulance is coming, John; it won't be long,' she says. 'Everything's going to be alright.' She is trying to sound calm, reassuring. 'You've fallen and I think you've hurt your head. Please try not to move around too much. I'm sorry I can't get down there to help you: I can't find the ladder anywhere. I promise that help will be coming soon.'

'*WHERE'S MY DAUGHTER?*' I ask again. 'What have you done with my daughter?' Nicola looks very pretty from this angle. I can almost see up her nose.

'She's dead, John,' she says suddenly. 'I'm so sorry. They both are, but you know that. You're just concussed and have forgotten temporarily. Your wife skidded on black ice on Christmas Day two winters before last on the road into Stroud trying to avoid a deer, they think. It was in all the local papers.'

I can hear sirens coming from somewhere far away. I go

back to the grille and look out at the blades of grass. The exquisite voice of a thrush is singing somewhere out there in the trees. It is so beautiful, the wood today. I have loved this place. I have loved it in the deepest fibres of my heart, down to the very marrow of my bones. I never want to leave the woods, the Stone House, these valleys. I do not want to be taken away from here: I will not go. I will not go quietly.

There are light footsteps in the garden. I can hear Bryony's sweet voice. I swear that it is as real as you or I. 'Mum,' she is saying, 'I heard him. I think he's down there somewhere. I heard him calling out to us.'

I shout and shout but her voice disappears into the undergrowth again. The sound of the siren is getting louder and louder. There are slamming metal doors and running feet. They have come for me. They have come to save me.

Acknowledgements

I would like to thank my agents, Jacqueline Korn and Alice Williams at David Higham Associates in London, for their support, advice and encouragement while I was writing this book, the 'difficult second novel'.

Tony Cook at www.abctales.com was particularly helpful in his ongoing feedback as the final draft of the novel took shape over the course of one long year and this version of the book was posted, chapter by chapter, onto that invaluable writer's website.

Last, but by no means least, I would like to thank my father, my stepmother, my wife and my brothers for always being there.

Richard Aronowitz was born in 1970 and grew up in rural Gloucestershire. He studied at the universities of Durham, Heidelberg and London and works at Sotheby's. He is married and lives in Cambridge.

His debut novel, *Five Amber Beads*, was published by Flambard in 2006. His poems have appeared in *The Guardian* and *The Independent*, as well as in numerous journals, and are anthologised in *Anvil New Poets 3*. He was a poetry runner-up in the 1999 Bridport Prize.